A GOOD GIRL

Johnnie Bernhard

Texas Review Press
Huntsville, Texas

FIRST EDITION
Requests for permission to acknowledge material from this work should
be sent to:

> Permissions
> Texas Review Press
> English Department
> Sam Houston State University
> Huntsville, TX 77341-2146

ACKNOWLEDGMENTS: I am indebted to Patricia Sproat for geneal-
ogy research that served as a spring board in the development of this
book. Many of the historic facts used within *A Good Girl* came from *The
Handbook of Texas Online* produced by the Texas State Historical Association and from on-line articles in the *Galway Advertiser* of Galway, Ireland.

My heart overflows with gratitude to my husband Bryant Bernhard, who
took every step with me, with loving patience.

Cover Art by Grady Byrd
Cover Design by Nancy Parsons
Author Photograph by Judi Altman

Library of Congress Cataloging-in-Publication Data
Names: Bernhard, Johnnie, 1962- author.
Title: A good girl / Johnnie Bernhard.
Description: First edition. | Texas Review Press : Huntsville, Texas, [2017]
Identifiers: LCCN 2016046603 (print) | LCCN 2016048545 (ebook) | ISBN
  9781680031218 (pbk.) | ISBN 9781680031225 (ebook)
Subjects: LCSH: Families--Fiction. | Irish American families--Fiction |
  Fathers--Death--Fiction. | Alcoholics--Family relationships--Fiction. |
  Gulf Coast (Tex.)--Fiction. | LCGFT: Domestic fiction. | Historical
  fiction. | Novels.
Classification: LCC PS3602.E75966 G66 2017 (print) | LCC PS3602.E75966
  (ebook) | DDC 813/.6--dc23
LC record available at https://lccn.loc.gov/2016046603

The LORD, the LORD, a God merciful and gracious, slow to anger, and abounding in steadfast love and faithfulness, keeping steadfast love for the thousandth generation, forgiving iniquity and transgression and sin, yet by no means clearing the guilty, but visiting the iniquity of the parents upon the children and the children's children, to the third and the fourth generation.

Exodus 34:7

A GOOD GIRL

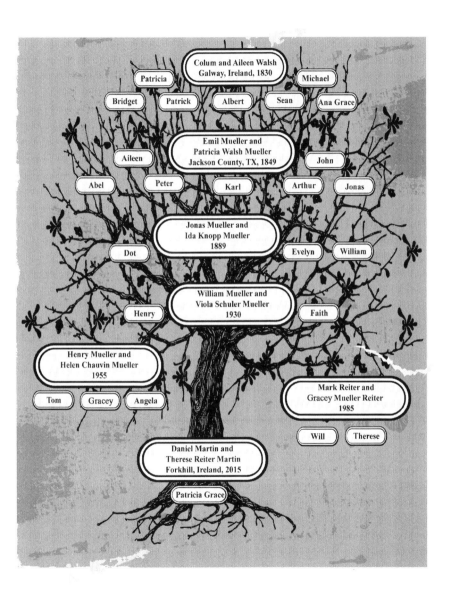

Chapter One
Lonesome Road

"I am lost."

With the drone of asphalt beneath her and a caffeine headache, Gracey Reiter murmured to herself as she scanned for the next exit off I-10. She veered to the right, exiting toward a truck stop. A rusted clothesline with attached shrunken alligator heads separated the gator farm from the truck stop. It was an amusement park for the natives; one of many dotting the South's wasteland perched on the Gulf of Mexico.

For thirty years she made the pilgrimage from Mississippi to South Texas. To Gracey, I-10 West was a 500-mile umbilical cord leading her home.

She parked the Honda in a side lot shared with a twenty-four-hour adult video store. In a pasture to her right, cows chewed among the carcasses of abandoned vehicles, as oil field rocking horses pumped away.

"This is as close as we get to Mecca, boys and girls," she said, scanning the parking lot and the choices before her. "It's a giant petri dish." She bathed her hands in liquid sanitizer and pushed the car door open with her foot.

Gracey navigated through the truck stop with one hand across her chest and the other resting against her purse. Amid counters offering pickled quail eggs and pigs' feet floating in pink broth, she found the restroom at the back, near the barbeque pork rind display.

She dried her hands at the spit-spackled mirror above the sink and thought of him.

Henry's death won't be that of a life well spent. I can count on it. It'll drag all of us by the knees every inch of the way. But I keep hoping this time will be different. This time we're going to get that Norman Rockwell moment with bowed heads and funeral wreaths that never wilt. This time . . . No, Daddy, you're not going out that way; didn't live the straight and true, did you? I'd expect no less from you than to kick and scream every inch of the way to the grave.

She sighed out loud, nudged the door open with her hip, and exited the bathroom without touching the door handle swarming with the unseen. Back in the Honda, she revved the small car's engine and headed to the onramp to merge with the interstate traffic flowing at seventy-five mph.

It had not been a good day for Gracey, but neither was yesterday. It took one phone call to disrupt the predictable, controllable world she held dear. "Your father is dying. You need to come home." The two sentences put her on a nine-hour road trip to a place she spent a lifetime running from. She knew the route, but not how to survive the journey.

She thought and thought again of the doctor's phone call as she weaved in and out of traffic, occasionally jolted by a gust of wind from a passing eighteen wheeler that sent her little car shaking into the slower lane of traffic.

She questioned the Fates as to why the doctor called her and not her brother and sister. Surely Angela, thin and wrinkle-free, would have managed better. Even Tom would have nipped it all in the bud, before the start of football season. But Gracey, the middle-child, the peacemaker, was chosen. Then, like a faint whisper, somewhere in her mind awashed in black coffee and Diet Coke, she heard it. It was Henry.

"Gracey, you're gonna be my medical power of attorney. I know you won't let them pull the plug on me before I'm ready to go."

She couldn't remember if she thanked him for his token of trust delivered as a title, but it secretly pleased her at the time. She felt like she pulled rank in the family's pecking order. But the feeling, like so many other things she felt in the past, quickly came and went. She was too tired to be the peacemaker. Titles and tokens were clearly over ranked.

What did that doctor say? I could barely hear him on my cell. There's absolutely no privacy at work. Everyone is either standing around, looking at your computer screen or eavesdropping on phone calls, waiting to see your face crumble . . . Got to get that conversation right, because title or not, Tom and Angela are going to be asking a lot of questions, and there I am caught in the middle, same old, same old . . .

"Ms. Reiter, your father, Henry Mueller, is in our care at Victoria Medical Center. Our tests are conclusive. Your father has stage IV colon cancer. Unfortunately, his blood pressure is dangerously high, and I don't think his heart can survive stents to alleviate that. There is fluid in the lungs. You will need to notify your family members."

Sitting at her desk at work with her cell phone pushed against her ear, Gracey stared at the open door of her office and the opened mouths of her two co-workers standing in the hall, staring at her.

"Yes, yes, I am his daughter. Yes, yes . . . But this is going to be hard. Just hard. It always is. I have a very unusual family, Doctor. This conversation is between me and you only. Hold on a minute . . ." She stood up from her desk and closed the door on the two opened mouths with a quick swing of her right hip.

"Mrs. Reiter, we are protected by law in issues of privacy."

"Yes, yes. It's . . . I've done this before, and I was sucker punched for two weeks while my mother lay in ICU, her kids standing around her, fighting about her quality of life. My dad folded, just folded. I'll not go through that again. You make Henry comfortable. That's all. There's no need to prolong any of this."

"Yes, Mrs. Reiter. I understand . . . "

Henry Mueller, the last surviving patriarch of a chaotic gene pool, with one leg left and a body oozing with cancer, was dying. He knew and didn't care; he had accepted it with the resignation of the tired and bored man he was.

If anyone had asked his children if they expected him to make it to eighty-four, the oldest and only son, Tom would be the first to answer, "Henry's a marvel of medical science! He might have made Guinness had he not smoked and drank three-fourths of his life away."

Outside of the Houston Downtown Loop, Gracey thought of the family lineage and was sure there was some unstated, century-old decorum to follow in such matters.

Guess I'll call Tom first. He gets three rings, no more. If he doesn't pick up, I'm not calling him back. It will be on his head to find out.

Gracey slowed the car to seventy mph and picked up her cell phone. Tom answered on the second ring. Before he could say hello, she delivered the news, taking confidence from the bestowed title.

"Henry's dying."

"Damn, and how are you, Gracey? Actually, I'm surprised Henry lasted this long," said Tom. "When did you get the call?"

"Yesterday at work. Sorry, I didn't call right away." *Why am I apologizing? Don't cry, damn it.* "Tom, I wanted to get my head straight before I called you. I'm headed to the hospital now. He's in Victoria. I want you to meet me there, Tom."

"The man smoked Camels and drank whiskey from a bottle for over sixty-five years. Yep, he's been on borrowed time."

Henry Mueller's only son became Henry's adversary the day he was born. At fifty-eight, Tom, the image of his father with the same sky blue eyes, lived his life proving he was nothing like his father.

"That's the thing that always amazed me about Henry. Lived his life like a country song. Get drunk Friday night, rip the house to shreds and up again Saturday morning for work. There was Mom, never drinking, eating her vegetables . . . she drops dead at sixty."

"She was dead at sixty, Tom, because she pushed a rock up a hill every day of her life. A rock called Henry."

Ignoring Gracey, Tom continued, "Let me call you later.

I'm teaching both sessions of summer school plus working on the football schedule. Don't know when I can come."

"You got to tell him goodbye. He's dying."

"He doesn't want a goodbye from me. He wants an audience; he wants us to rally around the hospital bed, so he can remind us he's the last of the Mohicans."

"All right. Forget it. I'll see you when I see you," Gracey said, hanging up on him before he could hang up on her.

Henry Mueller was the last of the Mohicans; the last surviving member of a tribe who lived hard, worked hard, and loved in vain. Their lives were do or die contests, living paycheck to paycheck until they dropped dead. Henry's eighty-four years were no exception.

I guess I'm alone in this. Who knows what Angela will do? Forget it. I have to keep my mind on what has to be done. Does he even own a decent suit? Who's going to give that eulogy? God help me, there are the stories Henry told about his life, and then there's the truth about his life.

She guided the car through multiple lanes of traffic as I-10 became Highway 59 South.

"Damn it, people drive like they're on some farm market road in the middle of nowhere. Whipping in and out of traffic like bats out of hell, riding up my backend," she cursed, gripping the steering wheel tighter and turning off the radio.

The sudden silence jolted her. She was giving in to it. The raw emotion that came upon her when her routine with predictable outcomes was taken away. It left her small; small as the little tear that squeezed its way down her cheek and dropped on the cell phone in her lap.

Gracey didn't want to go home. She didn't want to be the medical power of attorney. She didn't want to plan a funeral. But the expansion of the open road, as Highway 59 South cut a concrete ribbon through horse pastures, maize fields, and little towns in South Texas, she became immersed in the smells and sights of who she used to be.

Gracey was a good girl, sitting with her father in the kitchen. They were together in the house in Loti. The house with the walls painted a pale yellow and the curtains made from bed sheets. She swung her bare legs back and forth under the table. She watched him with her little girl eyes and heard him with her young perfect ears.

Henry was singing and tapping his fingers against the Formica kitchen table. She saw a bottle of Canadian Club and a Coke can lined up in front of him. He drank from a cut glass jelly jar with two cubes of ice, held by hands cracked with drywall mud. A metal ashtray held his cigarette, waiting for him to emphasize a point with a quick drag and exhale.

"Little girl, did I ever tell you about my time in the service? It took me all the way to upper state New York. Even went east of the camp to get a look at the Adirondack Mountains. They was somethin' to see . . . "

His words, his South Texas drawl raw and chafed from a lifetime of smoking and drinking, resonated in her head.

She bit her lip to stop the memories of Henry and a childhood spent watching him drink himself to death at the kitchen table.

She began piecing together the facts of Henry's life for the eulogy she must write. A simple chronological listing of birth, living, and death would be the safest thing to do, she thought. So much of her father's life was hearsay. The stories told to her as a child were often fueled by whiskey or delivered by blue-haired women clutching black purses at funerals and church socials. Both were reliable tools for distorting the truth.

Henry was drafted and sent to boot camp in New York during the Korean War. He'd never even been out of Calhoun County before. The only thing he knew about the military was his daddy was a Sea Bee stationed in Africa during the Second War.

But that's what poor boys did, they got drafted, saw some country and felt lucky not to come home in a box. That story is easy to tell, thought Gracey.

Life ran its course for Daddy. Eighty-odd years marked by the fact he survived them. I guess he loved us. He worked hard and had nothing to show for it. He knew he was dying, and like everybody else, he was glad it was almost over.

Steadied by less traffic and familiar sights, Gracey exited 59 South toward Victoria. She reminded herself to call Angela. She cradled the cell phone against her right shoulder. The number went straight to voice mail.

"Hey, Angela. I'm on my way to Victoria. Dad's in South Texas Medical. Call me. It's important."

Hanging up, Gracey thought about the word important. It held two different meanings for sisters separated by a decade and income.

I'd better get every detail straight before she calls me back. What did the doctor say? What tests did they run? Who made what decision? Like I'm one of her damn employees. That's the real stress. It's not that Dad is dying, that's been coming for years. It's the family. All their expectations of who they think I am and what I'm supposed to do. They don't even know me. That's what hurts the most.

She would make a plan for Angela. A simple day-by-day account of their father's decline. She remembered calling him early one morning last month . . .

"How you doin' today, Daddy?"

"Didn't sleep, at all. Up and down, up and down, all night in the bathroom. I'm in a lot of pain, Sister."

"What did you have for supper last night?

"I ate some potatoes and sausage. Had a little night cap before I went to bed."

The one constant in Henry's life was his diet. Whiskey, red meat, potatoes and the occasional banana for good will sustained him for years, but the gnawing effects of diabetes came closer to eating his core. He temporarily silenced it, and the alarming blood sugar level drops, with a handful of peppermint drops, crunching a few against his back teeth and swallowing the rest whole. When his body screamed in rebellion, he drank from the bottle he kept in the kitchen cupboard, behind the flour and sugar canisters.

But the bloating of his gut and his phantom leg, begging to be scratched, would not go away.

"Oh Daddy, do I need to call someone? You think it's that bad?"

"I don't know, Gracey. Damn it, my stomach hurts."

"Dad, calm down. It'll make it worse if you get upset."

"Don't tell me that. I can't make it go away. Went to the doctor last week and he gave me some pills for indigestion. They don't help. Nothin' helps."

"Sit in your chair by the window. I'm calling Joann. She'll be right over."

"Don't bother Joann. She's got her own problems."

"Dad, I want her to take a look at you."

Joann Ramirez, one of many retirees on the street, was a former nurse whose daily routine was to notice when the garage door opened and closed at her neighbor's house. She answered on the second ring.

"Hello."

"Hey, Joann, it's Gracey. Something's up with Daddy. He sounds bad. He didn't sleep last night and says the pain is constant. Can you run over and take a look at him? Call me back?"

Joann returned the call within minutes.

"Gracey, he doesn't look good at all. I can't pick him up to get him in the car. I'm not strong enough, too weak, and your dad can't stand even on the one leg. He's thrown up all over the place. I've called an ambulance. Sorry, honey. I'll see you when you get here."

Twenty-four hours later, the death march began for Henry Mueller. The Medevac Flight to a larger hospital and a private room was ordered. Tests were conducted to rule out possibilities of law suits, proving Henry Mueller was given everything modern medicine had to offer. A heart monitor reported what had been known for years: a heart shriveled with disease and disappointment . . .

Gracey cried as the highway opened into the coastal plains of South Texas and her childhood home.

Angela and Tom had better call me back. Is it too much to ask that my own flesh and blood help me?

Chapter Two
Lost Love

"Where are you?" Gracey's husband questioned on the receiving end of her cell phone.

"About ten miles from Victoria."

"Almost there. Good. You doing okay?"

"Yes, I'm okay. What else would I be?" Gracey replied with a sigh.

"You don't sound okay, Grace."

"Well, Mark. What do you want me to say? You don't want to deal with Henry's latest, so here I am dealing with it by myself."

"What do you want me to do? Tell me what you want and I'll do it, but don't expect me to sit around for days and talk about things that can't be fixed. I refuse to do that."

"I know that. I also know your absence is interpreted as someone who really doesn't care."

"I'm trying to make a living for us, remember? I can't drop everything and run to Texas."

"Work versus me. Well, I know I won't win that one. But you know what you don't seem to understand? When you drop dead in that office, your replacement will walk over your corpse and business will continue as usual. But me? Well, we both know where I am in your list of priorities."

"Damn it, Gracey. You're probably flying down the road with a million thoughts in your head before you even walk into the hospital room. I'm worried about you."

It was a toe dip into the emotional abyss of a three-decade-old marriage. Time, that ancient healer, taught them to survive by playing their assigned roles. Gracey's job was to fix, fix, fix. Henry was the first man to teach her that. Mark's job was to work, work, work. The safety of a redundant routine taught him that. Somewhere between fixing and working, for better or worse, Mark and Gracey stayed married.

They were opposites, and just like the adage, it was what attracted them to each other in the early years. Mark was a methodical, aloof thinker. To push him into doing anything without a clear outcome was a mistake. It took the first ten years of marriage for Gracey, who viewed life as a house on fire, to understand that. When she fought it, the same tired argument occurred. It began and ended the same way: "Tell me what you want me to do and I'll do it, but don't expect me to be there."

That was never an option for Gracey. Always there, in her mind, was an endless list of things to do. Despite each task she completed with a satisfying check, another task would magically appear. She accepted it as her lot in life. Her father had taught her to be a good girl. That well-learned lesson for approval became a reflex by the time she was twelve. Layers and layers of illogical demands, false responsibilities, and bad habits put her and her demons in the car heading west on I-10 for years.

"Never mind. Forget it, Mark. I don't know what I want. The one thing I do know is I don't want to be here. I don't want to deal with any of this. Can you at least show some sympathy? That's what I need. I need you to be my friend. Can you muster that? I got the reality of the situation down to an art form. Can't you at least pretend to be concerned?"

"Come on. Let's not do this."

"Neither one of us needs this, so let me do what I need to do, okay? I hate it, and I'm not even there yet."

"Call me once you see him and talk to the doctor, at least the nursing staff. You know, these things change by the hour. It might be a different story than what you originally heard. Call me. I'll come if you want me to."

"Yeah, it might not be until tonight. I'll go to the hospital then back to Dad's to clean-up and get some sleep."

"Okay, baby. Talk tonight," he said, then hung up.

Their marriage, like their conversations, had frayed into pieces of information and suggestions over time. It allowed Mark to hide in his work and Gracey to cling to her children. Always present, yet unsaid, was the expectation each had of the other— you will never leave me.

When Gracey thought about the life they built, she pictured a long, winding road, where detours and exits never offered an advantage, only a temporary illusion, which in the end only served to put them back on the same road they had travelled their entire marriage.

She followed his career from government contract to government contract for large naval shipyards. Mark was a brilliant engineer with an inexhaustible work ethic. He was one of the few in his craft who could design a ship hull in the engineering bull pen, then show the welders how to put it together on the shop floor. Those were his real loves: working with men and creating things with his mind and hands. The final satisfaction for him was watching his ships in the water, the clean lines, the curve of their bows piercing oceans around the world.

She loved and hated these things in him. She respected his success, but knew she was a low priority in his life. She saw it on his face every morning when he got up. That first realization of the day, after the coffee, after the paper, the words hung in the air, "Oh yes, you're still here and I'm still here, but I haven't the guts to change any of it."

She felt it too, but she was too tired to try the next new something that would erase all the bad. There had been occasions where she bought a new bedspread or cooked the right meal at the right temperature with the right wine. She had even pushed herself into Victoria's Secret for a matching lace panty and bra, only to leave angry and dejected by the number of teenagers buying the same items in smaller sizes.

She accepted the simple fact she was no longer his lover.

His mistress was every ship he designed; they were the perfect coupling of speed and weight. Any sailing vessel, any craft moved by engine and diesel, no matter how old they became, continued to please and satisfy him.

Gracey noted the highway sign: SOUTH TEXAS MEDICAL CENTER EXIT 67. She knew she should prepare herself for what was to come. *Not now, not now. I'm not ready.* She pushed the thought back in her mind, and thought of how duty replaced passion in her marriage . . .

Mark was a good father and provider. Gracey was a good mother and an average journalist, covering small town school boards and city halls from Venice, Florida to Biloxi, Mississippi, wherever the latest government contract landed them. She adjusted her career to fit the family's schedule, with one hand tied behind her back. The other hand was doling out lunch money, breakfast on a paper towel, dance costumes from the laundry basket and excuses to her husband.

"Please just let me sleep. God, I'm exhausted," she'd begged whenever he reached for her. When he didn't reply, she'd felt relieved. With a quick adjustment of the pillow, she slightly grazed her lips across his cheek with, "Good night," and turned to face the wall.

Gracey's was the first generation of American women who tried to do it all. The only thing she accomplished was a seat in dead center. Because she was not a full-time, stay-at-home mom, she was snubbed by suburban moms for contributing to a generation of latchkey children. Because she chose career moves based on her family's needs, she was not taken seriously by career women, or men, for that matter. Neither a full-time mother nor a serious career woman, Gracey remained in the middle, mediocre and marginalized by women of both camps. She lavishly heaped the guilt of never measuring up to the work force, motherhood, and being a wife, year after year, after year.

Even a marriage can become bearable given enough time. The years brought Gracey and Mark healthy children and beautiful things they felt privileged to own, but it didn't bring them the love they once knew. That love died to an understanding, a thing promised out of a sense of duty, an obligation out of kindness and simple dignity. Gracey and Mark did a good job of caring for everyone in their lives, except each other. Their mistake was accepting they were not as important as everyone else.

But sometimes, alone and aging, watching her children discover love, Gracey felt a sense of loss; a sadness that she was no longer a participating member of that world; the world of Friday night movies, bouquets of flowers and little love notes found in a car seat or on a bed pillow.

There was a time she and Mark owned that world. Drinking wine and laughing together. Holding hands, touching, touching, she had to be touching him every minute, every hour of the day. If he left for work, she'd simply stop breathing, waiting for the moment he would walk through the door, so she could smell him, and touch, touch, touch him. Gracey remembered every moment of passion she and Mark once knew. Like an addict, her entire body craved that stunted time in their very young lives.

Mark at twenty-four with black hair and chocolate brown eyes was everything to Gracey at twenty-one. His hands, his smile, his mouth were immeasurable gifts she never thought herself lucky enough to receive. For someone to return her love as passionately as she gave it was a balm to her soul. And for many years, it healed the sense of loss she'd carried since her childhood.

They met in 1984 at the Caribbean, a college bar near Rice University in Houston. Gracey was completing her senior year at the University of Houston. Mark was writing his graduate thesis at Rice.

It was her Friday routine to catch a live Reggae band during the three-for-one happy hour with her friends from the staff of *The Daily Cougar*. Gracey and her journalism colleagues wore their usual attire of jeans and tee shirts screaming political statements across the chest. Gracey wore her favorite shirt, a black tee shirt with the words SAN ROMERO in white print.

She saw him standing at the bar. He was wearing a pair of Birdwell Beach Britches, a navy tank top, and a pair of Chinese coolie slippers.

God, what an odd combination, Gracey mentally evaluated. *Either this guy is setting a new fashion trend or he really doesn't give a flip what anyone else thinks. If that's a can of Copenhagen in his back pocket, all bets are off. That'd be too weird for me; a socialist, surfer redneck? Or would that be a communist, surfer cowboy?*

He kept staring and smiling at her. By the third rum and Coke, she approached him.

"I've been watching you watch me since I came in here. What's so damn amusing?"

"People are amusing. Then there are the exceptional who are amusing and beautiful," he replied, smiling at her.

"You're obviously another genius from Rice with that line and the get-up you're wearing."

He laughed and looked down at his shirt, shorts and shoes, as if he was pleasantly surprised by what he was wearing, as if he had just discovered the colors and fabric draped on his body and feet for the first time today.

"I'm a slave to fashion," he laughed.

"I can see that. What's that in your back pocket, probably the reason why you've been standing at the bar most the night. I imagine it's uncomfortable, sitting on a can of Copenhagen."

"Oh, that's sex wax."

I knew it. Come to a bar and that's what you get. Conversation with a weirdo. Gracey gave him a blank stare.

"Wait a minute. It's wax with a stupid name. Wax for my surfboard. I try to surf in Galveston. Try is the choice word, between dodging oil tankers and praying for a swell."

"Oh."

"Yeah. Now, where were we? I had you for a minute there. Yeah, I was telling you how beautiful you were and you were telling me you hated what I was wearing."

"It's good to be an individual. Could be a sign of genius, you know, the Rice University thing and abstract thoughts in fashion."

"Genius has nothing to do with it. Any man would be attracted to a beautiful woman with a sense of justice."

"What? Oh, the tee shirt. Bishop Romero. I'm a coward. It's

easy to put on a tee shirt and ask for social justice, but he, he . . . well, I love the man for his faith and bravery."

"He was the priest shot while giving Mass in El Salvador, right?"

"Yes. Some days I actually have enough guts and think I will go there and help. But I don't."

"You've got a big heart. What's your name?"

"Gracey. No, big heart here, but I do wear it on my sleeve a lot."

"Social worker?"

"No, I prefer to create a reality I can live with, rather than fight it every day."

"Okay, Tinker Bell. Mark, my name's Mark. Let me buy you a drink."

"Big spender! You know as well as I do this place is the cheapest drunk in Houston. I've had my three for one already!"

"Couldn't bribe you with a two dollar cocktail. Scruples, too," Mark said, and they both laughed.

"That's right. Journalism major. Scruples, at least until I can no longer feed myself on the lousy pay of a liberal arts degree."

"I appreciate a woman who can think on her feet. Better prepare yourself for the future by letting me buy you another drink."

Their first date had left her completely in love with him.

"Welcome to Mr. D'Angelo's. Now, it's not a sexy place, but I promised you a good pizza and some wine," he laughed, opening the door to plastic flowers billowing from the arms of plaster statues of goddesses, gods and cupids. A thin layer of red-and-white-checkered plastic covered the seat cushions and table tops.

"Who would have thought a place with this much taste was waiting for me on Wayside Drive. Vintage Italian. Right here in the barrio."

"You're going to love this place, Gracey." Mark smiled. "Now, let's sit over there between Venus and Bacchus. Can't go wrong with the god of wine and the goddess of love."

They ate too much. They drank too much. They laughed too much. The night ended in his bed, where she stayed the next thirty years. When they were younger, their bed was the sweetest entanglement of legs thrown across hips, hands immersed in hair, and the singular breathing of two. They were inseparable following the first date . . .

I still love you, Mark. I still want you as much as I did when I was twenty-one.

Gracey wanted to tell her husband those exact words at fifty-two, but she didn't. Instead, she made a right turn into the parking lot of the facility that held her dying father and pushed the thought of her husband into the back of her mind, where it had been for quite a while.

The hospital sat in the middle of Victoria, like a bored, spoiled woman, unmoved by any surprises, arrogant in her self-importance. It was the same, day-in and day-out, people coming and going, no one any more special than the other; once the flesh is revealed and the mystery of life is reduced to routine.

A sadness seeped from the hospital's square structure; the same sadness that engulfed the whole town. Wide-open and grey, it served the oil fields. Victoria fanned itself through the few remaining family farms and ranches into an encroaching web of commerce and box stores. A past, consisting of cowboys and herds of cattle, declined in 150 years to a concrete jungle of apartment complexes, convenience stores, and used car lots; all to accommodate the masses feeding from the same bloodline—oil.

Gracey parked in the back lot of the medical complex, relieved to stretch her legs after the nine-hour drive. With each step, she felt her stomach rising into her throat.

I've got to get a hold of myself. I'm not even there yet and my nerves are shot.

She saw the receptionist desk to the left of the elevators.

"Could you tell me what room Henry Mueller is in?"

"Room 605. Visiting hours are over at 9 PM," chirped the grey-headed bird of a woman, who quickly returned to her Diet Coke and crossword puzzle.

Gracey opened the door to room 605, and the first person she saw was sixty-eight-year-old Irma Novosad. Sitting directly in front of Henry, clad in a pant suit with large pockets in front, Irma had arranged her body as a brace to keep Henry from slipping out of a green vinyl chair. Her pockets were bulging with used Kleenexes, a jewel-tone cigarette purse, peppermints, and tooth picks. On her head was a blue sun visor with a yellow rose embroidered above the words, "Yellow Rose of Texas." In the eight years Gracey had known her, she'd never seen Irma without a sun visor, rain or shine, summer or winter; it was a permanent part of her wardrobe.

"I can't lift him into the bed and he can't stand on the one leg anymore. There's no one to help us here on the floor. I keep buzzing and buzzing that nursing station and no one comes," Irma said looking at Gracey as she entered the room.

Gracey did not acknowledge her. Everything in her body refused to let her turn and address the woman speaking to her.

As she had explained to Mark several years ago when Henry's girlfriend first entered their lives . . .

"Irma Novosad is no more difficult to deal with than pulling a weed from a flower bed or moving a piece of furniture out of my way. Don't interpret my silence around Irma as stoicism, Mark. It's not that I hate her, how do you hate an old woman you won't take the time to know? Anything she says or does is inconsequential to me. I'll never call her mom or put her on the same level as a family member. I'm not going to torture Henry for having someone. At least he's not alone sitting in front of the TV all day. I'm grateful for that. But that's it. There's no room for her in my life."

"Come on, Grace. That's a bit harsh. She's very polite to me."

"Of course she is. She's the type of woman who is good to any man in the room and treats every female in the room, girl or woman, as an enemy. That's how women like that survive. They feed the male ego and eliminate the competition whether it be a mother, wife, or child, anyone who can divert a man from caring for anyone but her. Ask any child from a divorced family how easy it is to get along with Dad's latest wife."

"Okay. Draw the line in the sand. I'm sure this battle plan is going to work well for everyone involved."

Indifference. That was the emotion Gracey felt for Irma. It was the gift she gave herself on her 50th birthday. Indifference. She was surprised how easy it was to turn her heart completely off from people who hurt her. She let go of the "perfect mother," the "dutiful wife," and the "model employee" titles when she blew out the candles on the birthday cake. She called it her life insurance policy.

Irma returned each slight, each snub as easily as Gracey dished them out. The women held each other at arm's length, only far enough away to insult each other without Henry noticing. Unaware, Henry thanked his lucky stars for finding true love late in life; a woman who loved him and his adult children.

Irma and Henry became companions several years after his wife died. Typical of the hard luck tale of the Mueller gene pool and all those who cohabit with the clan, Helen Mueller was diagnosed on a cold February day with acute Myelogenous Leukemia. She was buried in June of the same year. In between, she languished in cold showers to quell the fever of the leukemia. The last two weeks of her life she lay in the sterile environment of MD Anderson Hospital's infectious ward, communicating with her children through plate glass and a telephone.

Henry retreated from life the day Helen died. He simply gave up, shut up and disappeared into his recliner.

"Dad, you're going to have to call the funeral home to pick Mom up from the hospital. The hospital is calling me in Mississippi. Call them, Dad. Call them. I don't know about Mom's burial policy. You've got to get it out and call Clegg's Funeral Home," Gracey begged him on the phone. His faint response was barely audible over the roar of the TV in the background.

"Angela can do that."

"What are you saying, Dad? What? I can't hear you over the damn TV. Turn it off. Turn it off right now."

"You call Angela. She's in the same state as me. She knows how to do that sort of thing."

"No, she's not doing it. You're doing it. She's eight months pregnant and her mama just died. Don't you know . . . don't you know how she . . . Dad, it's your job. You call them right now. Do it," she said hanging up the phone.

Angela, feet swollen and eight months pregnant, took care of the funeral arrangements; Tom picked out his mother's coffin, and Gracey dragged herself across I-10 to bury her mother and prepare Henry for bachelorhood.

Henry emerged a new man less than a year later. He quit drinking and smoking and began speaking to his children.

"Why now?" Gracey asked her brother at the first family dinner Henry scheduled for Thanksgiving. "Why did he wait so long to be a better man? He's even rolled the silverware in paper towels and placed them next to our plates."

"You think this is real for Henry? The man's never lived the straight and true in sixty years. Hell, I doubt if he's paid income taxes in forty years," Tom said in between sips of a whiskey tumbler.

"Tom, you better watch that," Gracey said, pointing to his glass. "Genetically, the cards are stacked against you in this family. We come from a long line of crazy drunks."

"You know what I think, little sister. I think you should mind your own damn business."

Angela walked into the dining room with a turkey on a platter. She slammed it on the table with a thud.

"Look you two," she said pointing the carving knife at Tom and Gracey. "You're not about to ruin this holiday for me and Dad."

"I have one thing to ask, Angela. Just one thing. Did you purposely match the apron to your outfit?" Tom snickered into the whiskey tumbler and left the room.

Angela turned and glared at Gracey.

"What? I was just saying—"

"Don't say it, Gracey. Don't even think it. Dad deserves a decent Thanksgiving. Now, get the kids together. Let's eat before y'all ruin it for me."

So began Henry's metamorphosis for Angela, celebrated with her heart, soul and money.

The shelf life of the new and improved Henry lasted several years, until a new neighbor moved next door, quickly followed by visits from his single, sixty-eight-year-old sister. It was a love affair that began with a feud across a six-foot privacy fence.

"Oh, the irony of two small worlds colliding," roared Tom, recalling the courtship of Henry Mueller and Irma Novosad.

During his brief stint of living the straight and true, Henry discovered he was living next door to a gay man. The property line separating the two neighbors soon served as Henry's "38th Parallel."

But Henry's new neighbor was a patient man. His lawyer boyfriend from Houston took up much of his time and so failed to notice his neighbor's escalation in exclusion.

Henry installed a six-foot privacy fence when he saw the two men planting an herb garden in the back yard. He then closed his kitchen curtains permanently, deploying the clothes pin he had been using to secure a bag of bread lying on the counter.

"I don't want to look at that shit," Henry spat every time he got a cup of coffee and looked at the clothes pin keeping the curtain closed.

"Who made you God?" Tom whispered under his breath every time Henry launched another insult across the six-foot fence.

"Dad is still a member of the Mean Jesus Church. That church hasn't discovered the doctrine of love and forgiveness, yet. It's been stuck for the last 200 years on hell, fire, and damnation. Apparently, there's a lot more entertainment value in hate and discontent, than in preaching about love for your neighbor," replied Gracey.

Henry's private war continued until the day he saw a gold-colored Oldsmobile pull up to the curb of his enemy's home.

Irma Novosad, married four times, widowed twice, and divorced twice, was making the first of many meal deliveries to her brother's front door. Henry recognized a trim woman in her mid-sixties who could cook and clean within two yards of his fingertips. The clothes pin was promptly removed and the curtain was generously parted.

Henry fell in love with Irma. Irma fell in love with Henry. The union was celebrated with a return to Canadian Mist cocktails and Camels. Henry kept his house. Irma kept hers. Together, they kept their individual social security checks. They spent their days frequenting the buffets of South Texas and each other's homes, referring to Henry's as the winter estate, and Irma's as the summer cottage.

Tom was the first to say, "I told you so . . . "

All of it, the years of disappointment, the silence between Henry and his children, the best intentions laid to waste with a single word, all of it came together in Room 605 in the South Texas Medical Center. An old man, with one leg, reeking of cancer and diabetes, was stuck in a vinyl chair in a hospital room. All the sins of yesterday became the chair and the man. Ugly and immovable.

She didn't cry. The realization of what was before her was far too painful for that. Instead she found her cocoon, the safe place she first found as a little girl. It was where she separated her heart from the rest of her body. She replaced the emptiness with action. She would fix this. She would make it better. She didn't care if each step she took was redundant. She was only thankful to not think about it, the impossible hopelessness of sitting and thinking . . . If she gave into it, she would simply disappear. No one would be able to find her again. Not even herself. She'd be lost . . .

Gracey dialed the nurses' station and requested two people to lift her father into the bed. She avoided Irma's eyes and turned toward Henry.

"Daddy, you tired of sitting up?"

"I'm hurtin', Sister. I need to be on my back."

Henry had twisted the hospital gown around his waist and swollen stomach in his attempts to rise from the vinyl chair. His nakedness in the macabre scene was cruel humility for a daughter and a father. Gracey turned away and stared at the floor.

Oh God, is this where life eventually lands us? It's so cruel, so cruel. Why am I so weak? Why can't I pick him up in my arms and put him in the bed?

Two male nurses entered the room, rearranged the web of tubes, righted Henry's hospital gown, and placed him on the bed. A deep moan escaped from his body as he turned to face the wall.

Silence filled the room as the two women stood over the bed looking at him.

I can't deal with the quiet. I'll lose my mind if I have to sit here with Irma and stare at Dad.

"I brought you some things, Daddy," she said, the sound of her voice startling her.

Out of an oversized gift bag, she produced a Houston Astros ball cap, *The Victoria Advocate*, and a roll of Copenhagen snuff. The irony of feeding a dying man tobacco with the warning "This product can cause gum disease and tooth loss" made her laugh out loud.

Alcohol, diabetes, and tobacco took a leg, might as well take the last few teeth in his head.

Irma glared at her.

"I got something for you, too, Irma."

Gracey handed her a paperback book with its title in bold green, orange, and white print, *Famous Irish Pub Jokes*. "Thought you might like reading about Ireland with Therese and Daniel's wedding right around the corner."

Irma extended her hand to receive the book without looking at Gracey. She kept her eyes on Henry.

"Honey, I'll be back later. You need to visit with your daughter," she said, touching Henry's shoulder. She placed the book on the vinyl chair Henry had sat in for six hours and walked out the door.

It was Gracey's turn to sit in the chair. She did for a while, thumbing through the newspaper. Then being the optimistic fool she accepted herself to be, she rose from the chair and lightly placed her hand on Henry's head.

"Our Father who art in Heaven, hallowed be Thy name. Thy Kingdom come, Thy will be done on Earth as it is in Heaven.

Give us this day our daily bread," she whispered in the darkened room, making the sign of the cross.

"Sit down."

Gracey's face burned with humiliation. She sat in the vinyl chair as he ordered. The familiar rejection from her father smarted, still.

I know this feeling. I know it, Henry. You've made me feel like this my entire life. You never once stopped to think how hard it was for me to try and love you. You never thought about what guts it took for me to reach out and want you to be my father. The whole town knew how crazy our house was. The whole town. I'm a fool to keep coming back for more, to keep offering my love when you simply slap it away. You've dismissed me, like, like, I was nothing to you.

When she stood up to search for her purse and a Kleenex, Henry spoke, without turning from the wall.

"They have good nurses here. Last night a beautiful black woman, about forty, came in here and told me everything was going to be okay. She kissed me on the mouth."

Gracey didn't say anything. She wondered if he was hallucinating from the pain medication or if the Angel of Death was a middle-aged black woman.

"She said I would pull out of this without any problem. I should be home in a few days."

"That's good news, Dad."

Silence enclosed her last word as she sat back down in the chair, staring at the floor.

"Where's your brother and sister?"

"They'll be here soon. Tom's got summer school, and Angela's been out of town. She's trying to get the first flight to Austin now."

"They're always out of town. They live pretty big lives, flying here and there, never home. She hasn't called me in a month. You know anything about that?"

"She didn't say anything to me. I think she's got a lot going on with the business and taking care of her family."

"For God's sake, she's got one kid. How hard can that be?"

"I don't know, Dad. Don't frustrate yourself. It'll make the pain worse."

"Well, she needs to get here. Get her on the phone now and tell her what's going on. She might not understand it all. She might be confused about what hospital I'm in. Hell, she could be looking for me at the hospital in Loti for all we know. I need her here."

Gracey looked at the floor and nodded her head. She felt the urge to jump from the vinyl chair and shout at him.

But I'm here, Dad. I'm right in front of you. I live the farthest away and was the first one here, doesn't that mean anything? Doesn't it count for something? Why can't you tell me that? Why can't we hold each other's hands and cry for all the sadness your miserable life has been? But you keep playing your little games. I know exactly how it's played; every bit of it. Except for the first time in your life, your play time is running out.

But the good girl didn't say anything. She simply rose from her chair and grabbed her purse.

"I'll go out in the hall and call her, so you can get some rest."

Gracey walked down the corridor to the visitors' room. She drank half a cup of black coffee before taking her cell phone out of her purse. The call immediately went to voice mail.

"Angela, it's Grace. I'm at South Texas Medical Complex with Dad. Give me a call."

When she walked back into the room, Henry was facing the door.

"Did you get a hold of her?"

"No, Dad, I left a message. She's probably in flight."

"What the hell am I supposed to think about them not being here? My own flesh and blood. Hell, this is what I've come to expect. No one has ever given me a damn thing, no one. When your mama and I were first married, I took any work I could. I worked in a canning factory at night. I've even lifted railroad ties and stacked them, as a day laborer. The money was enough to feed us for a day. We owned our clothes, our car, some dishes, an iron, and an alarm clock. That's it. But, when my baby sister got sick, I hitchhiked to Dallas to see her. Had five dollars in my pocket.

Had to last me a week. Bet you ain't ever been hungry, not one day in your life; the same as your brother and sister. Gave my kids everything. This is what I get in return."

"Dad. Please. I know they're coming, I just don't know when. Come on, now. This isn't doing you any good. I got the paper here. Let's figure out who's in first place in the National League."

The feel of a newspaper in her hands was tangible and real to Gracey. Even after all the years of fighting small town publishers for her pay, bad wages to begin with, she still loved the profession. The newspaper in her hands steadied her nerves as she turned the pages, reading the headlines to Henry.

For a moment, she lost herself reading out loud to her father. But when she paused to take a breath, she felt it. It was still there, looming over them in the small hospital room, even in the newspaper she held with both hands. Death. The small town newspapers, like Henry's generation, were dying a slow death. With their last breath, the newspaper, the small bookstore, the small shop owner, and Henry's generation, cursed the living, "Why, why do we have to go?"

"Girl, what did Atlanta do yesterday?" Henry offered.

"Well, let's see. They're up one from the beating they gave the Miami Marlins."

Henry laughed and pushed the sheet off his chest.

A nurse entered the room to check Henry's vitals.

"Mr. Mueller, I'm going to give you a little something to help you relax and take a nap."

Gracey watched her father's eyes close, as the morphine spread like a warm blanket across his body.

"I've been dreaming about Mama," he whispered to Gracey. "She was somethin' wasn't she, girl? She keeps telling me in my dreams not too worry, that I'll pull through this. She sang to me in my dream, like she sung to me when I was a kid. Mama probably had every song in the Baptist Hymnal memorized."

Gracey remembered her grandmother, Viola Mueller Bauer. She remembered how effortlessly she changed from mother to grandmother, depending on the ever changing dynamics in Henry and Helen's marriage . . .

Even in her sixties, Viola was a beautiful woman. That was the time Gracey remembered best. Up and down Highway 35, Gracey and Tom traveled with their father, all of them pressed together on the bench seat of the 1959 Chevy truck, the only sound in the truck coming from the radio. On her lap was a brown paper bag holding her clothes. Tom threw his paper bag on the floor board as soon as he got in the truck. It was time for Viola to be their mother.

Henry drove until he saw the Dairy Dream flat roof at the intersection of Highway 90 and Highway 36. This was their meeting place. This was the place where Henry dropped her and Tom off. It never changed through the years. Gracey could recall every detail about the Dairy Dream; the oak tree that stood between the road and the restaurant; the feel of her sweating hands clutching the paper bag of clothes, and Tom throwing oyster shells against the side of the building. The final scene was Henry making a U-turn in the oyster shell parking lot and driving away.

Viola would tuck Tom and Gracey in the back seat of her waiting Impala.

"Wave goodbye to your Daddy. Wave goodbye," she sang out to Tom and Gracey. The smell of peppermint and Estee Lauder Youth Dew surrounded her. For the rest of her life, Gracey associated that smell with love and security.

To Gracey, Viola was the most perfect human being she had ever known. The only mistake her grandmother had ever made was marrying Henry's father, William Mueller.

"The first time William Mueller left me, I had just had your daddy. We was living on a little cotton farm in Francitas. It was April of 1931. The Depression had begun. People were hungry and mean then." The facts were that simple to Viola.

When she told Gracey the story of her failed first marriage, Gracey was still in high school. They sat at the kitchen table drinking iced tea and eating sliced pears from the tree in Viola's back yard.

"The second time he left me, I picked cotton. It was the only thing I could do to make money. We had to eat. I was young and strong then. I could pick a hundred pounds a day. Didn't have time to worry about anything; never wondered if he'd come home or not. The August heat and rattlesnakes kept me from missing William Mueller. I let that man come and go so many years in our marriage.

"My mother-in-law was good to me and tried to make up for what her son couldn't do for his own family. But she had spoiled that boy. Those old Irish and German mamas were just like that. Did too much for 'em, about crippled their boys with too much love. There wasn't a day in that woman's life when she wasn't fixing, mending, and loaning money she didn't have to give to him. Don't always make for a strong man." Viola sighed heavily. She picked up a green pear from a bowl on the kitchen table and removed the fruit's skin with a metal potato peeler. She cut four perfect slices and placed them on a white plate in front of Gracey.

"The one time I had any hope for that marriage was in World War II. He enlisted, and thank God, for the first time we had some peace in the house, and a steady paycheck. Henry was so proud of his daddy because of that. But, Gracey, happiness never lasts. Seems like God tests us in many ways. When William came back from the war, he took up the bottle again. It was worse than ever. No one knows what he saw over there. Don't even know if he killed any Germans. All that meanness ate him up. His daddy was the same when he got back from the Spanish-American War. How do you take poor country boys and make them killers without destroying the good in them? They was pointing guns at Germans, our own people; we spoke the same language. But it ain't the poor that start war, they just fight it. Never understood the sense of any of it. But, I knew one thing, I didn't want to live that same, old life with him. I left him and moved to Palacios. Got a little waitressing job. Had no trouble taking care of my kids and working. The move tore your daddy up. Faith was just a little thing then. She didn't hardly know who her daddy was. William was either gone drinking or gone in the war," Viola said, reaching for a pear slice and putting it in her mouth. Gracey took a long drank from the tea glass in front of her. She didn't want to hear any more stories about her grandfather, but she could never tell her grandmother to stop talking. She couldn't bear to hurt her like that.

Viola's only other story of William Mueller was how he died. She told her granddaughter the next evening as she stood at the kitchen sink, washing the supper dishes by hand, staring out at the open kitchen window. Gracey stood next to her grandmother, drying each plate Viola placed in the dish rack on the kitchen counter.

"His family took him to the state hospital in San Antone. He was in his late forties by then and a real bad drunk. Living in the woods in a little shack, away from town. His family brought him food and tried to clean him up. I was already remarried and didn't see none of them. Henry would tell me everything. There was nothing anyone could do to help that man. He ended up dying in that San Antone hospital. Poor, old fool, he turned on the hot water in the bath tub and couldn't turn it back off or even get himself out of the tub. He scalded himself to death," Viola said like a school girl reciting a memorized fact . . .

William Mueller died in a hospital like his son would. Gracey stood next to Henry's bed in the South Texas Medical Center and thought of her grandmother.

"I loved her, Dad. I loved everything about her."

The last time Gracey saw her alive was in a nursing home in Schulenburg. It was only a few weeks later that Alzheimer's erased the need for Viola to swallow and eat . . .

"Hi, Grandma," Gracey whispered, pulling a metal chair next to her grandma's bed.

"Helen, is that you?"

"No, Grandma. It's Gracey, your granddaughter. I'm your oldest granddaughter. Helen and Henry's girl."

"I don't know any Graceys," she said looking at her with clear, violet eyes.

Those words would stay with Gracey for the rest of her life. It was done. Someone who had known and loved her as a child was gone forever, never to return.

Gracey reached for her grandmother's hand to place it in hers. "Mrs. Viola. How are you today?"

"I'm doing all right today, honey. Do you know that nice railroad man? He said he was coming for me today. We're getting married," Viola said, like a girl, a very young girl who still believed in love and marriage.

"I'm happy for you" were the last words Gracey said to the tiny woman, evaporating by the minute into the sheets and blankets of the nursing home bed . . .

Like his mother, Henry grew smaller and less significant as the disease grew larger. Like his mother, he wandered the recesses of his mind, searching for the reason his greatest love would also be his greatest sorrow.

"I had a lot of trouble in my married life, Gracey," Henry said to her, when he awoke from his drug-induced sleep.

"Daddy," Gracey said, turning to look at him and then her watch. Nearly three hours had slipped away since she first sat in the chair next to his bed.

"Mama didn't come to my own wedding. That church was right down the road, and she still didn't come. She never liked your mama. Helen was only seventeen when I met her. Me and my cousin was doing seismic work near Morgan City, Louisiana for a drilling company. Went to a Fais do-do in Abbeville one Saturday night, and there she was. I'd never seen a girl with such long, black hair. I took her across the state line to get married. The back seat of my car was full of shoes and dresses."

Gracey couldn't see if Henry was crying. With much effort he had turned to face the wall, away from her.

"Dad?"

"You can be in a place in your life, Gracey, where there's no more doors to open. There's no more startin' over for you. Now, girl . . . you go on to the house. I need to rest. There'll be somethin' to eat in the fridge." He didn't turn around to face her.

Gracey picked up her purse, touched his shoulder, and walked out the door. When she walked out of the hospital into the ninety-seven degree heat and blinding sunlight of August, she felt disoriented.

I've lost the car. How the hell do I get out of here?

Chapter Three
Welcome Home

Gracey scanned the hospital parking lot and walked toward the south entrance.

I remember parking near those crepe myrtles. Now, where's the damn car?

She spotted the white Honda Accord parked behind a row of oleander bushes and walked quickly toward it.

Oleanders, crepe myrtles—well, at least the blooms are hot pink on both of them. I've got to get a hold of myself.

She made a right turn out of the hospital parking lot and headed west on Highway 77. She hadn't eaten since stopping outside of Lafayette. She looked at herself in the rearview mirror. She ran her fingers across the lines on her forehead and at the smeared mascara underneath her eyes.

Too rough for walking into a restaurant. I'd like to keep this car moving until I'm parked in front of Henry's house.

She saw a Sonic Drive-In a few yards to her left, an easy exit off 77 without crossing too many lanes of traffic. She pulled in and scanned the menu.

"I'd like two corn dogs and a large Diet Coke. Extra napkins and mustard," she shouted into the little metal box underneath the menu.

"Yes, ma'am. We'll have it right out."

"I'm eating garbage because I feel like garbage, in case the chef is concerned," she mumbled back to the little metal box after she heard the line go dead.

Ten minutes later, a waitress on roller skates, sixteen, maybe seventeen, with hair neither blond nor brown, handed her a paper bag with a grease-soaked bottom.

Gracey read her tee shirt as she reached for the bag. AUSTINTATIOUS. An orange-and-white Longhorn stood underneath the bold white letters.

"Is that a pun or a new sorority at UT?" Gracey asked the waitress.

"Ma'am?"

Let it go, Gracey. She'll think you're a nut. Gracey handed the girl a $20 bill and gave her the best smile she could manage. "Thank you, dear. Keep the change."

The kid doesn't have a chance. She'd be lucky to make it to junior college, even luckier to get a decent job with benefits. That's how it was for poor girls who aren't very pretty in South Texas. Pretty girls get a huge punch card in life for shopping and lunching. The happiest days of this girl's life will be in high school, and then she'll get married and it'll be downhill from there.

Gracey ripped open the mustard packet with her teeth and slid its contents along the sides of the corn dog. She backed the car up with one hand on the steering wheel; her other held the mustard-covered corn dog like a wand. Waiting to turn on Highway 77, she ate it in three bites. She left the other corn dog in the bag.

The blur of varying shades of green, grey, and brown through the windshield brought her back to where she lived as a child. The flat two-lane roads of the coastal plains opened into rolling hills, small towns, and family farms. Neat rows of corn and soybean fields swept passed the car. An occasional field of gas wells separated the farms from the towns.

At one time in her life, Gracey thought she would live that life and for years she questioned herself. Would it have been a happier life?

The physical labor of a working farm and the monotony of small town life might have offered a certain peace Corporate America hadn't. I might have stayed younger a lot longer. I might have been a better wife to a farmer than I was to a corporate man.

But she had failed the first litmus test for that life when she didn't marry her high school sweetheart. She never had a high school sweetheart. While her friends were planning their weddings, Gracey was packing the suitcase she received as a graduation gift. She had not been an unlucky girl; the mistakes she made were her own.

God, if I could put a label on that time in my life, maybe I'd understand it better. I still can't figure out if it was ignorance or arrogance. Is there a difference between the two? But did he really have to be so cruel?

Andrew Bellows had inherited a house in Loti from his grandfather, and had no intention of ever living in Loti. He only visited on weekends, driving from Houston to make sure the pipes hadn't burst and the roof wasn't leaking.

"Who is that guy?" Gracey had asked her best friend, Carol Rosner as they sat together on the bleachers at a long ago Friday night football game.

"I think that's Mr. Bellows' grandson. You probably don't know them. They had the Farm Bureau Insurance Agency for years. I can remember his grandpa bringing him out to talk to my dad when I was a kid."

"God, he's really cute. I love how his hair's a little longer, not buzzed above his ears like everyone else's."

"Yeah, I wonder how old he is."

Gracey didn't think of that when she was seventeen. She only knew what she felt the first time he kissed her. The months of mumbled promises and fumbling in the dark were what she mistook as love.

It was nothing more than a man taking advantage of a stupid, small-town girl. It was more than embarrassing, it was humiliating. Then, for my mother to find out from those old women at church. What else could I do but move to Houston the first chance I got?

The last time she had talked to Andrew Bellows was the night she graduated from high school. What he told her before she left Loti at eighteen was the only thing that still made sense to her.

"Gracey, they're going to eat you alive out there."

Yep, Andrew, you were right. They did eat me alive.

She still heard rumors about his life from her high school girlfriends. Andrew Bellows was still living in Houston. He never moved into the house he inherited from his grandfather. Twice divorced, he continued to spend an occasional weekend in Loti, checking the roof for leaks and sleeping with local girls.

He scorched the heart of an eighteen-year-old girl. That girl, me . . . well, she's gone forever. I never allowed myself that vulnerability with a man, again. I guess Andrew did teach me something—don't trust a man.

Gracey saw her parents' house in front of her. She pulled into the driveway and let the car run. The large oak tree from the back yard towered near the two-story bedroom window she once slept near. The three peach trees she had planted with her mother stood in a neat row in the side yard. It was twilight and the temperature was still in the nineties. Gracey's heart stopped for a moment at the shock of seeing it all in front of her.

I shouldn't have come here alone.

She turned off the key in the ignition and stepped out of the car. She saw the morning's newspaper lying in the driveway and letters in the opened mail box standing at the curb.

I'm too damn tired. It will have to wait.

Each step she took toward the house took tremendous effort from her. She walked slowly on the narrow sidewalk leading to the front porch. Bordering the sidewalk were the daylilies her mother had planted years ago. They had become straw during the drought. The porch swing sat motionless in the heat of the evening. The WELCOME mat by the front door mocked her.

She unlocked the door to the dark house. The ghost of the family that once lived here breathed heavily when she closed the door behind her. It was the life of a man, woman, their son, and two daughters. "No more," the house whispered. That life evaporated over the years, as each child married, as the parents became old and sick, and as each grandchild moved away, forgetting there had been this house. There had been this one life for five people.

The house stood like a dark box slowly opening its content, revealing those memories within its stillness. The walls of the house illustrated each former occupant. Framed pictures showed a school boy, a baby, a graduate, a newly married couple, a family. The pictures disclosed the days of perfect happiness and also of unbearable tragedy for Henry and Helen Mueller, and their three offspring brought into this world.

Gracey walked through the house, turning on lights in the living room, den, kitchen, bathroom, and the bedroom she would sleep in. She circuited back to flip on the front porch light and the motion detector floodlight for the back yard, then hit the remote for the television, inserting background noise.

I need to call Joann. She might be alarmed if she saw all the lights on across the street.

Joann had been a good neighbor for Henry, picking up the mail when he was out of town, carrying plates of food across the street, and dragging the lone garbage can to the road when Henry no longer could. She often called weekends if she noticed Irma's Oldsmobile was not in the driveway.

Gracey used the black rotary phone by Henry's recliner in the living room.

"Joann, it's Grace. I didn't want to alarm you with all the lights on across the street at Dad's. I'm going to be here for a few days."

"I'm glad you called, honey. I've been thinkin' about all y'all. Such a bad time for you. Did you see your daddy in Victoria?"

"Yes, ma'am. It doesn't look so good. He's sleeping a lot, but we were able to talk a little while. He knows I'm here, so I hope that will give him some comfort. Maybe he won't feel so alone with all this."

"Well, poor Henry. He fought it a long time, and you're right, he done pretty good by himself all these years. Can I bring you somethin' to eat? I cooked a big meal tonight. Still in the habit of cookin' for an army! Won't take a second to heat it up for you."

"No ma'am. I got something on the way home from the hospital. I may stop by in the morning, though. I'll call first."

"That'll be fine. I'm praying for all of you, Gracey. I love you like you was my own. All you got to do is call me, and I'll come over and sit with you."

"Thank you for your kindness, Joann. You've been a good neighbor, really the best through the years. I'll be all right tonight. I'll give you a call in the morning. Thanks again for everything. Good night."

She hung up, and began to call Mark, then decided against it.

I'm too tired for that conversation. Of course, he didn't think to call me either. Well, there you have it.

She hung up the phone and went upstairs to take a shower.

Wrapping her hair in a towel, she padded downstairs for a glass of milk to settle her stomach, as it churned black coffee, Diet Coke, and corn dogs. Opening the refrigerator, she saw a five-pound box of corn dogs from Sam's Club for $5.99. She lifted the box and peered inside. One corn dog left.

She laughed out loud until she began crying.

Oh, Daddy. Did you happen to spend the last two weeks eating corn dogs? I guess we're keeping it in the family. Not really tasting it, just swallowing it down.

She found a half gallon of two-percent milk shoved in the back of the fridge. She smelled its contents. Looking in the cabinet for a clean glass, she found a coffee cup next to Irma's collection of pot pie tins. She put the coffee cup down, seized the tower of aluminum tins within her reach and threw them into the garbage. She then opened the next cabinet and threw away all the ketchup packets, artificial sweeteners, and plastic cutlery. In the bottom cabinet, she found three shelves of plastic margarine tubs in various sizes. Pausing for a second, they, too, joined the masses.

"Some would call you thrifty, Irma. But I'd call you a hoarder. Yeah, a hoarder, you crazy old woman," Gracey shouted to the purged kitchen cabinets.

She tied a knot in the garbage bag and took it to the can outside. Forgetting about the milk, she went to the living room and sat in Henry's recliner, directly in front of the television. Gracey stared at the screen, neither listening nor comprehending.

She turned to look at the curio cabinet in the corner. Her mother's tea set was on the top shelf, where it sat untouched from the day Helen purchased it with twenty S&H stamp books. Gracey was with her mother that day, forty-one years ago.

The white porcelain tea set, sprinkled with orange flowers on matching cup, saucer, creamer, and sugar bowl, made her mother happy the day it was finally hers. There would be a day, Helen promised herself, she would sit and enjoy a cup of tea with sugar and milk from the white porcelain set. That day never came.

The mantle clock struck eleven.

Henry, I guess you sat here every night, trying to stay awake until that clock told you it was okay to go to bed. If you stayed up that late, maybe you could force your body to sleep four or five hours . . . maybe, but you still had to make that long walk, while you could walk, down the hallway, to an empty bed. Irma might have been here. It didn't matter. She was drunk or dead asleep. But not you. You sat in that chair, with a broken body and a mind that would not let you sleep. Thinking, reliving it. Every wrong or right you ever did.

She got up from the recliner and walked upstairs to sleep. Passing the long hallway at the foot of the stairs, she looked at every picture on the wall.

Lining the wall were framed photographs of Tom in a baseball uniform, in a football jersey holding a football, and in line with other boys holding blue ribbons in his fist.

Tom was always so good in sports, any sport. Here's another picture of him missing his front tooth. Here he is holding a certificate for being a model student in the third grade. Oh, but that little boy, that little boy grew up to be a very sad man.

Here I am, graduating from Loti High School in a cap and gown and a huge high school ring on my finger.

The other photographs were of Mark and her on their wedding day.

"My God, we were so young. I was pretty," she said out loud, surprised the thought escaped her, making a hollow sound in the empty house.

There were photographs of Will and Therese, their children.

She continued to stare at them, touching the frame and glass slightly with her hand, loving them with her entire being.

And here's our girl, Angela.

The picture captured Angela as a twirler in high school, wearing white leather boots and a matching fringed leotard. Her forever-sixteen-year-old smile was engaging, but it was her enormous green eyes that caught the observer. The picture next to it showed Angela holding her college diploma with Henry's arm around her shoulder.

They were always close. Always. She seemed to love him more than the rest of us. She still does.

Gracey turned away from the pictures and climbed the stairs to her room.

In the same bed she slept in as a child, Gracey lay. She looked out the curtainless window at the lone street light illuminating the empty asphalt street. The branches of the oak tree stretched to the second story window where they rested and hugged the house.

On a wooden shelf next to the window were the mementoes of the young girl she once was. A small trophy reading FIRST CHAIR CLARINET, LHS, 1979 anchored six long ribbons of maroon and white. Glitter letters proclaimed HOMECOMING, 1980. The ends of the ribbons were tied to miniature cow bells.

Next to her bed, a small statue of the Virgin Mary stood on the night stand. A puddle of rosary beads rested at her feet. It was a gift from her mother on her First Communion.

Gracey turned to her side. With her back to the window and the outside world, she closed her eyes. The drowning sense of loss would not leave her. She missed her mother.

Mary, pray for me, I can't . . . I can't do it anymore. Nothing in me can utter the simplest of prayers. I am a bitter, miserable woman. I'll never, never forgive my father. That woman. Irma. She's a cruel joke for my mother's replacement . . .

With her pixie haircut, a shock of straight white-and-black hair combed forward as bangs, and her blue sun visor worn indoors and outdoors, at all hours, Irma was a bizarre mixture of post-WWII working woman and redneck hoarder.

She's the only person I have met in my life who travels with her own ashtray. Who does that? Where do you even buy those mini bean bag things? She probably buys them in bulk.

Two years ago, Gracey visited Henry in early spring. She came to meet the woman her father was in love with. Arriving at night, they ate a light meal together before Gracey excused herself. She could not bear another hour of watching them together in the small kitchen. He lighting her cigarettes. She wrapping a paper towel around a fresh cocktail. The intimacy between Henry and Irma told her she was now a guest in the home she grew up in.

It wasn't that they didn't invite her to join them in their evening routine. Irma offered her a glass of wine. Henry asked her opinion on music.

"Pick out some music, Sis. Whatever you want to listen to."

"That's okay, Dad. I'm really tired. I'll see you in the morning," she said as she rose from the Formica table, littered with cigarettes, jewel-toned lighters, a fifth of Canadian Club and a liter of Coke.

Gracey heard the music and their voices behind the closed bedroom door. Her breath quickened. She became a little girl again, lying in the same bed, afraid as she listened to the voices downstairs, waiting for the laughter to turn into accusations. But this time, there was no change. The laughter and singing of Henry and Irma continued until she fell asleep.

The next morning Irma poured a cup of coffee and placed it in front of her at the kitchen table.

"Your daddy and me thought you might want to visit your mama's grave while you're here. He needs to get a haircut, so I thought we could get her some flowers while he's taking care of that. We'll meet back at the house for some lunch and drive out to the cemetery together."

"That was nice of you to think of my mom, Irma. Sure, I'll go. I haven't been out to the grave site in a while. We might want to bring a hoe and some bags to clean-up around the area. I don't know if Dad gets out there very often."

Gracey was relieved by the suggestion. A plan was made for the day.

All I've got to do is enjoy Irma and Henry for who they are, not who I want them to be. We'll stay busy. It's hard to hit a moving target. A day of physical activity would leave no time or energy for those two to do anything else. All I have to do is be friendly and non-committal. I've spent a life time doing that in the workforce. I can handle it for a weekend.

Gracey and Irma spent the morning driving around in Irma's gold Oldsmobile in downtown Loti. The first stop was Bill's Dollar Store, one of the few small shops left in town once Wal-Mart was built.

"Well, there you go, I learn something new every day," Gracey announced, walking into the dollar store and observing an entire wall dedicated to plastic and Styrofoam funeral arrangements. There were pink crosses, blue crosses, praying hands, and a cardboard Bible outlined in plastic red roses.

She chose white hydrangea stems and whirling ropes of plastic ivy glued on a Styrofoam wreath. Irma insisted on paying for the flowers, but Gracey left a $20 bill at the cash register and walked out of the store.

Her hands were shaking when she sat inside Irma's car.

"How about some fried chicken for lunch," Irma suggested. "You look a little pale. We didn't have much for breakfast."

"Sure," Gracey said half-heartedly. She could feel it engulfing her, like black water rising, above her shoulder, to her chin, the drowning depression of realizing nothing, nothing is ever what she wanted it to be.

I should be in this car with my mother, not with her, not with my Dad's girlfriend, with the back seat full of Styrofoam and plastic flowers for my mother's grave.

Irma gave her order to a woman whose head protruded from a sliding window at the Rusty Rooster Fried Chicken drive-thru. Gracey looked at her, then closed her eyes, allowing the black water to go over her head.

The late afternoon trip to the Loti Cemetery was a blur

of colors and words for Gracey. She sat in the backseat of Irma's Oldsmobile with bags of plastic flowers on the floor board, resting in a carbon whirl of white on top of her feet. Her view was of Henry and Irma's heads, or rather, Henry's blue Atlanta Braves ball cap and Irma's blue visor. The bean bag portable ashtray sat on the arm rest between them.

"God, I'm the kid in the back seat on a little family outing," Gracey said underneath her breath.

"What? You need more air back there?"

"It's good, Dad." Gracey stared out at the flashing scenery through the passenger window. She saw the cemetery entrance before they did. "I think we're here."

Henry maneuvered the car next to the hurricane fence lining the north entrance of the cemetery. Two cedar trees served as citadels at the entrance gate.

The father and daughter walked to the grave site together. Gracey turned and looked at Irma in the car. Her arm rested against the open passenger window with a lit cigarette in her extended hand. They stared at each other. Neither one of them exchanged smiles.

Gracey saw her mother's grave before Henry did. She immediately stepped away from him. She could not bow her head and pray. She could not kneel next to the grave site. She could not read the words on the headstone. She moved closer. She read her mother's name, over and over again. HELEN OPHELIA MUELLER. HELEN OPHELIA MUELLER. HELEN OPHELIA MUELLER.

Henry was standing behind her with his head bowed. He spoke and the paralyzing anger within her rose to the surface.

"We sure won't forget her, will we Grace?"

"No, Dad. I haven't forgotten her. Not one day has gone by that I didn't, didn't wish she was still here . . . I can't, I can't even tell you how much I hate seeing old ladies with their daughters. Why couldn't that have happened for me? We failed her, every one of us. In her life, in her dying . . . she deserved better."

Gracey opened the plastic bag she clutched in her hand. She separated the twisted bunch of hydrangeas and roses, wiping her tears against her shirt sleeve, smoothing the wire stems with her fingers, determined to make them look different from what they were, dollar store flowers made in China.

"Little girl, ain't nothing we can do about what life brings us." Henry placed a hand on his daughter's shoulder.

Gracey turned around and faced him.

"No, I don't believe that. I don't believe we're here to only survive. We're here to make it better. Better than what we got."

She turned away from her father and reached into the plastic bag for the wreath, absentmindedly letting the bag flitter to the ground. She propped the wreath against the urn and marched back to the waiting Oldsmobile. A dejected Henry followed behind, carrying the empty dollar store bag . . .

Lying in bed in her old room, the pain of that day, like so many others, was renewed with the fact Henry was dying. Gracey pulled the bedspread on the single bed closer to her neck. It was quiet in her parents' house.

I've got to get some rest. Tomorrow may bring Irma collecting her share of Henry's goods before he's dead. Maybe Tom and Angela will emerge from pre-funeral limbo. Maybe, maybe Mark will come. Mark, and the kids . . .

But Gracey couldn't sleep. Her mind was filled with the past and the family she was once a part of. She was alone, alone in her thoughts of the life they could have lived.

Henry and Helen's marriage had an expiration date clearly marked, but they ignored it. They shared a bed, a son, and two daughters. But those hearts, they were divided. It was a war. No one knew every campaign, every strategy of that war better than Tom, me, and Angela.

Henry was either at work, eating in front of the TV, or mad. That's all I remember. Henry was always mad at us. His classic line we could always count on was, 'Why in the hell isn't there anything decent to eat in this house? Then he'd start pulling out dishes, pots and pans, food from the fridge and cupboard. Next, came the silverware

drawer yanked completely out of the cabinet. I'd lie perfectly still up-
stairs in my bed listening for the sounds of his footsteps on the stairs.
I'd pray over and over, 'Please God, let him go to bed. Make him go
to bed, God.'

The next morning, no one would say anything. Like nothing
had happened. Mom cleaned up the mess long before we even got up
for school the next morning.

I'd come home from school that afternoon and she'd be in the
same place I saw her that morning. Sitting alone on the back porch,
drinking coffee and smoking cigarettes, staring at something I could
not see.

I know now what you were staring at, Mom. You were staring
at the reality of a woman at fifty, a woman without an education,
without any money, a woman who couldn't leave. You kept staring
ahead, praying you could find a way out. It never came.

Now, there's Henry and Irma. And he, he gives this woman
every allowance, every bit of kindness he never offered my mother . . .

Gracey's last trip to see her father, before the current diagnosis,
was on Christmas Eve. She was out of the car for an hour after
arriving when Henry approached her with a $50 bill.

"Go to town and buy Irma something nice for Christmas,
Sister."

"What?"

"She'd probably like a new purse or a nice scarf. You know
what she'd like."

She took the money.

You're unbelievable, old man. You never bought a birthday gift
or a Christmas gift for Mom, and she was your wife. You never did
anything like that, Dad, and now, you want me to buy a gift for your
girlfriend and say it's from you? Well, this one has just topped the list
of all time craziness.

Gracey got back in the car and drove to the mall in Victoria.
She bought Irma a spiral, red-and-white candle and a red pair of
slippers. For some reason she couldn't explain, the thought of Irma

wearing her red slippers and watching the candy-cane candle glow at the same time made her laugh out loud in the store. The nervous, uncontrollable laughter was not appreciated by the girl at the cash register, who frowned at Gracey, jerking her credit card from her shaking, outstretched fingers.

That night, opening each other's gifts in front of the Christmas tree, Henry and Irma drank themselves into a stupor. Irma passed out, sitting on the toilet in the downstairs half bath. Henry woke Gracey up to help carry her to bed.

"Come on, Gracey. Help me get her to bed. She had a little too much Christmas cheer." Gracey followed her father down the hallway to the bathroom. Irma was a queen on the throne. Her snowman dangling earrings with miniature bells were silent against her ears. Her blue visor accented with a green rhinestone Christmas tree sat awry on the side of her head; a lone bobby pin kept it from falling into her lap.

"She's out like a light with her mouth wide open," Henry laughed.

Gracey wondered if she needed her dentures removed before being put in bed.

Do people sleep in dentures? What if she chokes on them? Dear God, please don't give me that job.

"Maybe I should get her some water," said Henry.

"Don't wake her, Dad. She needs her sleep." Gracey stifled a laugh. *Maybe she'll choke on her dentures in her sleep and the saga of Irma and Henry will be over . . .*

Months later, as winter turned into spring, and spring into another drought-filled summer in South Texas, Gracey lay alone in her childhood room, wondering why Henry loved Irma more than her mother.

There we all were waiting for her to take her last breath, and he walks away; walks away leaving his children to pick up the pieces. And we did, just like we always do.

The house was very quiet as she strained to hear any sounds

downstairs or outside the bedroom window. There was nothing but her loneliness. No one was talking. No one was playing music. No one was sitting on the back porch, drinking coffee and smoking cigarettes.

"I guess I got what I wanted," she said out loud and rose from the bed. She found the prescription bottle in her purse. She swallowed two bullets of indifference without water and prayed for a dreamless sleep.

But the dreams came.

She dreamt of her mother, younger than Gracey could remember her. Her hair was black, her eyes soft and brown. The angry, deep crease in her forehead and the anxiety of over-plucked eyebrows had not found her yet. She was dressed in a nylon slip and thin white cotton house shoes that slapped against the linoleum kitchen floor. She stopped at the kitchen sink, dried her hands on a dish towel and looked at Gracey.

"Gracey, try to forgive your father and allow yourself to love him. It's all that really matters, honey. Forgive him and you'll be able to let go of the pain."

When Gracey's alarm from her cell phone went off, she fought the urge to get out of bed and start the day. She wanted to go back to sleep. Maybe she would find her mother in another dream.

"Mama, I'm so lost," she whispered in the dark room.

Chapter Four
Baby Girl

Groggy from the sleeping pills, Gracey made a pot of strong coffee and boiled two eggs for breakfast. She sat at the kitchen table holding the coffee mug and staring out the window until the ringing telephone hanging on the kitchen wall jarred her back to reality.

"Mom, how are you?" asked Therese, her twenty-seven-year-old daughter. "I'm sorry you're there by yourself. If I were still in the States, we could have driven together."

Mark must have called the children. I wonder how much she knows. She really doesn't need this burden.

"Hi, baby. I'm okay. You shouldn't feel bad. We all knew this day would come. How are things going with the wedding? I did get the invitations mailed before I came."

"Daniel made the deposit for the reception at Darver. It's expensive, but we both love it. Y'all will, too. Google it. It's near Dundalk. I'm looking at the menu now. Maybe you can help me with the American list and any special diet foods they need. I know Grandma has been on the gluten-free kick for a while. But, we really got it, Mom. Don't worry about any of it right now."

"Everything sounds beautiful. It's not any work for me to help with the wedding, Therese. Actually, it takes my mind off of things here."

"You sound so sad, Mom. I hate this for you."

"That's life. It's something we all have to face sooner or later. I don't know how I could change it or make it any easier. I think you have to get through it, live through it. You know, strength through adversity."

"Right. Well, I'll call you in a couple of days to see how you're doing. Daniel says hello. We're all looking forward to a happier time for the family, Mom. We'll be in good form then."

She never mentioned her grandfather, Gracey thought as she hung up the phone. Her daughter's life was no longer in the States.

Therese met an Irishman her second year of law school at the University of Mississippi, and life changed for all of them. Daniel Martin of County Armagh, Northern Ireland was making his way through the interior of the state, studying organic tomato farming as part of an agricultural exchange between farmers in the US and Europe. His travel plans included the small farms in Lafayette and Panola counties. That travel itinerary changed when he met Therese Reiter in the Blind Pig Pub in Oxford. Her first words to him became part of their story, they told together, for the rest of their lives.

"Where are you from with that accent?" Therese asked, interrupting his conversation with another coed in the pub.

He turned around to answer and saw a 5'6" American girl wearing a tee shirt with a whale on it and the caption underneath reading SAVE THE HUMANS. Her hair was plaited into two chestnut braids. She wore a pair of blue jean cut-offs and white huarache sandals on her feet. Her eyes were the color of the summer sky.

"Ireland."

For the first two months of the relationship, Gracey listened to her daughter's stories of Daniel without worrying it would progress beyond fascination between two people from two very different cultures. She knew the heartache would eventually come for her daughter, and the Irishman would be a memory of a love she once knew. The miles between them would destroy the fragile novelty they held for each other.

Therese never feared the relationship wouldn't last. After a year of transatlantic flights and working waitressing jobs on the weekend to cover the airfare, Therese would not let go. Gracey began to worry.

With trepidation, Gracey told her friends and relatives about the relationship. It was easy to assume they had met at school and he was a foreign exchange student, but to believe he was an organic farmer in Ireland was difficult for a culture that based its world views on cable news and elementary-level geography lessons.

Most of her friends didn't believe her. The whispers droned in Gracey's small circle.

"Hey, girl." Wanda Kidd stopped her one Sunday morning before Mass at St. Patrick Catholic Church.

"How are you doing, Wanda?"

"Better than you, I suppose. I've heard the news about Therese. Good Lord, it can't be true, such a nice girl."

Gracey froze and prepared herself for the assault.

"Saw Beth Richton last night at Winn Dixie. Your daughter is moving to Greece and working in an import business, I hear."

"No, my daughter is moving to Ireland, Wanda. And, wrong again, she's working for a solicitor." Gracey had a quick visual of Therese hoisting barrels of smuggled diesel for the Eurozone on the back of a fishing boat. The captain of the vessel looked a lot like Anthony Quinn with one hand in a massive jar of olives and the other on the ship's wheel, pitching recklessly in the surf off a Greek isle.

"I knew there was an Ireland connection, but I must have gotten it all mixed up. Any who, it's been on the news almost every night how the Eurozone was a big mistake. All those people looking for a handout from the Germans. Smuggling drugs and diesel into Dublin. Don't be so proud, girl. We've been friends a long time. I can talk some sense into that daughter of yours. Keep her from throwing her life away."

"Thanks, Wanda. I appreciate your sincere concern for my family." Gracey turned quickly, searching for a pew. She left Wanda standing with her mouth open and two fingers dipped in holy water at the entrance stoup.

Two days later, her next door neighbor, seventy-two-year-old

Judy Doran, approached her, when both women were gardening in their front yards.

"Are they still blowing each other up over what church they attend?" Judy hollered over at Gracey, as she was bending over in her front flower bed, dividing daylilies for transplanting.

"I think Bill Clinton helped them with that a few decades ago," Gracey dead panned.

"Are you sure? Those people tried to blow up the Queen a few years ago."

"Judy, Irish Republican militants tried to blow up Margaret Thatcher in 1984. As for the Queen, she finally apologized to the Irish for centuries of servitude and ethnic cleansing."

"Now, Grace, I know you're worried about Therese and the rash decisions she is making, but don't ignore the facts," Judy said, pointing her gardening spade at Gracey. "I hope to God she keeps her citizenship to the United States of America."

"Right," Gracey replied, remembering what Henry had taught her as a child. 'Don't get into a mud-slinging contest with a pig. You'll wind up with mud all over you and the pig will love it,' sayeth Henry, The Wise.

Funny how that has stayed with me all these years. I've got to change the subject here before I tell Judy what I really think. Why am I surrounded by crazy old women thinly disguised as caring friends?

"Where are you moving those daylilies, Judy?"

The first time Gracey talked to her sister about her daughter's Irish lover, Angela laughed. "You would have a daughter marry an Irishman into organic farming and free range ranching. Sis, it's going to be a great wedding, but it's a long way to travel to see your girl."

Gracey didn't quite understand how this situation was typical behavior for her family. She was too afraid to ask her sister to explain. She was grateful, however, for Angela's kindness. It was typical of Angela to be generous in her love. She greeted each stage of the relationship as a huge event that called for celebration.

Angela was the perfect hostess for Therese's wedding shower. The food was Gulf Coast gourmet: blue crab cakes, Royal Red Shrimp, and fresh oysters on the half shell served on chilled silver platters. The guests drank champagne and California wines. Individual desserts were delivered on a tea cart, pushed to the many white linen tables floating around the guests sitting in the terraced back yard.

"I wish you wouldn't have gone to so much trouble," Gracey had offered.

"Therese's my niece. She's my family. I love her. It's really that simple, Gracey." Angela said while paying the servers at the end of the evening. Her hair, her make-up, the scent on her skin, all were perfect, elegant, expensive.

"You've always been like that, Angela. So giving to the family. You enjoy it, too. You're just open with your love," Gracey said, feeling a tightness in her own heart, realizing Angela was everything she wasn't.

Oh I gave, I worked for all of them at one time or another, but I didn't give with a smile on my face. I gave because it was just another obligation to fulfill.

"Well, Sis, it's going to be a great wedding. Each day gets us closer to the big event. "

Gracey greeted each day as a day closer to losing her daughter. The countdown she kept in her heart began the day she met Daniel Martin.

The Reiter family's initial meeting with Daniel was in Therese's tiny student apartment in Oxford. When Gracey, Will, and Mark left the hotel to drive over to the apartment, Gracey tripped over the parking curb, skinned both knees, and began crying.

"I'm such a wreck."

"Mom," said Will, reaching to help her up.

At 6'4", twenty-five-year-old Will was always first to help her and encourage her, but also the first in the family to challenge her. With his sandy blond hair and green eyes, he had inherited his father's looks and brilliance, but his heart was generous and proud like the Mueller's.

"Get hold of yourself," he said before opening the truck door for her. "You can't meet this guy with red eyes. Do you want me to take you for a drink before we go over there? I'll send Therese a text that we're running late."

Mark sat behind the steering wheel in the truck, watching his son and wife.

"Grace, you don't have to do this right now," he said giving her a nervous glance.

"No, I'm all right. I think this is it. I didn't realize she was really this age, and I'm really 'this age.' It's too much for me right now."

The three of them piled into the cab of Mark's truck and drove to Therese's apartment.

Therese and Daniel opened the door when they knocked. They were all facing each other. He, with black Irish hair and blue eyes, and her daughter, in braids, tee shirt, and yoga pants.

Gracey extended her hand to him for a friendly, yet non-committal shake.

You'll get no hug from me. You gotta earn that. Look at him sweat! I've never seen anyone sweat like that in my entire life. Wonder if he even realizes he is taking my little flower away, my little Therese.

Unfamiliar to paying attention when most people talked, a residual effect of early menopause, Gracey strained every nerve in her body to hear Daniel. Not only because he was speaking so fast, but every word out of his mouth was a matter of life or death to her.

Mark pulled Gracey into the kitchen. "What the hell is he saying? He's talking too fast. Keeps saying something about the pissin' rain."

"It's a general statement on the weather, Mark. Watch his lips. You'll pick up what he's saying."

"How do we know this guy isn't with the IRA? Tell him I have a high level security clearance. The Feds are going to investigate him before he even leaves this apartment. It will all come out who he really is and what he wants from us."

"For God's sake! He doesn't want anything from us. He's in

love with our daughter, and she's in love with him. What was she supposed to do, wait until one of the rednecks or frat daddies hit her over the head with a beer bottle and dragged her back into the cave? She's not a little girl anymore. Let it take its course."

"I know that, Gracey, but it's mistakes of this proportion that can ruin her life."

She turned around and faced him.

"Why don't you ask him if he'd like a beer?"

Will walked into the kitchen and stared at both of them.

"Really?" said Will. "I'm going to the store and buying every kind of meat they have and grilling it on the patio. We're going to eat, drink, and be merry. You two are going to chill."

Later that night with plates of barbeque balanced on their knees, they sat in front of the television watching the New Orleans Saints toss the Baltimore Ravens off the field.

The following May with an engagement ring on her finger and a juris doctorate diploma in her suitcase, Therese said goodbye to Mark and Gracey at the airport.

"Don't be sad, Mom. I love you and Dad so much, but it's time for me to have my own life. For the last five years, I kept thinking when is it going to happen for me? When am I going to meet a wonderful person, and that person is going to think that I'm wonderful, too? When you see how he lives and meet his family, you'll understand. It's finally my turn to be happy. Please be happy for me."

All Gracey could think was how small and young Therese looked.

"Therese, you tell him you won't wait forever for a wedding date. Irish men are like that. I've read it on the Internet. They've been known to be engaged to women for over ten years."

"Mom. It'll be all right."

"If it isn't, you make sure he understands what you mean to us. That we love you. If I had to, if you needed me, I could swim to Ireland, then run all the way to County Armagh. I could do it in a heartbeat for you."

"I know that, Mom. I've always known that," Therese said, kissing her mother and hugging her father before walking away.

Therese walked through the security clearance at the airport. She didn't look back. Suddenly, twenty-seven years were gone forever.

"What would make her do this?" Gracey said.

"The same reason why you married a poor man who was thousands of dollars in debt with school loans. There was actually a time when we didn't think we could live without each other," said Mark, walking away from her.

They drove home in silence.

Gracey spent the night trying to understand why her only daughter chose the life she did. She knew it was more than the allure of Ireland with its wild beauty and pastoral life. She knew somewhere in those years of raising her, she had planted a seed in her daughter's mind.

"You are worth so much more than that, Therese," she'd whispered to her when she was a girl, hurt from the disappointments of friends and the small injuries of a middle class American girl. "You are worth this world, and it is a very big world with many, many people who will love you for you. Don't be afraid to be yourself. The cowards of the world will hate you for it, but the freedom you will gain in self-respect will open many doors."

Therese found that world in a village in Ireland. It was a world where women were allowed to grow old, where their worth was so much more than their bra size or the purse they carried. Therese was escaping America's culture famine. Not so unlike her Grandmother Walsh Mueller, who escaped the Irish famine of the 1840s. Therese, like her grandmother, wanted more than to endure or exist; she wanted to live.

The ancestral blood that moved through Therese's veins set her course, like it had done for her grandmothers before her. They were women who loved without the fear of loss.

For months after Therese's leaving, Gracey sat in the kitchen at night, staring at the blackness outside, knowing it was morning for her daughter. She wondered if the night before had been one of perfect sleep and happiness for her.

"Why, God, why is it so hard to let her go?" Gracey cried to the kitchen walls.

Chapter Five
Eire, Oh Eire

Gracey and Mark sat in a bar in the international terminal at JFK airport waiting to board the plane for Dublin. She hadn't seen her daughter in four months. Telephone calls and Skype viewings failed to relieve her anxiety. She had to touch her. She had to smell her. She had to breathe the very air her daughter did to know the world was still spinning on its axis, and she would not simply fly off into another galaxy, never to be found again.

"Here, birthday girl. I got you some champagne," Mark said, handing her a champagne flute.

"Thanks. I was thinking . . ." Gracey said, taking the glass from him. "How many people do you think actually immigrate to Northern Ireland in a year compared to the thousands that come here? Maybe half of a percent? Why is our daughter that half of a percent? We're all immigrants in this world, if you really want to think about it."

"Come on, Grace, this trip could be fun. Seeing Therese and celebrating your fiftieth should make you happy. Relax a little."

"There's nothing fun about turning fifty, Mark. But I do appreciate you trying to convince me. You know, this trip to Ireland is the first of many, for the rest of our lives. We can't even get a direct flight from Gulfport to Dublin. We've been through three airports already, and we still have the Atlantic to cross. How are we going to do this when we're eighty?"

"Why don't you concentrate on being fifty right now?"

Mark replied, ordering his second cocktail right as the gate agent announced first-class boarding.

"We're next. Hurry up with your drink." Gracey swallowed the rest of the champagne in a single gulp followed by heartburn. "Now, where's the boarding pass?"

Once boarded, she removed her shoes, chewed two antacids, and clutched her rosary beads in her fist.

"Guess we're flying the friendly skies with Jesus today," Mark said.

"Is that supposed to be a joke or a smart-alecky remark? So hard to figure out an engineer's sense of humor," replied Gracey.

Mark laughed, patting her thigh next to his.

"Try to get some sleep, Grace. When you wake up, you'll be in Ireland with your daughter."

What Mark and Gracey found in Ireland was what their daughter found earlier, a beautiful life. They spent their days in Forkhill walking in the summer rain that fell in every direction, only to be chased by the sun twenty minutes later. The country lanes with hedgerows and summer roses crowded the tiny paths, taking them to the farms and homes of Daniel's family. They were greeted with smiles and a chair close to the fire, though the host and hostess were sweating in the sixty-degree temperature of a June night. Every comfort for their Southern guests was considered. The craic was good.

The food and drink offered was of a Thanksgiving abundance. Irish beef, root vegetables, and potatoes served three ways—mashed, roasted, and boiled—crowded the kitchen table with a strawberry-rhubarb pie served with fresh cream for dessert. The nights were long in the Irish summer and filled with laughter.

Every evening during her visit, Gracey ended the day with a cup of tea with Therese. The mother and daughter sat on the couch together, facing a small coal-lit fire. Mark and Daniel brought the cows into the barn from the pasture, giving the two women a chance to be alone.

"You're happy here. It's so easy to see," Gracey said, adding a splash of milk to her cup of tea.

"He makes me happy, Mom. It's a good life. If I'd stayed in the states, I'd be working as a junior lawyer for some firm, putting in a sixty-hour week, trying to justify my existence with the ability to buy a $1,500 purse."

"I know. You don't have to explain it to me. You chose happiness over status quo."

"You're still my mother, even if Ireland is my home. I'm not going to forget you and Dad. You shouldn't ever let that be a worry."

"Honey, I know that, too," said Gracey, reaching over to enfold Therese's hands in hers.

The mother and daughter heard the fence gate close at the road and knew the men were done with their work. Gracey squeezed her daughter's hand.

"I'm glad I came, Therese. It's been one of the best weeks of my life."

The next morning, Mark and Gracey stood in line at the Dublin Airport waiting to check their baggage for the return flight to the States.

"Therese found the life I dreamed of as a girl," Gracey said, packing her sweater in her carry-on bag. "The house, the farm animals, and Daniel. Mark, he's crazy in love with her. That's all we get in this. We get to see her happy. And you know . . . that's enough for me. It's enough to help me live with the pain of missing her every single day for the rest of my life."

"I already miss her," Mark said, removing his shoes to go through the X-ray security portal, but Gracey didn't hear him. She was thinking of someone else, someone who would never see Ireland.

Henry loved to tell stories about the Irish side of the family. All his stories about Grandma Walsh meeting Grandpa Mueller. He was the sole heir of the family Bible, Grandma Walsh's Bible . . . two hundred years of prayers and tears in that Bible. Two hundred years of a chaotic family history began with an Irish girl, Patricia Walsh of County Galway, Ireland.

Chapter Six
Trading Fate

Fourteen-year-old Patricia Walsh, her mother, father, and six siblings, scratched out a living in the stone fields of County Galway, Ireland.

Colum Walsh supported the family as a stone mason building estate structures and repairing the fences of an Anglo-Irish landlord. He rented a windowless cottage with a patch of wet, black dirt his wife and children dug in, producing their only crop, potatoes.

The family had always known the anxiety of hunger. His wife birthed their first son in 1831, the fourth year of the food shortages in Galway. When the second son came in 1842, there were food riots in the city. When their last child, a daughter, was born in 1845, the first potato crop failed.

"I swear, Aileen, they was loading potatoes at the docks today. Potatoes, grain, sheep, I seen it with my own eyes. You can't buy a potato in Galway, but crate upon crate was loaded at the dock for England. Red coats and our own people holding loaded guns on us, like we was bank robbers, common thieves, daring us to come any closer to the boat. Our own people, Aileen. Feckless fools. There'll be blood on their hands as sure as they pulled the trigger. Shipping food out, food raised by Irishmen, the same men starving in the streets like dogs."

"Don't fight them, Colum. Stay away from the docks. I hear talk leaving Mass on Sunday, people are stealing to get arrested and fed a meal in jail. Criminals, we'll all be, God help us. The Fever Hospital on Beggar's Bridge won't take any more. There be no empty beds for the dying. People lying about the steps there and in the streets, dying of the hunger. What will winter bring? Ah, the miseries." Aileen placed one-year-old Bridget to her breast, silently praying her body would produce enough milk for the child, although Aileen hadn't eaten in a day.

By 1847, the unholy trinity of cholera, typhoid fever, and dysentery raged across the countryside, leaving a hundred wasted bodies a week in the streets of Galway. Those who survived the fevers, were tortured by the hunger. "Where's God?" they cried in the street.

Over seven thousand were fed each day in the soup kitchens of the Protestants, Dominicans, Convent of Mercy, St. Vincent's Convent, and the Monastery School. The irony of receiving "Daily Bread" from the churches of Galway was lost on the parishioners, listless and hallucinating from days without food.

"I'll be more than a Cottiee, Aileen! I swear to Our Lady, I'll not dig my children's graves in the rotting soil of Ireland. There's no money to be had, and I won't wait to be evicted and turned on the road with the others. My family worked for the Stokes for as long as we've been here, my father and grandfather toiling for them. Our blood and sweat made them rich. They owe us . . . they owe us our lives."

"You're a bold man, Colum Walsh! There's nothing for us from the likes of them. Let the Devil take William Stokes. Don't you be starting any trouble."

William Stokes, the owner of the land and the people starving on it, was more than willing to remove the carriers of pestilence from his family's land. Two exit routes secured the family name and land for generations to come—bury the dead and launch the half dead to America. It cost him nine tickets on a freight ship leaving Dublin for New York. To ensure the clan would never return to Galway, William Stokes invented a cousin in America, who eagerly awaited the family for employment and housing on his cotton plantation near Charleston, South Carolina. For 600 shillings and a lie, Colum Walsh was removed from Ireland forever;

the bones of his father, grandfather, and great-grandfather cried out from their shallow graves on the Stokes Estate.

The family of nine walked to Dublin, eating molded bread and stolen eggs. What they found waiting for them on Dublin's Docklands only Satan could conjure. The begging children, the schoolgirl prostitutes, the aged and dying, the staggering drunks—together, a slow moving mass of ragged people clamoring, clawing, and scratching their way to the freight ships like a massive grey shroud from hell.

What Colum Walsh, his wife and seven children received for the portal to the land of milk and honey, was third class accommodations on a coffin ship sailing under the Union Jack. Colum, his daughter, Bridget, and his five-year-old son, Michael, were dead within the first ten days. Typhus, carried by the lice-infected straw used for bedding by the third-class passengers, took their last breath. In the delirium of his raging fever, Colum begged to go home.

"My Mam. Mam is calling me. She's calling me home. I can swim to her, Aileen, if you help me, I can swim home to Ireland."

Their burial at sea was held in the faint morning light with the receiving Atlantic rowing beneath them. A third mate positioned the three corpses, wrapped in canvass with weights attached to their feet. The plank was raised. A sound. Bubbles. The black ocean swallowed them whole. Aileen and her five children returned to the bowels of the ship, cold, wet, and hungry.

The surviving members of the Walsh family moved through the immigration process dripping in disease. Quarantined in New York Harbor, they eventually made their way to South Carolina, where work, housing, and plentiful food awaited them.

The last of William Stokes' money took them to the docks of Charleston. But no one there on the docks knew of a cotton plantation west of town or a man named Magnus Stokes.

Sleeping in an abandoned shed near the docks and eating fish soup with the heads and spines of gutted flounder, the family was starving to death. Aileen Walsh's prayers remained unanswered.

She did not find God in America. Instead, she found the

same human story she had left in Ireland, men fighting for a wage and women fighting to feed their children.

In the public houses on Broad Street, she approached men gathered for beer and local news. She could clean. Her three sons had strong backs. Her daughters could cook. A fair wage for a day's work was an extravagance. A sack of rice stolen from the docks and a bucket of fish guts for soup were the reality.

The sympathy of drunks fed her children for a month. But she knew it would not last. Each bite of food she begged from strangers brought the ghost closer and closer to her. It was her dead husband, Colum Walsh, crying to her from the Atlantic, pleading that his life had not been lived in vain.

She heard there was a group of sympathetic Ulster Scots-Irishmen at the newly built Hibernia Hall in town. She took the only two possessions she had left, her husband's gold watch and her wedding band, and sold them for $50 to a merchant at the Hibernia Hall.

She walked back to the shed her children were huddled in and gave her oldest daughter the money.

"There'll be no work for you here, girl. You take this and you get yourself onboard a boat that leaves tomorrow for Texas. You'll take Ana Grace. She is young, but a good worker. They tell me there's work for Irish girls as scullery maids in the new hotels and boarding houses. The Germans are going to Texas now. They'll have plenty money to build houses and farms. God be with you, Patricia. Be a good girl."

The next morning Patricia and her seven-year-old sister boarded a three-masted sailing vessel leaving for Galveston. Her final destination would be Indian Point on Matagorda Bay. Nearly eighty miles from Corpus Christi, the small port sat on a peninsula separated from the Gulf of Mexico, where the mouths of the Lavaca and Colorado rivers fed the adjoining coastal flat lands.

She waved goodbye to her mother and three brothers on the docks of Charleston. She grabbed Ana Grace's hand and held it tightly in hers as the ship pulled from the dock. Her last image of her family was four figures in rags with hunched shoulders walking toward the lean-to shed. She would never see nor hear from them again.

Patricia did not find a town or even a village when she

landed in Indian Point. Her view from the bow of the boat was of mud, wagons stuck in mud, and a clapboard building with a sign reading HOTEL rising from the mud. Even the water was muddy. The town looked nothing like Charleston. From as far as she could see, people were loading wagons and walking in mud, leaving Indian Point as fast as they could.

"Hold my hand, Ana. I don't want someone to take you."

The two sisters walked hand-in-hand to the hotel. Beside it, people stood on the porch of the small post office with letters and packages in hand. The only package Patricia held was hidden within the folds of her coat. She patted it quickly to make sure it was still there. It was the only thing of value the sisters owned—a loaf of bread wrapped in a dirty cloth. Stolen from the ship's galley the night before, the third mate handed it to Patricia before they landed at the tiny port town.

The feel of it beneath her coat reminded Patricia there would be nothing to eat after the bread was gone. She gripped her sister's hand tightly and pulled her close to her as they stood in front of the hotel.

"Ana, we've no money at all, at all. We will ask for work here. To be sure, tis our only chance. Don't be afraid. God will provide. I won't ever leave your side, but you must be brave. Do not let them see you cry."

"They won't see me cry. I'll be good."

Patricia smiled at her sister, whose frail body of less than four feet, covered in tattered cloth, once resembling a dress, trembled next to her. There was no color in her small, pale face. But her eyes, they were as deep and blue as the ocean that held their father.

"That's my girl. Now smile and hold my hand. I will take care of us. That will never be a concern of yours."

In exchange for cleaning, the two sisters were given food and a quilt to sleep on in the hotel kitchen by the owner's wife, Mary Elizabeth Ott. The Otts built their hotel and general store when they landed in Indian Point three years earlier.

The Otts were part of an immigration plan by a German prince who brought artisans and peasants to the Texas frontier by way of Galveston and Indian Point. Briefly called Karlshafen by the Germans, the initial port of Indian Point, was the beginning of a western journey for the new immigrants into the hilly and rocky terrain surrounding San Antonio and Austin.

The royal courtier and soldier, Prince Carl of Solms Braunfels and fellow European nobility attempted to create a new Fatherland within the Texas wilderness. Their Adelsverein Society purchased land and negotiated land grants from the Republic of Texas to establish colonies.

The new immigrants would build "new crowns to old glory" for generations to come. The carefully chosen words of nobility never spoke of the hellish summer heat or lack of rain fall in their new Germany. There were no paper notices of elegant script describing the Karankawa, Apache, and Tonkawa Indians fearing death of their culture and starvation. No one wrote about the bandits who stole livestock and children. Their nightly raids into the newly built homes and farms of immigrants resounded with horror.

But, that is the immigrant's story. The cruelest of lies is to plant hope in the desperate. As it was for Colum and Patricia Walsh, and the thousands before and after them leaving one misery to encounter another. The Germans and the daughters of Colum and Patricia Walsh would survive or die trying.

The Germans built a life in Texas with their bare hands, one farm, one house, one school at a time. Across the hills of Central Texas, their work was accomplished without slave labor; a principle that would see many of them hanged from trees and murdered by mobs once the new Fatherland was bloodied by the Civil War.

But the first night two Irish girls slept in Texas, a year-long nightmare ended with full stomachs and fitful sleep. They laid on the cotton quilt placed near the kitchen stove in the hotel. They held hands and whispered to each other in the dark at the good fortune they had found in the fine establishment owned by the Otts.

Mrs. Ott made them plates of hot food, with steam rising above the mounds of pinto beans and pieces of fried venison back strap. The bread she served was yellow and sweet, almost like a cake. The girls had never tasted corn and surely never a bread called corn bread. They swallowed it down quickly and drank glasses of fresh cow's milk. It was their first taste of milk since before the food riots in Galway several years ago.

They were given a bucket of hot water and a bar of soap. Patricia washed her sister's body, carefully, lovingly. The miles of travel, the nights of hunger, the days of fear were removed by her hand and the soap. On the kitchen table, two nightgowns made from flour sacks were folded neatly. They were Mrs. Ott's. The girls fell into the clean, soft cloth, twisting the material around, and around, like a cocoon under the quilt.

"We must say our prayers, Ana. We'll pray for Mr. and Mrs. Ott, as well. Surely, they be saints."

The two sisters spoke the words they had been taught by their mother long ago in a place they hadn't the heart to remember.

"Hail Mary, full of grace. The Lord is with thee.
Blessed art thou amongst women,
and blessed is the fruit of thy womb, Jesus.

Holy Mary, Mother of God,
pray for us sinners,
now and at the hour of our death. Amen.

"Blessed Virgin, we pray our mother and brothers know the good fortune we have found in Texas. We thank you for the Ott family and ask you to bless them." Patricia made the sign of the cross and pulled her sister's small frame next to her. She slept deeply, neither dreaming nor trembling from fear.

Spring came to the little port. With it came more immigrants, buildings, and hope for the future. In time, Indian Point became Indianola, the seat of Calhoun County. A stagecoach service, hospital, newspaper, and churches replaced the outpost, and the resemblance of a civilized community brought the joys of daily routine to the two sisters. Patricia and Ana Grace had a home. They belonged to a town. People knew them by name. Only in their hearts were they the orphan girls from Ireland.

They worked long hours at the Indianola Hotel, serving

the German immigrants who seemed to come by the hundreds as the ships came weekly from Galveston. In time, a New Yorker would bring a steamship line to Matagorda Bay, covering three miles from the beach to Powerhorn Bayou. Indianola was quickly becoming Galveston's rival as Texas' leading port.

That spring brought twenty-two-year-old Emil Mueller, a first-generation Texan from German parents in Houston, over a hundred miles away. Working for the Neue Welt Transportation Company, Emil led a wagon train for the Germans, moving to the settlements of New Braunfels and Sisterdale, nearly fifty miles outside of Austin and San Antonio.

Over six feet tall with broad shoulders, blond hair and blue eyes, Emil noticed the two sisters with black hair and pale skin. They appeared frail in comparison to the Germans and Mexicans working in the town. The youngest smiled at the customers in the dining room, but the older girl was more reserved. She was quick to scold her sister in the hallway if she became too familiar with the hotel guests.

"What's your name, girl?' he asked, when the youngest girl filled his glass with water in the dining room of the small hotel.

"Ana Grace, sir."

"A pretty name for a girl a long way from home, yes." He handed her a stick of hard candy from his waistcoat pocket.

"Thank you, sir. My home is across the ocean. It takes many, many days, months and months to go there. I be from County Galway, Ireland."

"What's your sister's name?"

"Patricia Walsh." The child smiled at Emil, adding a rose of color to her pale skin. He gave her another stick of candy. He made a promise to himself that he'd learn more about the sisters when he returned from New Braunfels next month.

A month turned into a summer before the German-Texan would return to Indianola. By then the town had buried the little Irish girl with the black hair and blue eyes. Emil Mueller would never know the story of Ana Grace Walsh, and the eight years she fought to live the simplest of lives.

"It was terrible, so terrible, Emil," Mary Elizabeth Ott said, wiping her blistered hands across the front of her apron before writing his name in the hotel registry. "It was the Yellow Fever. We all knew it came off one of those boats from Galveston. They'd been burying their dead by the hundreds there. Horrible death, horrible. Townspeople wanted to quarantine the ships."

"It be the mounds of garbage and open sewer ditches they keep at the dock, Mary. That place is full of insects, mosquitos. It is death, itself. I saw it coming into town today. It's the laziness of men making us sick."

"Poor child. She was gone quickly, quickly. Her vomit was black. God help me. To see that sight, I'll not ever forget it."

"How long, Mary? Did she suffer long?"

"About three days. That white skin and blue eyes were lost forever. Yellow, yellow she was."

"Did she have a proper burial?"

"Yes, oh yes, the whole town came. We loved her, Emil. She was like a child to me. Like a baby. Her sister, poor girl, it was all I could do to keep her from jumping into the grave with her."

He stared at the woman. "The sister, Patricia Walsh. She's alone, now."

"Yes, heaven help her. Such a terrible, terrible tragedy for someone to know only hunger and death most of her young life. She still works here, works as hard as ever, but she talks to no one. Still lives here, too. Goes to bed each night without saying a word. Poor girl . . . those eyes of hers cast down all day long."

"Where did they bury the sister?"

"In the Indianola Cemetery. Back behind the hotel, no more than a mile. There's a little wooden fence around it. The gate is unlocked."

At the end of the day, when the stillness of the evening hours began with the falling of long shadows against the trees and buildings, Emil walked to the little cemetery.

He knew it was her grave from a distance. A small mound

of fresh earth rose from the grass. There was no cross or head stone for Ana Grace Walsh, but he knew she was there. Shaded by an oak tree bent by the winds off the Gulf of Mexico, she laid beneath a hand-picked blanket of Blue Bonnets and Indian paintbrushes.

He knelt on one knee.

"Father, your hand is heavy upon me. Teach me to understand your ways," Emil whispered into the finality of the grave. Rising, he sat beneath the oak tree until the evening's shadows turned into the faintest of stars in the infinite summer sky.

He slept lightly in the hotel bed that night. He could not stop thinking about the Irish sisters and the briefness of Ana's life. He struggled with the harshness of Patricia's fate. She was a stranger to him, but he could not stop thinking of her.

He had been awake, sitting on the edge of the bed when the roosters crowed at the light of day. He knew what he would do; he was only waiting for the world to awake, so he could begin his work.

She was standing in the back of the hotel dining room. A pot of coffee was in one hand and a flour sack cloth rested across the other.

"Morning."

"Coffee, sir?"

Patricia never met Emil's eyes.

"Yes, eggs and biscuits, as well. I'll be leaving for a few days. Is the mistress around?"

"I'll get her, sir." Patricia returned his question with her eyes fixated on the floor. Realizing another task was asked of her, she quickly turned and left the room. He watched her and thought, *Is it possible that she could be thinner than when I last saw her?*

"Good morning, Emil."

"I want you to keep my room. I'm going to Houston. I'll be back in two days."

"That's a hard ride for two days."

"Keep the room." He handed her two silver dollar coins from his vest pocket.

"No need for that. Your word is good."

"Take it, Mary. Give the girl something to eat besides beans and cornbread. I can see her bones through her dress."

Emil rode the hundred miles to Houston. He stopped the thundering in the horse's chest and his heart when he saw the banks of Buffalo Bayou. Man and beast drank from the grass and mud banks in frenzied gulps.

He tied the horse to a willow tree and sat on the bank of the bayou. When he was a child, he swam with Mexican children whose fathers and mothers worked the large farms west of the bayou. His boyhood summers were spent throwing rocks at the alligators seeking shade under the willows in the coolness of wet clay and mud. He smiled remembering the ease of those days. Language was not a barrier to the children who played on Buffalo Bayou. They were boys who only wanted to laugh and swim.

He stood up remembering the urgency of his adult life. At this distance, he could smell the new stockyards and slaughter-houses south of the muddy water. He saw store fronts and board-ing houses rising from the grass and mud. It was not the same place of his childhood. There was too much money to be made in Houston for it to remain small.

Once a capital for the Republic of Texas, Houston was quickly becoming a working man's town. When the Republic President Sam Houston lost the politically charged archive war, and the Republic's documents were moved to Austin, the city's fate was sealed. Austin became the state capital when the Republic was annexed to the US in 1845, and Houston became an interna-tional site of commerce.

Sam Houston's vision of capital buildings and congressio-nal libraries were replaced by investors' saw mills, slaughterhouses, iron foundries, and cotton warehouses. The Germans followed with skilled labor, mercantile store fronts, and churches.

Emil walked with his horse to the church on Congress. He was one of the first German-Texans to be baptized there. He spent considerable time praying in the stone building with his mother and father, along with other German immigrants. The hands that carved the limestone blocks of the East Dutch Evangeline Lutheran Church were some of the best stone masons of Germany. Their wives planted the rose gardens along the west lawn. These were his people and he'd always been able to come to them.

In a day, the small headstone was shaped and etched. It was made from white limestone brought by wagon from San Antonio. Emil wrapped it in a bolt of fabric he bought for Patricia. She would need a dress. He left Houston at daybreak with the stone tied to his saddle horn. His one free hand held it steady for the long ride back to Indianola.

After two days pushing the horse across prairie, marshes, and creeks, he arrived in the port town. An early summer rain from the night before patted the dust and sand to a fine silt that covered the hotel's front porch.

He waited for Mary Elizabeth to come in from the kitchen.

"You give this to the girl. Tell her I will place the headstone when she is ready."

"Emil," Mary Elizabeth whispered, pushing the cloth from the stone. "The color . . . so pure, so white. It's like snow. What is written? Let me see." She wiped her hands on her apron before picking up the stone.

Just as the Morning of her Life was Opening into Day,
Her Young and Lovely Spirit Passed From Earth and Grief Away.

Ana Grace Walsh
County Galway, Ireland

The woman accustomed to life in an immigrant outpost and the cruelties of watching people with nothing die with nothing, cried without restraint. Mary Elizabeth Ott's tears dissolved into the white stone as quickly as they fell.

As Patricia knelt at her sister's grave with one small white hand upon the headstone, Emil knew his heart would never be his own.

He loved her beyond anything or anyone he had ever known. The new dress, the thick, black plait of hair that fell to the center of her back quickened his breath. The colors within her face, the blistered, red lips and the deep blue eyes set against white skin, caused him pain with its stark beauty.

Emil made a solemn promise that day in the cemetery. *I will keep her near me for the rest of my life. She'll never suffer again.*

A month later the German-Texan and the Irish girl were married at St. Mary Catholic Church in Calhoun County. The husband and wife were moving to Jackson County, near Lavaca Bay, where the sister rivers of the Lavaca and Navidad joined hands.

An Irishman had obtained a Mexican land grant in the Red Bluff community of Jackson County. The land was good for cotton and running cattle. Gone were the Indians, pushed farther west. Many Anglos were moving there, starting small farms and ranches.

There would be no flood waters in Red Bluff. The town was named for the russet clay bluff towering nearly 100 feet above the Navidad River. Emil purchased thirty acres of land on the east bank of the river. He was determined to build a future for Patricia without the past.

But the memories of Ireland and Indianola followed his wife wherever she went. She would never forgive herself for leaving her sister behind in a graveyard.

The white headstone of Ana Grace was never meant to last, nor was the town of Indianola. The bones of the little Irish girl were washed to sea on August 20, 1886, when a 150 mph hurricane made landfall. What the howling winds did not blow away, a fifteen-foot storm surge from Matagorda Bay drowned. To ensure all traces of man were swept clean from the port city forever, a fire roared through the remaining buildings, trapping citizens in two-story structures and burning them alive. The recently built school by the Sisters of Mercy of New Orleans disappeared in a frenzy of wind and water. All that remained of the town were snakes and bloated bodies hanging from broken trees.

In 1938 the state of Texas erected a granite monument on the sands of the lost city of Indianola. The French explorer La Salle stands forever on the beach he called Fort St. Louis in 1685. Absent from the monument are the dead of Indianola, the founding pioneers and immigrants who forged a brief life in the port town. Gone forever are the names of Mary Elizabeth Ott and Ana Grace Walsh.

Chapter Seven
Storm Warning

Gracey stood in front of the kitchen sink in her father's house in Loti. She rinsed her coffee cup and placed it in the plastic dish drain on the counter. She returned to the kitchen table to finish her breakfast, folding her legs underneath her in the chair. She picked up a boiled egg on a saucer next to her great-great-grandmother's Bible. She ate the egg and stared at the open Bible that revealed a dog-eared page and the Walsh-Mueller family tree. A small linen handkerchief, yellowed with age and marked with the embroidered initial M, laid next to the Bible.

Patricia. Patricia Walsh. Just a little Irish girl set adrift in the world . . . Poor, dear Grandma. Too much loss for anyone to bear, despite Grandpa's love. Can't believe this little jewel has been tucked away in her Bible all these years. Gracey picked up the handkerchief and placed it in her open palm, moving her index finger slowly, lovingly against the black stitch of the M.

She sighed heavily and rose from the table. She closed the open Bible and placed it by her purse on the counter.

Maybe Grandma's intentions were to keep this handkerchief in her Bible until the day her granddaughter could take it home. Maybe she knew me somewhere in a dream or knew Therese . . . maybe she knew my name. I'm Ana Grace's namesake, Grandma. Your little sister hasn't been forgotten. You're not forgotten. We all live on in each other's heart. I'm taking your handkerchief to Ireland. I'll give it to my daughter on her wedding day. Your memory and your handkerchief will live in Forkhill.

Gracey grabbed the back of the kitchen chair with one hand and slid it underneath the table, then put both hands on her face, blocking out everything in front of her.

I've got to start this day. I need to find Henry's funeral policy and call Tom and Angela.

The lock turned on the back door, followed by a knock and a shrill, female voice shouting, "Yoo-hoo."

Gracey turned with a jolt toward the door, as Irma let herself in with her own key.

"I need to pick up a few things for Henry, before I head over to the hospital this mornin'," she announced, while surveying the kitchen counters, opening the refrigerator, and the cabinet doors to make sure nothing had been moved or taken in the last twenty-four hours. Her mouth formed a silent O when she noticed the pot pie tins, plastic tubs, and artificial sweetener packets were missing. She made her displeasure known by slamming the cabinet door closed.

"You're going to the hospital, now?" asked Gracey, ignoring Irma's strip search of her parents' home. "I'm moving slowly this morning. I need to check on some things, and then I'll head over."

"Did you check the mail?"

"No. I was too tired when I got in."

"I'll check it when I leave. Your father got Therese's wedding invitation before he went into the hospital. He wants to go. We talked about it. If he pulls out of this one, we're going together. He'll need me over there to help him."

"Well, OK, Irma. Do you and Dad have passports? It's not a matter of 'Yay! We're going' and then you arrive."

"I know that. That's why I am telling you now. If he pulls out of this, he is expecting you to take care of those things and get us both a ticket."

Gracey glared at her.

You're not worth $1,500 in airfare to me, Irma. Henry is dying, and typical of you, this is a ridiculous conversation. The one good thing that comes out of this mess is I'll never have to see you again. As for you, well, you'll move on to your next dying old man, hating his *children, and spending what little money he has left. It's been a good career path for you, old girl.*

Gracey looked directly at the old woman. "Sure, Irma, I'll look into that later on today."

Irma gave her a nod of approval and went upstairs to rummage through Henry's drawers, while Gracey stood at the kitchen sink, holding on to the countertop in a death grip, staring out the window.

Irma was back downstairs in a few minutes with a plastic Wal-Mart bag bulging with men's underwear, tee shirts, and white athletic socks—socks for a man with one foot who could no longer walk.

"I'll see you at the hospital," she said as she walked out the door. The house resonated for an hour with her voice. In its wake, the ghost of a family that once was moved through the empty rooms.

Gracey felt her mother's hand on her shoulder as she sat in front of Henry's desk, searching for the burial policy.

Mama, I don't want to manage this lost cause anymore.

In the massive roll top desk, she found her parents' marriage license, the children's report cards, Henry's military discharge papers, and Helen's birthday cards from her children stacked neatly in shoe boxes or arranged in folders.

Some folders were labeled in her father's handwriting. Some were labeled by her mother. She read the teacher's comments of the back of the report cards.

"Tom is a quiet boy who does very neat work." "Tom is a model citizen in the classroom."

Gracey noticed the days of absences on Tom's report cards. Some reported absences for five or six weeks with him returning within the last few weeks of the school year. She imagined these were days they spent with Viola or Helen's family in Louisiana.

Helen's brothers and sisters in Louisiana were the only relatives who didn't whisper to each other or exchange knowing looks when Tom and Gracey were dropped off with their paper bags of clothes for an unannounced visit.

Gracey's favorite aunt and uncle, Parrain and Tante Lovina, lived in a white asbestos siding house near a rice field southwest of Lafayette. She thought of them and the times she spent there as a child.

"Eat your rice and gravy and pray the Rosary before you go to bed, Boo" *were the words they said to me every day I spent with them. They were happy people. Happy in tending their garden in the backyard near the clothesline and Parrain's Jon Boat. Happy pulling weeds in the front flower bed with a statue of Mary by the mail box. They were happy to be alive and have each other.*

That enamel coffee pot of Tante Lovina's boiling on the stove and Parrain's pouch of Bugle Boy on his lap, ready to roll a smoke on the porch. To come from a home where I expected the bottom to drop out any minute . . . their home, how they lived, the way they loved me . . . it saved me.

She continued rummaging through the stacks of papers in Henry's desk. She found her report cards. There was nothing unusual. She might have been too young for a record noting the absences, the separation of a child from her mother and father.

There would be time to tell her what happened during those years once she was older, although she would never be old enough to understand the reasons why. There would be plenty of townspeople and relatives to tell her for the rest of her life—decades of Helen's daily confession of an unforgiveable sin and Henry's alcohol-fueled rages—to remind them all.

"I found it," Gracey said aloud, placing the burial policy and a copy of the will on top of the desk. She closed the drawers to the other relics of a past no one had enough heart to live through again.

She walked into Henry's bedroom and sat on the bed, thinking of him. Around the bedpost was a worn leather belt. Henry had used it to pull himself out of bed every morning.

It took some guts to start the day, realizing you had to fight your way out of bed each morning, Daddy. It was a hard way to live.

She rose from the bed and looked in the closet. There was nothing left of her mother's. It had been too long ago. Irma's clothes hung in there, now. A robe and nightgown hung together on a hanger. Irma's shirts and coordinated pants hung together. There wasn't a single dress in the closet.

My mother had a closet full of pretty dresses and shoes, so different from you, Irma, so different.

Gracey stared at the racks of cheap, polyester clothes in the closet.

When she was a girl, she'd count the dresses and shoes in her mother's closet. Helen would hang her slips and bras on the same hanger as her dresses. The cream bra and cream panties were bought especially for a favored dress. They would be separated from the work clothes Helen folded carelessly into the dresser drawer.

Her favorite dress was turquoise-colored, filmy, and pleated with a rhinestone belt. It smelled of the very ordinary perfume, Tabu. It was the perfume of a girl who left Louisiana at seventeen with the back seat of the car filled with dresses and shoes. The man driving that car was ten years older. She'd met him a month before in a dance hall.

When Helen and Henry received their marriage license from the court clerk in Jackson County, Texas, Helen mailed it to her mother in Lafayette. Her mother walked from house to house of shotgun shacks in her neighborhood. In her hand was the marriage license. "My daughter is legally married. My daughter has a wedding ring."

On the floor of Henry's closet was an artificial Christmas tree lying on its side with a box of ornaments next to it. Odd pairs of shoes were strewn around it. Irma had a pair of black SAS shoes next to Henry's tennis shoes, slippers, and boots. Some were paired together, as if Henry still had two feet and needed a pair of shoes to walk wherever he wanted to go.

She looked in the large, six-drawer chest, standing in the corner of the bedroom. His wallet was on top of a pile of folded, white handkerchiefs. As she opened it, she found an AARP card, a Shell gas card, and a piece of white notebook paper folded into tight, dirty squares.

Gracey unfolded the paper and sat on the bed. She recognized her mother's handwriting.

"I know you will never forgive me, Henry. Although I have forgiven you for all the years of pain we have caused each other. I think of when we were young, and all I wanted to do was please you. To iron your shirts, to cook your meals, I loved doing all of it for you, to please you, to see you smile. But we brought others into our home, strangers who poisoned our marriage bed, later poisoning everything around us, including our children. It has not been an easy life, but I have loved you. Our children have made it worth the pain."

Gracey refolded the letter and placed it back into the wallet.

I already know this story and the punch line. Henry, the unforgiveable, could not forgive. He wouldn't even talk about it. The "it" in our lives that seeped through his pores. It was a war fought with the rage of a betrayed man.

We were on the front line of that war, Daddy. All the miles in that truck, you shifting at the steering wheel, dead silent and staring straight ahead. What else could we be but obedient children, silent and as still as still could be. We were lined up on the bench seat next to you. In our minds, in our hearts, were the repeated questions: Where's our mother? Where's your wife? Maybe in Dallas, Houston, or New Orleans. We didn't know. All we knew was riding in that truck. All we knew to do was to keep looking.

Gracey walked back into the kitchen and picked up her grandmother's Bible from the kitchen counter and returned to her parents' bedroom. Closing the thin metal venetian blinds from the still heat of late morning, she laid down in the bed, propping the Bible on her stomach and began to read.

She lost herself in the small script of her grandmother's writing. Beneath the family tree and its dates of births, marriages, and deaths, she found her notes, her testimony to the life given her.

No choices, Grandma. No choices in your life, like the smallest of leaves, fragile and thin, blowing, drifting in the wind. Ah, but you did choose. You chose to stay with Grandpa. You chose to love your children.

The slants of light squeezing through the closed blinds darkened, as a clap of thunder pushed by the dry land and the liquid air boomed against the house. A summer storm played its temporary havoc against the little town of Loti, as Gracey laid in the dark room.

Fat raindrops driven by a wild wind, pelted against the bedroom window. Gracey stared towards the windows, listening to the ting, ting of dry dirt and gravel from the driveway strike the metal garbage can by the back door. She listened closely to the sounds outside, resting the opened Bible against her chest. The aluminum water can fell from its hook on the backyard gate and rattled its way across the brick path to the abandoned garden.

She turned the lamp on next to her and pulled her mother's crocheted afghan around her legs. Lightning cracked against the sky as she read her grandmother's faded recording of her life on a cotton farm in Red Bluff, Texas in the nineteenth century.

Chapter Eight
Two Sparrows in the Wind

The hurricane of 1886 was one tragedy Emil and Patricia Mueller escaped. Their life as husband and wife on the small cotton farm in Red Bluff, sixty miles inland from Indianola, began in 1849. It was a place where children died in infancy and young brides became old women overnight.

Despite Emil's vow to protect her, sorrow and loss surrounded them in Red Bluff. Patricia's only surviving possessions, a photograph of her sons and a Bible laden with the recorded births, deaths, and marriages she witnessed in her lifetime, told the tale of backbreaking labor and poverty for Emil and Patricia Mueller.

They barely survived the first year. The conditions made it nearly impossible to build a house or grow food. The clay soil of gray and black cracked without rain, becoming clumps of rock in July temperatures above ninety-five degrees. Patricia prayed for rain as she broke the clay rocks with her hands. She would have a fall garden.

They ate what the land provided. The mulberries, rabbits, and fish were plentiful, even in the hot summer months. She knew Emil to be a good shot.

Waterfowl and white-tailed deer were in clear sight every morning when she walked to the river for water. She was quick about her business. Cottonmouths swam in the black leaves and hollow trees of the muddy water. One bite ensured a painful death.

The young couple slept in a tent made from cow hide. One

side of the covering was attached to the wagon, creating height for ventilation. While there were no gulf breezes in the thick river bottom land, a cooler air moved through the tent in the early morning hours. The other end of the tent was pulled tightly to the ground and secured with wooden stakes. Ten-hour days in ninety-degree heat and suffocating humidity made the work of building a home and planting a garden difficult. Sleep came immediately for Patricia and Emil, despite the crude accommodations.

The dog-run house with a south side porch was completed before the baby was born. Emil hewned the framework from live oak trees, joining them with mortise and tenon joints held by wooden pegs. Patricia filled the spaces between the logs with moss from the oak trees and mud from the river.

Aileen Mueller, named in honor of Patricia's mother, was delivered by her father a month before she was due. The narrow hips of Patricia, the lack of food during childhood, and the years of physical labor done by a frail-boned and undernourished body, failed to deliver a healthy child.

On a cold and rainy morning in January, Patricia woke with a start. The baby hadn't cried to be fed. The young mother reached into the small crate next to the bed.

"Emil, Emil, she won't open her eyes. Open your eyes, sweet girl. Open your eyes for me."

Emil jumped from the bed. He took the motionless body from his wife's arms and pressed his ear against the baby's chest.

"She's gone. Her heart has stopped."

"No. No. Give her to me. Here. Here. If I can put her to my breast, she will nurse. Open your eyes, baby Aileen." Patricia touched the baby's closed eyes and her parted mouth. She rubbed her hands against the baby's stomach, as if sheer will could make it move with an inhaled breath.

Emil took the child from his wife's arms.

"Too, too frail . . . the poor babe was never meant for this life. Too soon, all of it. She was born too soon."

The small family, a father, mother and child, became one within the arms of Emil. He wept into the folds of his wife's black hair that fell against their child's body. He had failed his wife and his first-born child.

The fair hand of Patricia recorded the first death in her black leather Bible in 1850. The looped cursive writing of the mother carefully wrote the name of the only daughter she would bring into this world, Infant Aileen Mueller on the white space underneath DEATHS.

The baby was buried beneath a redbud tree near the garden fence. Once the danger of frost had passed and the warmth of early spring rose from the Earth, Patricia knelt in the orange and grey clay of the grave site and planted wild morning glory seeds near the small white cross marking the grave.

Patricia gave birth to six sons following the death of her daughter. From the moment she conceived each child, she gave her body and soul to his existence. Nothing was more important to her than her sons. She would never again live to see one of her children buried.

The happiest days of her life were spent picnicking with her sons on the banks of the Francitas River. Following the spring rains, Emil, Patricia, and their sons left the work of the cotton farm and travelled twenty miles by wagon to a clearing on the river.

Underneath the shade of willows, Patricia placed a cotton quilt and set a jar of figs, bread, fried chicken, tomatoes, and green onions on a wooden cutting board. She spent the day watching her sons swim in the river, while Emil slept on the quilt near her.

A tintype photo taken by a wealthy cattleman neighbor forever captured the sons of Emil and Patricia Mueller picnicking near the river. The picture revealed six boys, ranging in age and height, with their hands on their hips and their eyes squinted in the sunlight. They stood barefoot on the sandy banks. The bravado in their stance revealed the only true emotion poor men, sons of immigrants, would allow themselves; a reckless trait in all six sons, especially for the youngest son, Jonas. It secured a tragic fate for him despite the love of his mother.

Chapter Nine
Favored Son

Jonas Mueller was the last child born on the small cotton farm of Emil and Patricia Mueller. He arrived on a hot July afternoon following five hours of labor pains by his mother. His father delivered him on the south side porch of the dog-run house where a month before he placed a bed for his wife. The month of bed rest underneath the shaded ventilation of the porch ensured a safe delivery and a breathing male child for the mother who was too old and broken to deliver yet another baby.

"We will call him Jonas, like the great servant of God. Jonas, our dove. Pray with me, Emil. Pray God will protect our child from the wickedness of the Devil," Patricia said, reaching to take the bloody infant from him before he had cleaned the tiny body and wrapped him in a clean flour sack.

"Ahh, Patricia. God will protect this child, like all your boys, woman. That is not your worry."

Ignoring Emil's words, she placed the baby to her breast to suckle and began to pray. "Saint Patrick, intercede for us. May the strength of God pilot us. May the power of God preserve us. May the wisdom of God instruct us. May the hand of God protect us. May the way of God direct us. May the shield of God defend us. May the host of God guard us. Against the snares of the evil ones. Against temptations of the world. May Christ be with us! May Christ be before us! May Christ be in us. Christ be over all! May thy salvation, Lord, always be ours, this day, O Lord, and evermore. Amen."

Each word she spoke—feverishly, passionately—felt like the closing of a door, forever separating Emil from his wife. The words no longer were a prayer, but a pleading to God, begging for protection from any tragedy she no longer had the physical or mental strength to endure. He felt each word pound in unison with his heart. It served as a bitter reminder he had not cared for her as well as he should have. The boys who followed baby Aileen's death were frail. Yet, it was not from trying, Emil reasoned. He worked as hard as he could to provide for her and his children. It was their place in life to struggle in the fields to feed their children and themselves. The summer of 1849, their first year in Red Bluff, would be like every summer of their lives, laboring to eat and praying to survive.

His thoughtlessness killed their first child, as sure as he had strangled the infant's neck with his own hands. The day he knew he loved Patricia and wanted her for his wife was also the day he vowed she would never suffer again. He failed her. He failed their children. Fate's destiny was a bitter life of meager earnings and physical labor. Then fate delivered its final blow. It killed the love his wife once held for him.

Patricia was no longer his love, his own heart and soul. She was now the mother of six sons, and the youngest and the fairest, Jonas would be her favorite. There was no longer any room in her scarred heart for a husband. Her existence was for her last child and his brothers.

The final word of her prayer resounded throughout Emil's body, as he looked at her and the child. The door was closed. He knew he would never be a part of the bond forged that day between Patricia and Jonas Mueller.

God, bring Patricia back to me. I pray jealousy does not keep me from loving my son. Hold him in your care, Father, remove the jealousy and fear that may rob him of his innocence or cripple him as a man. Take away my wife's worries, the endless anxieties she bares each day. I have tried, but I've failed her. Oh, God . . . Jonas, she names him. Jonas, the fool who would not listen to God. Ahh, but the boys need tending. They are hungry and their mother needs to rest. I will not solve this heartache today.

His gaze lifted from the mother and child to peer all around him, taking in the overwhelming vista, knowing what he had to do now and until his last breath.

The early years between the mother and child served to further strengthen the bond between them. He was the only child of her six sons she would lavish with unwavering devotion.

Jonas learned to read and write sitting at his mother's kitchen table. With money Patricia made from selling eggs and butter in the Red Bluff community, she bought the McGuffey Reader. The mother and son spent hours indoors reciting the stories in the primary reader and practicing Jonas' handwriting on rags with a slate pencil.

"Jonas, you want to be like this grand boy in the story. He is good, kind, and honest. He does not tell lies or make people wait for him," Patricia lovingly prompted her son, while stealing a look at Emil and the other boys minding the cattle in a pasture behind the house. "You'll not work in the dirt to make a living, Jonas. You'll be a proper gentleman."

By the time he was nine years old, Jonas had completed his education. The Red Bluff community would not erect a schoolhouse until 1896. Patricia's grand plans for her son's future were stunted by her husband.

"You have to let him learn outdoors, Patricia. I've not the money to let him ride a fancy pony or join the turnvereins schools with the rich German ranchers. There'll be no university for your son, woman. He's got to learn to feed himself."

Jonas soon fell in line as the youngest son of the six brothers, working beside them weeding the garden and tending the cattle. For the first two years, Jonas would listen to his brothers and follow their instruction . . . but he soon became tired of the work outdoors.

He fell behind in following them to the pasture in the early mornings; he would become distracted by the sight of a sandhill crane in a pasture or a bright red cardinal sitting on a bald cypress branch. Sometimes he would even stop following them, so he could pick his mother a bouquet of wild flowers.

He often feigned a stomach ache or an aching back when it was his turn to hoe the garden. By the time he was thirteen, he simply would wait for them to leave for work in the morning and find a book to read. His favorite was a Christmas gift from his mother. He had read *Hard Times* by Mr. Charles Dickens at least ten times.

When his father and brothers were completely out of his sight, he would take his book and a biscuit left from breakfast and walk to the river. There he would eat, read, and sleep until one of his brothers would find him. With a quick kick to his leg, he would jump up and return to the house, just in time for supper.

The joy of his daily routine would soon change for Jonas. His brothers were told to no longer get him from the river after they returned from their day's work. Emil would go himself. The guilt of raising a family in poverty would not allow Emil to raise a hand to any of his children. Soon, Jonas would become the exception.

Emil heard the other farmers were planting watermelons and selling them at the post office in the Navidad Community in northwestern Jackson County. The melons were profitable and easy to grow. He began a watermelon patch with his youngest son near the unshaded west side of the property. He prayed the new garden would interest Jonas. He would make it Jonas' responsibility to grow and take the watermelons to market. At fifteen, the boy had the gift of gab and could easily sell the melons.

The father and son tilled the soil and planted the seed. By April the melons, green and round, emerged from the dirt in a tangle of green leaves and vines. But the weather was becoming hot, and Jonas soon became tired of the enterprise he shared with his father. The magical lure of going to the Navidad Community to sell watermelons was quickly forgotten in the haze of the sun and the pulling of milk-thistle weeds.

He'll not be back for a while with my brothers. That pasture is far from the house and the cattle move slow this time of year. I'll have one of these melons for myself. Take it to the river where I'll find a deep hole in the river bottom. It'll be just right to eat after some time in that cold water.

Emil returned with his five sons from the pasture. He found a hoe lying on the ground and uprooted vines in the watermelon patch.

"Go inside and get washed up. Tell your mother I've gone to find Jonas," he said, turning his back to them and walking towards the redbud tree, the tree his first child, his daughter, was buried beneath. He snapped a long, thin branch with leaves from the tree with his hands and walked toward the river.

He found his youngest son asleep at the river's edge; the remains of a watermelon, its green body broken in several pieces; its sweet, red fruit eaten. He whipped the sleeping boy on his arms and face. The boy awoke in disbelief.

"I'll not tolerate a thief or a lazy man. You either do your part in my house or I'll break you until you do," Emil said, yanking the boy up from the river bank and shaking his thin shoulders.

Jonas cried and ran from his father. He met his mother halfway to the homestead.

"What, Jonas, what did he do?" She touched the rising red whelps across his face. "You go home. Go to bed straight away. Don't follow me."

Emil saw the mother and son standing and talking together from a distance. He stood and waited for her. He held the tree switch in his hand. She walked quickly to him. She stopped suddenly, look into his eyes and then at the switch in his hand.

"No, you'll not beat him, Emil. My son will not be treated like one of your calves, whipped into place to suit you." She grabbed the switch from him and threw it to the ground. She walked back toward the house, never turning around to see if he was following her home. Emil closed his heart that day to Jonas, as Patricia had closed her heart to him the day their youngest son was born.

It took a day's ride by mule and wagon the first time Jonas left the homestead for the Navidad community. The wagon was loaded with the green melons, a tin of food his mother had made him, and a sleeping roll. In his pocket was the two dollar bill she gave him in case he came across any sort of trouble. During the slow, hot ride to the Navidad community, he would occasionally take the bill out and rub his thumb slowly across George Washington's face. He liked the feel of the money in his pocket. He liked being away from the homestead with its constant labor in the fields with the stinking cattle. Today was a good day for Jonas. Today, he felt like a man.

He arrived at dusk. He unhitched the mule and tied it to an oak tree west of the post office and general store. He placed his bedroll close to the wagon and mule, like his father had told him.

I can get under that wagon if it starts to rain during the night. Ain't nothing to protect me from bandits and drunk cowboys, though. They might take my money.

Jonas gave his pant pocket a quick pat with his hand, ensuring the bill was still there and closed his eyes to sleep. He awoke to the sound of a man singing.

"Róisín, have no sorrow for all that has happened to you
the Friars are out on the brine, they are travelling the sea
your pardon from the Pope will come, from Rome in the East
and we won't spare the Spanish wine for my Róisín Dubh
Far have we journeyed together, since days gone by.
I've crossed over mountains with her, and sailed the sea
I have cleared the Erne, though in spate, at a single leap
and like music of the strings all about me, my Róisín Dubh

You have driven me mad, fickle girl— may it do you no good!
My soul is in thrall, not just yesterday nor today
You have left me weary and weak in body and mind
O deceive not the one who loves you, my Róisín Dubh
I would walk in the dew beside you, or the bitter desert
in hopes I might have your affection, or part of your love

Fragrant small branch, you have given your word you love me
the choicest flower of Munster, my Róisín Dubh

If I had six horses, I would plough against the hill—
I'd make Róisín Dubh my Gospel in the middle of Mass—
I'd kiss the young girl who would grant me her maidenhead
and do deeds behind the lios with my Róisín Dubh!
The Erne will be strong in flood, the hills be torn
the ocean will be all red waves, the sky all blood,
every mountain and bog in Ireland will shake
one day, before she shall perish, my Róisín Dubh."

Jonas leaned over on his side and propped his head up with his arm, so he could get a better look at the singer of the Irish ballad. He was a lean man with coal black hair, who appeared as old as Jonas' oldest brother. He sat on the porch steps of the general store, gently tapping a stem of Johnson Grass against his thigh as he sang the ballad.

He might be Arthur's age, maybe twenty-five or twenty-six. Can't tell how tall he is, but looks to be over six foot. Those legs of his are all over the place. He don't look to be no bandit, maybe just a cowboy. He's not carrying a side arm.

The singer noticed the boy staring at him, but continued his song, nodding once in Jonas' direction. Jonas immediately saw a friend.

Hungry and lonesome, Jonas wiped the sleep from his eyes, patted his pocket for good luck, and approached his new found friend.

"How do you know that song? My own mother sings that. She was born in Ireland," he said.

"Ah, tis the 'Little Black Rose.' My mam taught it to me when I was a boy. She be from Cork. But, I left her and Ireland a long time ago. Ahh, but I have her song," Aedan Bowen replied, all the while taking in the mule tied to the tree and the wagon loaded with melons, a few feet from what appeared to be a fearless, naïve boy. Aedan immediately recognized a new partner and a means of delivery for his illegal whiskey business.

Jonas held out his hand and Aedan grasped it firmly, smiling at him with blue eyes.

"Aedan Bowen, sir. Please to meet you."

"Jonas Mueller. Came here all the way from the Red Bluff community near the Francitas River to sell my melons."

"Well, Mr. Mueller, you don't say? It's a fair day for selling melons. You're going to leave here a rich man."

"What's your trade, Aedan?"

"I'm a horse trader. When it's cow punching time, you'll find me in Victoria working for the Hahn's. They pay a good wage for handling the longhorns they keep. When things slow down there, I paint houses and barns, mend fences. I also do a bit of bare knuckle boxing and other paying entertainments to amuse myself and others."

"Boxing? I don't think I've seen that."

"It's a fine sport, young Jonas. Round late afternoon while there's still a bit of sun, I'm gonna box and win $100."

"How you gonna make $100 by doing that?" Jonas asked wide-eyed.

"You take care of your melon business, sir and I'll show you how to make some real money. Now, that's if you can stay that long. I'm sure you mam and daddy will expect you back in Red Bluff right away."

"Oh no, my mother knows it's a hard day travel with the wagon and mule. I might just spend another night here and leave at day break."

"Well now, you're a good man Jonas Mueller to want to make some real money for your family. I was about to go in the store and buy a biscuit and coffee. Would you care to join me?"

"No, sir, my mother packed me a breakfast. I need to get busy with the melons."

"I'll come check on you later then. Pleasure meeting you."

"Yes, sir. Same here."

By ten o'clock that morning, Jonas sold all his melons. He counted several dollars in coins. Proud of his work, he bought two pieces of dried beef and a slice of hard cheddar cheese from the little store and ate it with one of the biscuits his mother had made. He brought the mule some fresh water and gave him a handful of oats he kept in a bag underneath the seat in the wagon. Proud of what he had accomplished in a few short hours, Jonas took a nap under the shade of the wagon.

It seemed to him he had only been a sleep for a few minutes when he felt someone pulling his right foot that protruded from underneath the wagon.

"Get up, Mr. Mueller. You're burning day light underneath that wagon."

Jonas recognized the voice of his new friend. He rolled over on his side out from underneath the wagon and stood up. Aedan Bowen was bare-chested, wearing loose britches tied with a thin rope around his waist. He danced around Jonas, throwing punches into the stale air of a May afternoon.

"You're my new partner in a money-making enterprise, Jonas. Now, follow me around out back behind the store where I keep my wares. You're gonna get a real education today."

Jonas and Aedan walked half a mile behind the grey clapboard store building into a thicket of palmetto palms, briar, and scrub oak trees. In a clearing of Little Mexican Hat flowers of red and yellow, a heavy cotton tarp covered four wooden crates of quart-sized Mason jars.

"Now, Jonas, you're gonna be selling those jars for me right before I win my money from boxing. You make sure those men don't get thirsty, especially the men with money betting on this match. You give my opponent a jar for free. I'll point him out to you beforehand. Be friendly-like to him beforehand, so he'll know you are offering him a gift with gentlemanly manners."

"What's in those jars?" asked Jonas, picking one up and observing the dark liquid in the afternoon sun.

"That's the best I make. Charter moonshine. I keep it in charred oak barrels for a couple of days. Makes it dark like that. Gives it the rich taste of charcoal. If I'm running low on supplies, I cut it with some turpentine."

"I believe selling moonshine is against the law, Aedan. I don't need no trouble with the law. I came here to sell melons. I done that and I'm going home with my money." Jonas stood his ground bravely.

"You sold your melons, Jonas. Now, you're gonna make some real money. Don't worry about no lawman. He's done come around and got his whiskey for free." Aedan cocked his head and winked.

"How much does it cost?"

"For each jar, you take one Seated Liberty from a man. That's a fair price. One quarter of a dollar for a few hours of joy in this world. You get a nickel out of every Liberty you give me. You know your numbers, Jonas?"

"I do. I can read, write, and spell."

"That's good, Jonas. You also just learned you can make twice as much money helping men relieve their pain than digging in the dirt and sweating in the sun."

"Yes, sir," replied Jonas, as he counted the money he'd make in his head from all the glass bottles laying at his feet.

By four o'clock that afternoon, Patricia Mueller's youngest and fairest child had sold eighteen quarts of moonshine to farmers and cowboys in Jackson County. He'd also reserved a quart for himself, without paying for it, and drank it in the clearing in the woods, sitting on the tarp that had been used to cover the wooden crates. Shortly thereafter, he commenced to vomiting the store-bought food he ate for lunch, clutching the branch of a blueberry juniper to steady himself from falling into the vomit covering his shoes. He crawled back to the tarp with his head and heart pounding to the same cadence. The white clouds in the late afternoon sky swirled above him until he mercifully passed out.

After winning the bareknuckle boxing match against a drunk Mexican in five minutes, Aedan Bowen found his young partner asleep in the little clearing in the woods behind the store. He was covered in a veil of vomit with his pant pocket bulging with coins and a two dollar bill. Aedan laughed out loud at his good fortune. Careful not to wake the boy, he took the money made from selling melons and moonshine. The two dollar bill was the fine Jonas would pay for stealing from him. For good measure, Aedan kicked the sleeping boy with the toe of his boot. A faint groan rose from the ground as Jonas rolled to his side, feeling the pain somewhere in the recesses of his drunken mind.

He can have the damn mule and wagon. I've made enough to get myself to Galveston. In a day I'm gonna be eating oysters and drinking whiskey from a real glass. Gonna buy me a fine suit of clothes and see Mr. Jack Johnson box. Aedan grinned and walked away with a jaunty gait; dreams of fame and fortune danced around in his head.

Jonas woke up in the dark. He called for his mother, but she did not answer. He stood up only to fall on his knees when his stomach contracted with an explosion of mucus and vomit. He swiped his mouth with the sleeve of his shirt, then touched his right eye lightly with his forefinger. It was bulging. Sitting back down on the tarp, he felt his pocket for the coins and bill. Gone. Frantically, he spread his hands across the tarp, fingering in the dark for the feel of the money. The only substance encountered was crispy oak leaves falling to pieces at his touch. He cried and convulsed with dry heaves until day break.

Hitching the mule to the wagon, he left the Navidad community with his right eye swollen shut. He was broke, beaten and hung-over. It would become a familiar feeling for Jonas every time he left a place, vowing to never return . . . but he would again and again, with the same lonely feeling, and with the same Bible verse playing in his head, "Like a dog that returns to its vomit, is a fool who repeats his folly."

When he came to Mustang Creek, outside the Mustang Settlement, he stopped the mule, climbed down from the wagon, and immersed himself in the water, fully clothed. The stench of regurgitated hard liquor and the remains of the meal from the night before had become unbearable. Yet nothing would wash away his new knowledge. He began to think about his present situation as he floated on his back in the cool water, staring up into the vast blueness of the sky.

I'm as smart as that Aedan Bowen, if not smarter. He probably can't even read or spell. I can box and make whiskey, same as him. I'll get my money back and then some. It may take some time, but that's something I have. For now, all I got to worry about is getting home in time for supper. Then, I'll go to bed and think it all through tomorrow.

Patricia Mueller met her favorite son at the south gate of the homestead. She had slept against the fence post, wrapping herself against the cool morning dew with a woolen shawl. When she saw Jonas from the distance by late that afternoon, she no longer felt the pain in her joints and stooped back. Her son was home, and he was alive. Her heart leaped with joy.

"Mam, bandits, I counted five of them before they knocked me unconscious. They took the melons, the money and nearly my life. I came home straight way as I could manage the mule," Jonas called from the wagon seat.

"Thanks be to God, you've made it home, Jonas," Patricia cried, wrapping her arms around her son when he jumped down to greet her.

Emil watched them from the south side porch. He felt it in his bones. His son, the child God gave to him and his wife, was a miserable man. *Don't be a fool, Patricia. He's no prodigal son. Oh no, your educated boy is a liar and a thief. He will prove to be the scourge of our old age. He will be the one to kill you, woman. He'll just keep breaking your heart until you die."*

Once Jonas was nursed back to health by the loving hands of his mother, he began his plans for the future. By the time he was seventeen, he was the sole provider of moonshine on the southern edge of Jackson County and along the waterfront of Port Lavaca. There was no need for him to hide the money he made from his mother and father. He simply gambled and drank it away as quickly as he made it. Under the guise of delivering vegetables, eggs, and butter to the area store fronts, he loaded crates of Mason jars covered with a heavy cotton tarp in the back of the wagon.

He began his boxing career with a group of fishermen who lived along the wharves of Port Lavaca. The men would spar in the sand and oyster shell yards of the seafood warehouses facing the bay. The men-of-the-sea were strong from hauling nets. Jonas was no match for them, but he enjoyed the days away from the homestead.

One cool spring evening, Jonas sat on the dock overlooking the water with Albert Schmitt, playing cards and drinking mustang grape wine by the light of a kerosene lamp. Their drunken laughter and singing soared into the night sky like the flight of mad seagulls.

"Down around the corner
Of the street where I reside,
There lives the cutest little girl
That I have ever spied.
Her name is Rose O'Grady
And I don't mind telling you
That's she's the sweetest little rose
This garden ever grew
Sweet Rosie O'Grady,
My dear little Rose.
She's my steady lady,
Most ev'ryone knows;
And when we are married,
How happy we'll be;
I love Sweet Rosie O'Grady and
Rosie O'Grady loves me."

"You need a woman, Jonas. You got money, now. Go get yourself a wife, before you lose any more teeth in your head," laughed Albert, an oysterman who supplemented his income repairing small skiffs with his German-born father in towns up and down the coast line.

"That wouldn't be a worry of mine, Albert, if you was fair in boxing. You had no count hitting me like that earlier. Think it broke my front tooth."

"Now, now. We was all sportin'. No need to get angry. As I was saying, I've been thinking of a pretty little German girl who lives in town. Her father did a lot of work with that dredging company, the one which took care of all those sandbars. I've not a chance with her. I'm too shy to speak to such a grand lady."

"What's her name? The Queen of Calhoun County?" Jonas

shouted, standing up from the wooden crate he sat on, bowing in front of Albert. Both men roared with laughter.

"Ida Knopp, you fool. But you'll need to talk to her father first. He's strict with his girls." He puffed out his chest, took a deep breath and continued sharing his wisdom, like a man with much authority. "But alas, you have a true friend in me, Jonas. I can help you with old man Knopp. I know for a fact he likes mustang grape wine. Sometimes I deliver fish and oysters to their house in town. The old man drinks his wine out of the smallest, thinnest glass I've ever seen in my life. You might be better received by Emmett Knopp bearing a gift of wine."

"She best be a pretty girl to go to all that trouble for, Albert."

"Ida is tall and thin. On the bridge of her nose, a few freckles introduce you to her eyes. They are green, Jonas. Green as the grass, green as the leaves of a tree. Those eyes take you into her soul, and it is as fresh and tender as new grass. Old man Knopp educated his children. You'd be getting a good woman to raise your children and tend to you in your old age."

On a fine May morning in 1889, with a south westerly wind skipping off of Lavaca Bay, Jonas Mueller walked into the Kotz Emporium on Houston Avenue in downtown Port Lavaca and purchased a black waistcoat and matching vest, black pants, white shirt with a stiff front decorated with shirt studs, a four-in-hand black necktie, and a black bowler. On his feet he wore a new pair of black stove pipe boots, with a cowboy walking heel and a narrow toe.

"The new clothes give you quite a striking appearance, Jonas," said Fritz Kotz, the owner and tailor of the Emporium. He knelt at Jonas' feet, tacking the pant legs with straight pins. "I've always said clothes make the man."

"Mr. Kotz, I sure hope so. I've spied a pretty girl with the biggest green eyes you've ever seen. I'm going to meet her father tomorrow."

"Who would that pretty girl be?"

"Ida Knopp. I've seen her around town, and we've exchanged pleasantries, but I've not been to her house."

"I know the Knopp family. They're good customers here. They have a respectable family name in town, Jonas. You be on your best behavior with Mr. Knopp. He's not a patient man, like your father. He's a hard worker, though, and fair in his business dealing. Mind your manners, and you'll have a good life ahead of you marrying into that family."

"Why that's no concern of yours," Jonas spouted back rudely. "You worry about hemming my pants. I've never had a problem making friends in my life. Don't expect to now," Jonas finished his little performance of indignation by throwing a $50 bill at Fritz's bent head, just as Fritz placed the last pin in the left trouser leg. "That should do for the clothes and your time. I'll pick up the pants by this evening. I'm sure you'll be done by then."

"By four o'clock, Jonas," Fritz replied, with his eyes on the $50 bill at his feet.

He watched Jonas as he walked down Houston Avenue in the early morning sun. It was the walk of a careless young man with an arrogant stride. Fritz placed his hand on his stomach to muffle the sound of gnawing indigestion as he saw Jonas turn the corner onto Alamo Street. He closed his eyes against the pain in his stomach . . . and the thought of Ida Knopp's future.

"*Schade!* That man has been nothing but heartache for his poor mother since the day he was born. I'm sure he'll break many a woman's heart before his time is up," he said to his wife, who was folding bolts of fabric behind the counter, as he handed her the dirty $50 bill.

"Don't mind him, Fritz. Mr. Knopp'll take care of him. Now, help me move this barrel of flour, away from the fabric. It's a bit too heavy for me alone. I'll get you some buttermilk for that stomach of yours once we're done with our work."

Fritz touched his stomach again and winced in pain, before dutifully helping her move the barrel next to the jugs of molasses.

By one o'clock the following day, Jonas was standing on the front porch of the Knopp residence; a two-story, white clapboard made of solid bald cypress, located on the prettiest street in town, Jackson Avenue.

Jonas turned to look at the front lawn before knocking on the door. It was anchored by two Chinese fan palms with their large fronds fluttering in the afternoon breeze off the bay. A thicket of leaves and yellow blooms from a confederate jasmine vine wrapped itself around the banister of the porch. Palmetto palms, juniper bushes, and an oleander bush with pink blooms sat beneath it. To the right of the porch, a persimmon tree loaded with yellow-orange fruit lead toward a small, white shed behind the house.

I've a mind to pick me some of those persimmons before I leave here. He tugged absentmindedly at his coat and vest, then smoothed the new fabric with the palm of his hand.

He looked up from the porch, admiring the ornate ginger-bread lining the first-story roof line. The second story featured two dormer windows. Jonas thought he saw the green-eyed Ida peering out of the one on the right, smiling at him through a parted lace curtain. The thought of her eyes gave him the courage to finally knock on the door.

In his left hand, he gripped a glass bottle of mustang grape wine, a gift brought especially for Emmett Knopp, who answered the door on the first knock. He had been watching Jonas through the window facing the front porch for quite some time. At six-feet, three-inches tall, his massive build engulfed the door frame with each shoulder grazing the sides.

"Good afternoon, Mr. Knopp," Jonas said, removing his hat and extending his right hand for a handshake. "I've come to visit your daughter, Ida."

The old German ignored his hand. "I know who you've come to see, man. But you will see me first," Knopp said, taking the bottle of wine from Jonas' left hand and directing him into a sitting area in the rear of the house.

Jonas sat down in a straight-back, caned chair by an open window. In clear view from where he was sitting, a large cruci-fix was nailed to the wall. Two pieces of palm crisscrossed each other behind the crucifix. Jonas turned away and looked out the window. He could smell the salt air from the bay; he could hear men returning from lunch to their jobs at the Foley Oyster Knife Factory. He turned to look at Emmett, who returned his look with a frown. Jonas wondered why Ida wasn't sitting with them.

Emmett Knopp watched him from his large upholstered chair; he knew very well the man sitting next to him. He had heard about Jonas Mueller for at least two years before he laid eyes on him. Emmett stared at the new shoes on Jonas' feet. *Only a fool would spend money like that on clothes and shoes. Money I know his mother and father don't have. Money he's made living like a criminal. As if a suit of clothes or new shoes would make him a gentleman! Ich Verachte Vorwand!*

"I suppose you want to marry my daughter, Jonas," he asked, pulling his chair closer to him.

Jonas instinctively sunk his spine into the small back of the chair he was sitting in.

"Yes, sir. She is a fine lady. I'd make her a good husband. I come from hard working people."

"I know your father and mother. Emil's worked hard on his cotton farm and runs a fair herd of cattle. Patricia has been a good wife to him, a good mother to her boys. But I also know something about her youngest. That be you, Jonas. I've not come from Germany to build a life in Texas, so my daughter can marry a bootlegger. I also hear you make your dirty money fightin' men along the wharves."

Jonas looked down at the floor and rubbed his sweaty palms against his new trousers. "Soon I'll be getting a job at the oyster knife factory. Those wild days are behind me, Mr. Knopp."

"That may be. But one thing you'll get straight today. *Kein Aber!* I'll not tolerate my daughter doing without. She's a clever mind. She'll not spend her life scratching a living with a man who can't support her. I'll make you stand by every word you say to me today. You'll take care of her and the children you bring into this world."

"Yes, sir. I intend to do right by her and our children. They'll not do without. My mama taught me to read and write. I'm good with my numbers. We've kept books in our house as I was growing up." Jonas extended his hand to shake Emmett's.

"Ida's been reading since she was a little girl. See those books there." Emmett ignored Jonas's extended hand and pointed to a row of leather bound books on a pecan wood shelf in a corner next to his upholstered chair. "We come from scholars, learned men and women in Germany. That is our history. And we'll keep that history, Jonas. My grandchildren will be scholars, too."

"Yes, sir, Mr. Knopp. There's nothing better than a book in the evening, after the chores are done. That's something my folks taught me. It's what separates us from the animals; we're creatures of reason. I own a book by Mr. Charles Dickens, myself."

"Very good, Jonas," the old man sighed. "I've got a few other things you need to understand. You'll not move her all over the country, either. She'll be near her mother and me." Emmett rose from the chair and took Jonas' hand. He squeezed it with every ounce of strength in his body. "Don't ever make the mistake of thinking I'm giving you my blessing. *Nicht vergessen!* I'm doing this for her, knowing full well the love she thinks she has for you is nothing but a schoolgirl crush. You be kind to her, boy or I'll kill you."

Emmett walked away from his chair and stood at the base of the stair railing and called for his daughter.

"Ida, your beau is here." Emmett turned and looked directly at Jonas. "You sit on the porch with her right in front here. No need to take her walking in town."

Emmett sat back down in the upholstered chair, so he could watch the only joy he knew in the world walk down the stairs. He watched her smile at the pouting man in the caned chair. Together, they walked toward the front door.

Emmett Knopp felt a great sadness when he looked at his daughter. He knew without a doubt that the man his daughter walked out the door with would never be anything more than what he was that day—a careless, arrogant man.

On the front porch, the afternoon sun danced through Ida's

hair, filling the chestnut strands with golden-red streaks. Her eyes were enormous, green globes framed in black lashes against her white skin. Jonas trembled inside looking at her.

"I've asked your father if I could marry you, Ida," Jonas said, touching a piece of hair that fell across her left cheek.

"Oh, Jonas," she smiled and turned her face toward him.

"I'll be a good husband for you, Ida. You, you will make me a better man, because of it."

"Jonas, look, look there on the juniper bush by the front of the porch steps. It's a cardinal. You know, the old Germans say when you see one, a red bird all alone, that someone in heaven is thinking of you. It's my grandmother. Papa's mother. They say I look just like her." Ida blushed and turned away from Jonas. She lowered her voice to a whisper. "I think this means she's happy for us. We'll have a good marriage. God's blessing is on us today."

"I love red birds. Just like I do you, Ida Knopp." He cupped her chin in his hand, turned her face to his and brushed his lips lightly across hers.

"Papa won't like that," she said, laughing and pushing him away.

"Your papa will get used to things in time," said Jonas, reaching toward her to steal another kiss.

In September, just as the harvest moon rose above the muddy waters of the bay, Jonas Mueller and Ida Knopp were married at St. Mary Catholic Church in Port Lavaca. The bride wore an ivory dress with puffed sleeves and a full skirt. A sash accented by a cream rosebud circled her small waist, then trailed along the front of her dress. She carried a bridal bouquet of milk lilies. The groom wore the suit he wore the day he met Emmett Knopp.

Patricia Mueller sat next to her husband and grown sons on the front pew. Emmett and Frieda Knopp sat in the opposite pew next to their two younger daughters. The family members exchanged smiles amongst themselves, all except Emmett. He offered Emil a stiff handshake before they walked into the church. To Patricia, he gave a polite nod of his head.

Not even Emmett Knopp's cold heart could stop Patricia's

joy. She could hardly believe she was sitting in the same church she came to as a young girl from Indianola with her husband-to-be by her side. Now, her youngest son, her favorite son, was marrying a good girl, a girl who could tend to her son as well as she had.

She saw it as a sign from heaven; hard times were over for her son. God had tested him and he delivered Jonas into grace. As a wedding gift, she gave her son and daughter-in-law a brand new one hundred-dollar bill. It was the first and last time Patricia would see that kind of money again.

Emil had taken her by horse and wagon to the National Bank in Port Lavaca a week before. Cautiously she carried the cloth bag of coins and assorted bills inside the bank and placed it ever so gently on the smooth marble counter. When the bank teller replaced the bag of money with a one hundred-dollar bill, it took Patricia's breath away.

"Woman, you're throwing good money after bad," Emil said, when he offered his hand to help her into the wagon.

"Shame, shame, Emil. To hear you speak of your own flesh and blood so," she replied, placing the empty cloth bag on her lap. They did not speak to each other on the ride home.

But none of that mattered anymore. Patricia Walsh Mueller was happy and her son, her Jonas would be, too.

The first months of Jonas and Ida Mueller's marriage held promise. Jonas tried his best to live the life Ida planned for them. Abandoning boxing and whiskey for a wife and a home, Jonas no longer carried crates of moonshine by wagon. Instead, he became a company man at the Foley Oyster Knife Factory, where he received a weekly wage for his efforts.

Ida brought a trunk of books to the three-room cottage she shared with Jonas. In the early months of their marriage, before Jonas' demons found them, they lay together on a white iron bed pushed against an open window. The moon and salt air from the bay bathed them each night, as Ida read to her husband. Jonas listened contently with his head on his wife's smooth, naked stomach.

But with the birth of his daughters, Ida no longer had time to console Jonas when he returned in the evening from the factory.

Soon he sought solace from crying babies and a sickly wife with brawly men and bottles of wine. First, he stayed away for a night. Thinking no one cared enough to look for him, he stayed gone a week.

When Emmett Knopp visited his daughter and grand-daughters in the three-room cottage, he found his precious girl thin and pale. Her eyes, no longer the bright stars of her soul, were anxious and sunken in worry. She had been working in a patch of dirt behind the cottage with a dull hoe. His granddaughters were soiled and smeared from head to toe in dirt and sweat from sitting at the feet of their mother while she worked in the garden.

"Father, I didn't know you'd be visiting. We're a sight to see, I'm sure."

"Ida, where's your husband?"

"He's tending to some business at the wharves. He can make extra money there helping the men mend nets and load the boats."

"You're lying, daughter. He hasn't worked at the factory or anywhere else for a week. I know what people have told me. Today, I see it with my own eyes. That man is neglecting his duties to his own family. I'll not stand for it."

"Father."

"No, Ida. This is out of your hands. Wash the dirt off of you and your daughters. I didn't raise you to dig in it so you could eat. It'll not be the life for you nor my grandchildren. I knew Jonas to be a weak man the day I set eyes on him, but I'll change him or . . . He'll be back home with you and his children this day, so help me God."

Emmett Knopp found Jonas asleep in a wooden chair propped against the back door of the Boehm Shrimp and Oyster Company. The light, salty breeze emanating from waters a few feet from the sleeping man made for a pleasant evening. At the shoreline, a lone man, holding a kerosene lamp in one hand and a floundering gig in the other, walked in the shallow water where piping plovers and egrets nested in the folds of salt grass.

The first blow knocked Jonas off the chair and startled two brown pelicans into flight from the nearby wharf. The second blow broke Jonas' nose. The man floundering turned from the water and shone the kerosene lamp in the direction of Jonas' cry.

"You get to your feet. I want to see your face before I hit it again," Emmett Knopp screamed, his entire six-foot-three-inch frame shaking with rage.

"No, Emmett. I'm your family. I'm your son-in-law."

"You are nothing to me. Nothing. But to my daughter and my granddaughters, you are everything. And I'll not have you break them, Jonas. I'll not have it." The old man grabbed Jonas' neck with one hand and up righted the wooden chair with his other. "Sit. Sit on your *aschel* and listen."

Jonas looked up at him through his swollen, bloodshot eyes, cupping his hand underneath his bleeding nose in a vain attempt to keep the blood from spilling onto his shirt and pants.

"You're a weak and cold-hearted man, Jonas. You feed yourself whiskey and tobacco and leave your wife and daughters penniless, working in the dirt for food. I'd kill you myself, but it seems the yellow journalism of Pulitzer and Hearst will do that for me. Friday morning, I'm taking you to the recruiting station myself. You want to live like an animal, well you'll get your chance. There's a war that'll teach you better than any bottle of rot-gut will. You tell your wife and daughters goodbye. And then you go and tell your mother goodbye. Make her believe she bore a son that's a true hero, a brave boy going off to war." Emmett grabbed Jonas by the throat and pulled him to his feet. "By God, if you run off again . . . *Kein Aber!* I'll kill you with my bare hands and let the crabs in Lavaca Bay feast on your body." He threw Jonas down in the chair with his last breath.

He would see his son-in-law one more time, the day Jonas enlisted in the US Army.

Jonas and his friend Albert joined Company E, First Regiment Infantry out of Corpus Christi. It was an adventure for the two young men who had never been out of Jackson and Lavaca counties. They could hardly imagine sailing through the Caribbean to

Cuba, let alone killing Spaniards. But they were soldiers, not politicians. It was not their war to develop; it was their war to fight.

Albert died in the mud, blood, and mosquitoes of San Juan Hill outside of Santiago. A single bullet shattered his skull. Most of the men who left Corpus with them ten weeks earlier died from yellow fever and heat exhaustion. Jonas survived and returned home to his waiting family.

Life was not the same in Calhoun County for Jonas, but Jonas was not the same careless, young man. He came home with the ghosts of the war in his head. He captured them and placed them in a bottle of whiskey. Together, they danced the waltz of the dead and dying in South Texas.

He buried his mother and father the first year he was home. Now, there was no one strong enough to will Jonas into sobriety. When his demons called, he abandoned his wife and daughters to the bars of South Texas, then followed a circuit of boxers from Houston to Corpus Christi. When his demons rested, he returned home to his wife and daughters, painting houses with lead paint and drinking bootleg whiskey cut with turpentine.

His last child, his only son, William Mueller, was delivered by his schoolgirl daughters and a neighbor following a hurricane that destroyed their home and the last bit of love Ida felt for a man she lost to whiskey and a war. William would grow into a boy who never saw his father sober. He thought that was how a man was supposed to live.

Chapter Ten
All These Years

Far away, tucked inside a dream, Gracey heard the ringing telephone in the kitchen. She sat up in her parents' bed, placed the opened Bible on the nightstand and ran her fingers through her hair. She blinked her eyes several times, pushing the fog of deep sleep aside, and ran into the kitchen, barefooted.

"Gracey?"

"Tom. Tom. I'm so glad you called. When are you coming? Would be so great to have you here. We can sit and talk, cook for each other, stuff we haven't done in so long."

"I'm not coming, Gracey."

"Why? Why can't you?"

"I've thought about it a long time . . . hold on a minute, it's hard to hear you in here."

"Where are you?"

"I'm just stepping outside, hold on . . . "

Gracey could hear her brother talking to someone and the muffled sounds of other voices and music.

"Gracey?"

"I'm here. Where the hell are you? It's too early to be at a bar. You're not at a bar, are you, Tom? I thought you were finishing summer school. That's what you told me last we talked. What's changed? I know nothing has changed over here. Nothing at all."

"I just stopped off the side of the road for a minute after leaving school. I was thinking of Dad and all his favorite haunts, those little beer joints he'd find up and down the highway, when he found work outside of Loti."

"Are you in Houston or not?"

"I am. There's still a few of those places off 45 South, heading toward Galveston. The suburbs and box stores haven't wiped everything out. Yeah, it's old school here. Henry's type of place."

Gracey felt her heart sink to her feet.

"Hey, you there?"

"Yeah, I'm here. I'm here at Dad's house by myself. By myself!"

"Take it easy, Gracey. Nobody's having fun with any of this, including me."

"Tom, you really shouldn't be hanging out in some dive in South Houston drinking alone. It's depressing. Things are bad enough. Either get here or go home. Those are the only places you should be."

"You're not my mother or my boss. And . . . and . . . you sure in the hell don't know how I feel . . . or know the things I know about our family, no one knows what I do, no one, so don't pull your self-righteous crap on me."

Gracey stared out the kitchen window watching two mockingbirds chase a cat in the neighbor's yard. She needed to pick up the rotten limbs from the oak tree the thunderstorm knocked to the ground, and close the open gate to the backyard. There were a million things she'd needed to do besides have this same-old, dead-tired conversation with her brother. *Just throw him a bone, Gracey and get this over with. He's not coming and that's that. You're it, girl!*

"Yes, you're right. I'm sorry. We all grieve in different ways; big difference in how men and women grieve. That whole Venus and Mars thing. Let's not fight, Tom. I just don't want you to hurt yourself; being alone, alone in a beer joint. Don't sit over there by yourself thinking and feeling. That isn't any good. Believe me, I've spent years doing that," she said, while continuing to search for the cat out of the kitchen window.

"It's the falseness. The damn falseness of it all that I can't bear. I'm not going to pretend it was a Cleaver Family experience for any of us. I guess I loved the man, but, but, that's all I can do right now. That's it. I'll be there soon, just not now. Don't be mad, Gracey."

"Oh, Tom. I'm not mad. It is what it is. Just get here soon. I'd like to see you, that's all. I just want to spend some time with you."

"Things will be better tomorrow. I'll come tomorrow."

"I'll be here."

Gracey hung up the phone. She poured a glass of water from a plastic jug in the refrigerator and wondered what happened to the cat the birds were chasing.

Maybe the cat just decided to hide somewhere dark and still, quiet underneath the neighbor's house, out of the heat and madness of the day. No one will bother him there. That cat just wants to be left alone.

She walked back into the bedroom and straightened the pillow and folded the afghan on her parents' bed. She ran her hand across Henry's dresser; just the thought of dusting left her exhausted. She picked up the wooden-framed, tin-type photo of Grandma Patricia's six boys, straightened the family portrait to the left of it and put it in place of the boy's photo.

She stared at each boy, searching for the promise in each of them, pulling the photograph closer to her face, so she could find something in their eyes, something that revealed who they were with years and years of life spread before them.

The smallest one must be Jonas. Jonas? Yes, I'm sure of it. He's standing just like Henry does. Just like Tom. Feet spread slightly apart and broad shouldered. Both hands on hips, with a slight turn of the head toward the camera. Father, son, father, son. Emil, Jonas, William, Henry, Tom. A long line of pain passing through those veins, setting the course. Then there's the women who loved them. All they could do was pray and register another birth or death in the family Bible. There's your reward for bringing children in the world and sticking it out in a bad marriage.

She opened the venetian blinds in the bedroom, allowing bright slices of sunlight to lighten the dark room. Peeping through the slats, she saw the two mockingbirds splashing in Henry's bird bath outside the bedroom window. Their spread wings were adjoined in a frantic dance of water and feathers in bright sunlight. She thought of the Emily Dickinson poem she memorized for a grade in her high school English class. She saw herself, thinner, prettier, pronouncing the words in front of the class. She had no idea at the time what any of it meant, but she knew now as she said each word out loud.

> "Hope is the thing with feathers
> That perches in the soul,
> And sings the tune without the words,
> And never stops at all,
>
> And sweetest in the gale is heard;
> And sore must be the storm
> That could abash the little bird
> That kept so many warm.
>
> I've heard it in the chillest land
> And on the strangest sea;
> Yet, never, in extremity,
> It asked a crumb of me."

The bird bath was purchased for Henry the year diabetes took his leg. Gracey thought of the hours he would spend in bed, with only the window in his bedroom to remind him of the living world outside. The view of birds, splashing in the cement bath would give Henry hope, he would recover and, like the little birds before him, fly away from the confines of his bed and disease.

Life and all its movement, its possibilities within reach, so close, so close, reach out and touch it, Henry, taste life outside the bedroom window.

Although the birds were the tiniest of creatures, the David against the Goliath in nature, they still continued to clean their bent wings in the water of the bird bath, despite the cat, despite the fear of falling from their little perch. The brilliance in their creation was their keen sense of sound and perception, so they could fly, far away; far away from any danger or pain.

God knew every bird in the field and their needs, as he knew every hair on Henry's head, every thought and sorrow that troubled him. Don't be afraid, Henry.

But that hope did not come for him. Gracey sighed as she sat on her parents' bed, placing the framed photo of Grandma Patricia's sons next to the Bible on the bedside table. She looked at them both for a long while, then opened the heirloom and turned to the page where the family tree was.

Tracing the birth dates of Jonas and William, she stopped and look at the tintype photo. Jonas and William were only stories and a collection of old photographs to her. Try as she might, she could not feel them, know them, no matter how long she stared at their pictures. The father and son she knew, Henry and Tom, were as familiar to her as the hands that held the Bible. She did not need to look up their birth date, just as she did not have to remind her heart to beat or her lungs to fill with air.

The only thing she felt in looking at her family tree was her grandmothers' disappointments and loss; their determination to endure; their capacity to love and forgive. Then there was her father, on a small branch of the family tree, grafted from the love of William and Viola. His name was penned on the line in the blackest ink, HENRY MUELLER.

It bled across the page, seeping the words "lost boy," "lost father." So she conjured him. The image was instantaneous for her. It was simply a matter of closing her eyes and there he was. Sitting alone, crying at the kitchen table, except for that bottle of whiskey and a cigarette burning in an ash tray.

She watched him, as a young girl in her nightgown, holding on to the door frame between the kitchen and living room, with one foot on top of the other, making herself as thin, as invisible as she could be. She folded her two arms, across each other and made them one. She pulled in her stomach, just in case it peeked outside of the door frame. He would be angry if he saw her there. She held her breath as long as she could, watching him relive all those years.

Henry grieved for his father, William, just as Gracey sat on the bed grieving for her father, Henry. Father, son. Father, daughter. Mother, son. Grandmother, granddaughter. It was the oldest of songs sung by the human race. It was as true as the family tree that held the story of the Walsh-Mueller family.

Chapter Eleven
Viola's Lament

William Jonas Mueller was born August 25, 1905 in Port Lavaca, Texas, following a hurricane that pushed a ten foot wall of water into Lavaca Bay, flooding the low-lying coastal plains and rendering the little town motionless in a quagmire of mud and debris. Wind gusts of 125 mph ripped the tin roof off the rent house he was delivered in. His mother Ida Mueller protected her newborn and two daughters from the August sun with sheets tied in knots across the exposed roof joist. William watched them flap in the humid breeze above his head as he lay in the apple crate his sister found for him to sleep in.

His father was not there.

He grew to be a handsome child with a gentle disposition. His mother read and sang to him as an infant, and his sisters carried him on their young girl hips when he was not on his mother's lap. He was almost fourteen months old before he learned to walk.

The baby preferred to view his world from the safety of the females in the family. A small cry from his pink mouth sent them running towards him with loving eyes and open arms. This did not make for a patient child nor man.

As he grew, he learned to distinguish the times his father was home with the family and when he left them without a note, money, or food. The smell of his father—tobacco, turpentine, sweat, and fish—were the smells of a world beyond the house William lived in, securely with his mother and two older sisters.

The sounds of his father's laughter, singing, crying, and cursing were sounds he learned to love and to hate.

He was christened at Saint Mary Catholic Church, where his grandmother and his mother had been married. He attended the parochial school behind the church and received a Saint Michael's medal for his mastery of the Baltimore Catechism while in the fifth grade. His mother cried with joy, realizing her son loved reading like she and her husband. But Jonas Mueller could not share his wife's joy in their son since he was living in some other town, somewhere along the Texas coast, lost to his family and himself.

In the fall of his twelfth year, William's father came home. Jonas returned from the boxing circuit in Corpus Christi with an envelope full of dollar bills and a new pair of brown leather boxing gloves. Jonas wanted to show his son how to make a living.

On an oyster shell lot near an abandoned warehouse on Lavaca Bay, Jonas stooped to his son's outstretched hands and pushed the gloves over his hands.

"You need to get away from your mama's apron strings, before she ruins you," Jonas laughed, noticing the boy's small pale hands against the dark leather gloves.

"Daddy, I'm doing good in school. I'm first in class with spelling and math," William said to the bent head of his father.

"Math is good. You need it to count your money. The money you'll make in boxing," said Jonas, tying the white strings of the boxing gloves around his son's wrists. "Now, you hit my open palm hard. Let's make sure you got these gloves on good."

The boy laughed and pushed the gloved hand against his father's palm. Jonas fell backwards in an exaggerated stumble from the blow delivered by William. The laughter of the boy and his father echoed against the walls of the abandoned warehouse.

"We'll do some sparring. Watch me." Jonas danced around his son, throwing quick punches into the air with his bare fist and ducking his head at imaginary hands. He jabbed his right fist into the air repeatedly. William watched him. He loved his father.

"Are you ready, William? Today you become a man."

The boy silently commanded his spine to lengthen at his father's words.

I am a man. I am taller. I am my father's son.

"Now, I want you to hit me as hard as you can in the face," coaxed Jonas.

"I don't want to hit you hard, Daddy."

"You must. Like your very life depends on it. Hit me."

Jonas began dancing around his son, throwing quick jabs into his thin shoulders, chest, and head.

"That hurts, Daddy."

"How can that hurt? Now, hit me back. Look, I'm right in front of you, boy. Hit my face."

William began to cry, covering his tears with the brown boxing gloves.

"Move those gloves away from your face and hit me!" Jonas yelled at the boy in front of him.

William cried louder, his small-boy shoulders shaking uncontrollably.

"God Almighty, I'll hit you harder. Maybe it will bring some life into you." Jonas jabbed his right fist into the side of his son's head. The punch was returned with a howl of protest and tears.

"Fight me back, William! Fight, boy!"

William returned a timid punch to his father's stomach. In a split second, instinct flooded Jonas' mind and he returned the slight blow with the force of a hammer. His son fell backwards on the oyster shells and rolled into a fetal position, his bare knees bleeding from where the oyster shells cut them; a whelp the size of his father's hand was rising on the side of his head.

"Don't make more of this than it is, William. We were sparring, that's all."

The boy looked through his tears and saw his father clearly for the first time. He was no different from him. He was a boy, weak and cowardly, hiding behind boxing gloves.

William turned away from him, nauseated at the thought rolling around in his head, ashamed of his father.

Jonas immediately felt that shame spread through his bones.

He looked closely at his son and recalled what he had known since his childhood in the Red Bluff community all those years ago.

Yes, I know, William. I first learned that look from my father, then your mother, and now, you. I know what I am. The world knows what I am.

Jonas grabbed his son's arm and helped him to his feet, avoiding his eyes.

"You won the match, fair and square, boy. I'm disqualified for not using proper gloves." He took a $5 bill from his pants pocket and handed it to him. "Take this fin with Mr. Lincoln on it. It's your purse for the match." Jonas took a deep breath, turned away from his son, and began walking in the direction of Corpus Christi.

William stood in the oyster shell lot with a throbbing head. He gripped the money in his brown leather fist, watching the figure of his father grow smaller and smaller in the haze of the September sun.

A year later William learned from his school friend his father had returned to Port Lavaca.

"I've seen him down at the bay, fishing in a little skiff. He's got a beard now, William," said Earl Janica as the two boys walked to the ice house near Houston Avenue by the railroad tracks. Earl swung a burlap bag across his shoulder to carry the ice home.

"Mama don't like for me to go around him, Earl, but he's my daddy."

"Maybe you can do some fishing with him on that skiff. Ain't nobody need to know about that but you and him."

The following Saturday morning, William woke before his mother and walked to the wharves on Lavaca Bay. He saw his father from a distance, smoking a cigarette and mending a broken net inside the wooden skiff.

"Can I go with you, Daddy?" William called to him from a distance.

Jonas looked up from the boat and saw his son. He tossed his cigarette in the water.

"Got enough bait and an extra pole. Come on."

They fished in the cool air of an April morning. The sky and the water were the same color that day. Their first casts using shrimp for bait hooked four sheepshead.

"We'll fry them in corn meal tonight," Jonas said when William pulled up the first one.

Encouraged by an early catch, they rowed in the direction of the grass flats for speckled trout.

"Need to be careful around the mud and oyster shell reefs here," cautioned Jonas.

He made the first cast in the new spot and quickly reeled in a sixteen-inch trout with its large mouth of sharp teeth and its olive body covered in black spots. The fish's silvery underside glistened in the morning sun.

"Come on, William. Get your shrimp in the water. We're in the right place now."

They caught twenty speckled trout that day. When they returned to the wharf, William lined the trout and the sheepshead on the wooden boards of the wharf, then gutted each one, throwing the entrails to the waiting cats pacing below them.

"I got a little place out back by that old warehouse. We'll cook 'em up there."

William followed his father to a tent standing in oyster shells, shaded by the building next to it. His father had made a little fire pit in front of the tent; a straight-back wooden chair without arms was the lone piece of furniture to be seen.

That evening they cooked the fish.

Jonas drank from a bottle of whiskey, leaning against the little wooden chair, while rolling the fish in corn meal and salt; he carefully placed them in an iron skillet of bubbling oil. William bent over the skillet slowly turning each piece of fish with the flat blade of his pocket knife.

They ate the fish off pages of newspaper his father kept in the tent. William licked the corn meal and oil off his fingers. He couldn't remember when he had tasted anything so good.

They didn't feel the need to talk. The father and son were

comfortable in the silence between them as the sun sank into Lavaca Bay. After they finished eating, Jonas took the remaining fish and wrapped it in the newspaper.

"You go on home, now. Don't make your mama worry. Take the fish and this." He handed the boy a piece of cloth wrapped with string. "You make sure she gets this money, William. She needs it a lot more than you."

"Can I come back tomorrow?"

"I have business tomorrow. You go to Mass with your mama and sisters. You can come see me next week."

William walked home in the dark. His mother and sisters were not there when he opened the door. A note on the kitchen table said they were at the neighbors shelling peas and would return home by eight o'clock. He placed the cloth tied with string on the kitchen table. He put the fried fish rolled in newspaper next to it.

He removed his pants standing in front of the bed and hung them across the headboard, leaving his shirt on in case he got cold during the night. He closed his eyes as soon as his head touched the pillow; he slept the dreamless, fitful sleep of those who are happy and loved.

After school and finishing the chores his mother had for him on Wednesday, William walked to the tent by the wharves. His father wasn't there. He walked to the shoreline of the bay and looked for his father's boat. The single-masted skiff was gone. He walked back to his mother's house and waited for another day to visit his father.

By evening, the unpredictable late spring weather of South Texas delivered black skies choked with lightning across the bay. The temperature plummeted twenty degrees within minutes. William watched his mother race to the clothesline behind the house. Just as she reached for the wooden clothespin holding the sheet on the line, cold rain fell from the skies.

William thought of his father and the boat. He ran outside to stare into the black sky. The winds spiked from twenty mph to nearly seventy mph in the few minutes he was outside.

"Go back in and get in the kitchen with your sisters. It's the only room in the house without windows. This storm might spur a tornado," Ida shouted at him as she forced her body to move against the wind into the open door of the house.

Inside the kitchen, near the wood-burning stove, Ida and her three children held hands and prayed as the wind and the rain hammered the little grey clapboard house.

"Graciously hear us, O Lord, when we call upon You, and grant unto our supplications a calm atmosphere, that we, who are justly afflicted for our sins, may, by Your protecting mercy, experience pardon. Through Christ our Lord. Amen."

As Jonas' wife and his three children made the sign of the cross, his little boat flipped into rolling, ten-foot waves. Jonas swam to the side of the boat and held on with both hands. He tried to upright the boat, but the wind and waves rocked it violently until he lost his grip. He watched it dip up and down in the water a few feet from him. It occurred to him he could swim to it if he gave it all his strength, but he didn't. Instead, he watched his lifeline dip up and down only a few yards from him. Still, he didn't swim to it. He laughed out loud when he realized he was bobbing up and down in the water just like the boat. Suddenly, he felt very tired and cold. He let his head slip underneath the black water. Below the surface, the world was calm with soft colors and muted sounds. He felt a peace he had not known in years as he closed his eyes to the same grave his grandfather Colum Walsh found in the Atlantic.

Two workers from the seafood processing plant found Jonas' body six days later on the grass flats he had fished with his son just a week before. His fingers and toes had been eaten by crabs. They knew it was Jonas Mueller, though . . . on his finger was his gold wedding band. When they pried it off and over the chewed flesh, they saw the name 'Ida' engraved inside the band of gold.

Charles Janica, Earl's father, came to the door of the little grey clapboard house and delivered finality and grief to Ida Mueller and her two daughters. For William, he delivered regret and rage. The boy took his regret and rage and ran with them to the tent his father had lived in on the shoreline of Lavaca Bay.

There he found a bundle of newspapers, the red leather-covered *Hard Times* by Charles Dickens, a pair of boxing gloves, and a bottle of whiskey. Inside of that bottle, he found what his father had found—a softening, a solace against the world and its pain and disappointments. Sitting on the wharf that night with the rotgut between his legs, and the boxing gloves tied together around his neck, William cried. No one heard his sorrow; no one understood his pain like the bottle of amber liquid between his legs.

At thirteen, William quit school and got a full time job at the WB Seafood Processing Plant with his two older sisters. On the weekends, he fished with Earl and sold bottles of iced Coke along the wharves to tourists from Houston and Victoria. He was proud to be able to help his mama.

In 1921 life was improving for the residents of Port Lavaca. A large seawall was built to protect them from storms, and the abundance of a successful shrimping season brought the town's first quick-freezing plant. In time, William would deliver shrimp to El Campo, Rosenburg, and Houston in a Dodge panel van. His routine was marked by the final fifty miles home to Port Lavaca, where he ceremonially took the last sip from the bottle of whiskey next to him.

At twenty-six years old, William still lived with his mother. And every Saturday night, Ida would starch and iron his shirt and pants, placing a five dollar bill in his shirt pocket with an unopened pack of Camel cigarettes.

They no longer lived in the grey clapboard rent house. William had found them another house in town, so Ida could walk to Mass at St. Mary's. His sisters had married and moved to Point Comfort, returning to Lavaca Bay daily for their jobs at the processing plant. His mother had the church to love and his sisters had their husbands, but William had no one.

There had been women, plenty of women along the road from Port Lavaca to Houston. He met them in beer joints in Rosenberg or cafés in El Campo. His interest in them was gone as quickly as the satisfaction he felt from taking them roughly in the back of the panel van parked along some country road.

But a feeling deep inside him awoke from a long sleep when he saw the back of a girl standing in front of the Allen Drug Store in Ganado, Texas on a Friday afternoon in early December. Her chestnut hair fell to the center of her back. The emerald-green wool coat she wore was cinched at the waist with its white fur collar nestled against her slender neck. The colors that enveloped the girl for a moment erased the grey poverty of the early 1930s.

He pulled the panel van next to Citizens Bank and walked into the drug store. She stood in front of the soda fountain and placed two small bottles on the glass counter top: a bottle of Bayer Aspirin and a bottle with a black crow on the label and the words Carter's Little Liver Pills ~ 'Make the Liver do its Duty.'

"Can I pay for this here, Mr. Schoen?"

"Of course, Viola. Looks like someone isn't feeling good."

"My papa."

The drug store clerk wrapped the two bottles in brown paper and tied them with a string.

"Here you are. Hope your daddy feels better."

"Thank you, Mr. Schoen."

When she turned around, William saw her face.

Viola with the violet-colored eyes. You're going to be my wife.

William stepped ahead of the violet-eyed girl, so he could open the door for her, tipping his hat and smiling broadly.

"Thank you."

"I'm sure you'd like to get that medicine home to your daddy right away, but maybe you'd have some time for a cup of coffee?" William queried.

The violet-eyed girl's face turned red.

"I came to town with my brother. You can walk with me back to his truck."

As William walked down Main Street with Viola Schuler, he

saw mothers with babies on their hips and older children linked hand-in-hand walking into Kacer Grocery Store, along with farmers standing in front of Mauritz Farming Equipment & Feed, discussing the weather and their crops. There was life all around him on the streets of Ganado. It was a good life. Predictable and quiet. William wanted that life. Viola would be the girl to give him that life, for a while.

"Here's my brother's truck. I didn't even ask you your name?"

"William. William Mueller. My folks are from Port Lavaca and Francitas."

"Please to meet you, William. Why don't you come out to my papa's place on Sunday?"

"Yes, ma'am. Where 'bout y'all live?"

"Twenty miles out, only road west of town. The Schuler place. You'll see a two-story farm house with rows of corn right in front of it."

"What time should I come?"

"Why don't you come for church service at 11 AM? You'll see the Antioch Baptist Church on the way, then we can all go out to the house together. You can meet my mama and papa."

"I'm Catholic, Viola, but I guess the church roof won't cave in when I walk through the door."

Viola laughed. "You don't need to worry my mama and papa by telling them you're Catholic. Just say you're a Christian. That's what really counts."

"I can be Baptist, Viola, if you wanted me to. And I can be a farmer, if that suits you. Just because I lived and worked on the water my whole life doesn't mean I can't do anything else," he said and opened the truck door for her. She stepped up into the truck cab and smoothed her dress and coat with her hand.

"I believe that to be true, William Mueller," smiling at him through the open truck window.

William met Mr. and Mrs. Schuler on the porch of the farm house following church service with their daughter at Antioch Baptist Church Sunday morning. He brought the mother and daughter a bouquet of yellow roses he purchased in Port Lavaca the night before. The old German farmer took one look at the flowers and the new shoes on William's feet and walked back into the house, letting the screen door slam behind him.

"Don't pay him no mind, Mr. Mueller. My husband is not a sentimental man," said Clara Schuler. "I'm gonna get a little lunch on for us. Why don't you and Viola have a look around while I do that." Five feet and three inches tall with her grey hair pulled into a bun, Clara Schuler appeared much older than her fifty-five years. The life of a farmer's wife, raising ten children and working alongside her husband in the fields, made her an old woman by the time she was thirty-five.

Viola and William held hands as they walked around the farm. She showed him the barn and the smoke house. Back behind a thicket of mustang grape vines, they sat on a wooden bench.

"This is a nice place y'all have here."

"It's quiet mostly. Papa works us pretty hard during the week. We go to town almost every Saturday. Sunday is for God."

"Do you get bored? Or maybe even lonely?'

Viola laughed. "Papa makes sure no one gets bored, much less sits still. I got my whole family here. Why would I be lonely?"

"I was just thinking out loud," he said, taking her hand into his. "I like music. How about you? Do you have a favorite song?"

"I have just about every song in the church hymnal memorized by heart. We do have a radio in the house, and Papa lets us listen to popular music."

"I want to sing you a little song right now, Miss Schuler. When I met you last week in town, I haven't stopped thinking about you. You remind me of this song."

Viola's face turned red as she looked down at their two hands folded into one, resting on the bench between them.

"Beautiful dreamer, wake unto me,
Starlight and dewdrops are waiting for thee;
Sounds of the rude world, heard in the day,
Lull'd by the moonlight have all pass'd away!

Beautiful dreamer, queen of my song,
List while I woo thee with soft melody;
Gone are the cares of life's busy throng,
Beautiful dreamer, awake unto me!
Beautiful dreamer, awake unto me!

Beautiful dreamer, out on the sea,
Mermaids are chanting the wild Lorely;
Over the streamlet vapors are borne,
Waiting to fade at the bright coming morn.
Beautiful dreamer, beam on my heart,
E'en as the morn on the streamlet and sea;
Then will all clouds of sorrow depart,
Beautiful dreamer, awake unto me!
Beautiful dreamer, awake unto me!"

When William finished singing, he brushed Viola's hair off her shoulder with one hand. Then turning her face toward his with the other, he pressed his lips against hers. A small sigh escaped from somewhere inside Viola.

In the distance, he heard a screen door slam and the voice of Clara Schuler: "Viola, y'all come on now. The food's ready."

William and Viola were married in May at the Antioch Baptist Church. Ida came with her daughters and son-in-laws from Port Lavaca and Point Comfort. She wore a navy dress, a black hat, and a new pair of black Swagger Sport Oxfords with a sensible heel. She cried when William pinned a white gardenia to her dress before the ceremony.

"I wish you a lifetime of happiness, William."

"Wouldn't that be nice, Mama? A lifetime of happiness. Seems we're all due for some of that," William said, hugging her with both arms.

Nearly sixty people stood to honor the bride as she walked down the aisle with her unsmiling father.

Viola wore a veil of white pinned behind her ears with bobby pins. The wedding dress her mother had made was cut from cotton percale with the bodice cinched at the waist and a full skirt. It fell to her ankles, revealing a pair of white high heels with peep holes on both sides of the shoe. She borrowed them from her sister-in-law the week before. She carried a bouquet of white calla lilies from her mother's garden.

The dreams of a young girl in love and the desperation of a young man to find peace brought Viola and William Mueller to a small cotton farm in Francitas the day after they were married.

Arthur Mueller sold his nephew a small parcel of land not far from the original homestead of his parents, Emil and Patricia Mueller. William used his uncle's tractor to plow the dry fields. He added a coat of new paint to the exterior of the farm house and painted the bedroom he shared with his young wife a pale blue. In the early months of the marriage, his energy was as boundless as the love he felt for the violet-eyed girl he married.

Gone were the days of the open road and the lost, fatherless boy from Port Lavaca. William would finally live the life he dreamed of as a child.

But trouble found him. The physical labors of a cotton farm were different than those of fishing and delivering shrimp. A day's work on the water produced good money. The cotton he raised sold for pennies. The growing Depression tightened the knot in his gut each day as he watched what little he had slip away in the heat and dust of a cotton farm.

His young wife was swollen with pregnancy eleven months into the marriage. He could go nowhere to ease his mind. When he made the drives in the panel van to Houston, he would soothe his aching head and gut in a cool, dark bar. If he were only back in Port Lavaca, he could fish and drink with Earl in the grass flats or throw a cast out from the wharves of Lavaca Bay. There was nothing in Francitas for him; nothing but work, responsibility, and a future with more of the same.

"I'm going to town for supplies. Might cross on over to Port Lavaca to see Mama," he told his wife one evening after supper.

"But William, the baby will be here any day now. I'm scared alone," said Viola, picking up his plate and fork and placing them in an enamel bowl of soapy water on a rickety table next to the stove.

"Viola, you're a farm girl. Having a baby ain't nothing for you and your people," William laughed.

"Well, all right, if it's only for a day, but stop and tell Mrs. Zajeck on your way out, so she can check on me while you're gone. I don't think I can walk all the way to her house being pregnant and all."

"It's less than a mile. Stop your worrying."

"You're a cold man to leave his wife right before she has your baby," Viola said, bursting into tears.

"I don't need a seventeen-year-old, snot-nose girl to tell me how to come and go. Much less tell me what kind of man I am. You wouldn't know a man or what to do with him, country girl, if he stood right in front of you, like I'm doing right now."

"Why are you being so mean, William? Don't you love me? I'm your wife," Viola cried into her cupped hands placed over her eyes.

"I can't take you bossing me around all day. You learn how to be a wife and I'll come back and be a husband," he said, slamming the door behind him. He found himself running to the 1929 Ford truck he kept parked in the barn. When he turned the key, his heart leaped with the engine.

I'm going to do some fishing and drinking with Earl. Gonna do some living. I ain't gonna spend every hour of my life sweating on a cotton farm and listening to that woman tear me down.

William was thinking about a song he heard on a radio in a little bar just south of Houston when he sped past Mrs. Zajeck's house. He sang it out loud against the hum of the tires on the road to Port Lavaca. "I got no worries on my mind. Left my troubles far behind."

The second night William was gone Viola's water broke. She touched her stomach to reassure herself and her unborn child, then removed her wet panties. She dressed in the dark, pulling on William's cowboy boots he kept in the corner of the bedroom. She was afraid of walking on a snake at night. She knew they liked to come out when the weather was cooler and lie in the open road. She could kill it with the boot heel if she had to. She lit the kerosene lamp from a match box she kept on the stove, and closed the door to the house behind her.

She was thankful for the moon-filled light that cast shadows on the road to Mrs. Zajeck's house. By the first half-mile, her labor pains had increased and she began to worry.

I can't give in to fear. Won't do me no bit of good. I just have to keep putting one foot in front of the other. Jesus, guide me, guide me to Mrs. Zajeck's door. Help me and my little baby.

By the time she walked two miles, her breathing was shaky and the labor pains had increased in violent waves across her hips, back, and stomach.

Help me, Lord. Help me. Please don't let my innocent baby be born in the dark. Lead me there. Take my hand, Jesus.

In the distance she heard a dog bark. With each step she took, the barking became louder. A light appeared before her. She saw the silhouette of an old woman in a nightgown, bending over, talking to a dog standing next to her.

"Who's out there?" shouted the old woman from the front porch. "Hush, your barking, Lily. Hush."

"Mrs. Zajeck. It's me. Viola. I'm gonna have my baby."

"Oh, heavens! Stay there, honey, I'll come for you. Don't be afraid of Lily. She's just excited. She won't bite."

Henry Mueller, the first child and only son of William and Viola Mueller, was delivered by Frances Zajeck on April 2, 1931 in Francitas, Texas.

Viola laid in Mrs. Zajeck's bed, covered lightly with a thin sheet, nursing her child at her breast. Frances sat in a kitchen chair next to the bed, with a cold washcloth, tracing Viola's tears and sweat across her brow and cheeks, to the crevices of her thin neck and innocent ears.

"Mrs. Zajeck, you'll need to find my husband. He had work in Port Lavaca and had to leave. Find William and tell him I gave him a son, a sweet little baby. He's just perfect, every finger and toe in place, two eyes to see God's world, a straight noise and little round mouth. He's perfect, perfect as only God could make him. Our Henry. Our son."

Chapter Twelve
Keeper of Secrets

Gracey returned the Bible to the bedside table and walked into her bedroom. She pulled a sundress from the suitcase on the bed and began to get ready for her trip to the hospital. On a shelf near the bed was a photograph of her in a lavender prom dress with a boy she knew in high school.

Well, it must have been serious. Look at the orchid corsage on my wrist. It's the size of a truck tire. That dress! Lavender and a lavender sash around the waist. Mama and I bought it in Victoria. What a day that was, right before the junior prom. What could have been so good, changed, changed so quickly. Everything changed, forever.

Gracey looked around the room, but her eyes came back to the photograph; she didn't want to remember, but the girl in the lavender dress, she knew so long ago, spoke to her through the years.

Mama took me right away to the mall. I remember every detail of that day, but can't remember the name of the boy in the picture to save my life. I was a different girl then, before that day. I had to stop being just Gracey. I had to become the protector of my mother. I was the keeper of her secrets . . .

Mother and daughter were alone in the car, returning from Victoria. They'd spent the day shopping for a prom dress; they ate lunch at Luby's with other mothers and daughters who had been shopping. The middle-class rite of passage gave Helen and Gracey an intimacy they didn't dare hope for in Loti. Helen's timing was perfect. There would never be a better day to tell her side of the story.

Helen let Gracey drive. "You're a big girl, now, honey. You get us home." She watched the side of her daughter's face, searching for any hint of rejection. She turned off the car radio and took another drag of her cigarette.

"Honey, I need to tell you something. You're a woman now, and you need to understand some things." Helen turned again to study her sixteen-year-old daughter's face. She took another long drag off her cigarette, and exhaled the smoke in jagged fumes.

"There's things between a man and a woman that can happen so quickly, without you even knowing it. It can change you, make you do things you don't ever think you're capable of doing," Helen sighed. "I'm not a perfect person, Gracey. I want you to understand me before, before you leave the house and go out on your own."

"Mom?" Gracey turned to face her.

"I had just delivered you. I was tired, basically exhausted, and your father, well, he was never home. When he did come home, he was drunk." Helen didn't turn to look at her daughter; instead, she blankly stared straight ahead at the two lanes of asphalt in front of her. "I hated living in Houston; we had an apartment in the Heights. I missed my family, missed Louisiana. No one to talk to all day in that apartment. Hell, I was a kid myself, taking care of two kids."

Gracey gripped the steering wheel with two wet palms. *Don't do it, Mom. Don't ruin it. Please, one normal day.*

Helen stabbed the burning cigarette into the car ashtray and slammed the little metal door closed. A stream of white smoke spilled through the perfect metal seams, evaporating into the floor board.

"I wasn't taking care of myself. Living on coffee and cigarettes to keep myself going. There was a man who lived in the apartment complex. He was kind." Helen began to cry. "We took you and Tom to my brother's house in Lafayette, and I left. I drove off in that car, left my babies, and drove away. It wasn't for the sex—you'll understand some day—it was so I could live . . . live a little bit."

"Why, why are you telling me this?" shouted Gracey. "I don't want to know! I don't want to know!"

Helen ignored her and continued talking, only faster now. She had waited a lifetime to tell this story. She couldn't stop now, though she heard the sound of her daughter's adolescent heart beating louder and louder next to her.

"Your daddy stayed gone a long time after that. Of course, nothing lasted with that man. I went back and got you and Tom. Had the same little apartment. The church down the street helped us out with groceries. Found your daddy, eventually. No big surprise, found him in a bar one night. Left you and Tom in the locked car and walked on in there." Helen gave a nervous laugh and lit another cigarette. "I had two kids who needed a daddy. I really didn't care what anyone thought. Walked right up to him sitting on a bar stool. He slapped me in front of his friends, but he left with me. Even drove us all home. He never said another word about it that night. Not one word about the whole thing."

Gracey looked straight ahead at the highway before her. She fought the urge to drive the car off the freeway into the cement culverts in the drainage ditch serving as a shoulder. She wanted her mother to shut her mouth.

"Dreams are broken when you marry at seventeen, Gracey. Funny, I loved Henry then, just as I do now. But marriage, it's a lot of work. Day-to-day living can kill love." Helen leaned toward her daughter and patted her thigh. She released a little sigh, then inhaled a ragged breath.

"I may have been disappointed in my marriage, but never in my kids. I want you to have a better life. Get an education, so you never have to depend on a man for money. Make your own. There's no need to live the same life I've lived. Best to learn from my mistakes and don't repeat 'em."

Gracey stared at the road ahead of her.

"Are you lost, Goosey? You passed the Loti exit."

"Sorry, Mama. I'll turn around."

Gracey took one thing from her mother's lesson that day, and she repeated it every day until it became second nature.

I have to try and be good, a good girl, and never, ever be a bother or get into any trouble. One stupid mistake can cost you and everyone around you any chance at happiness.

Gracey never told her brother and sister what their mother had shared with her. Her mother had been right. She was a woman, now. She understood the importance of keeping secrets and reading people's faces.

Gracey thought of her childhood traveling with Tom and Henry in the truck, looking for her mother . . .

That her mother would leave again was the only consistent pattern Gracey knew in their lives. If Helen left during the week, Henry took a draw on his paycheck, then collected his children from the neighbors where Helen had left them the night before. Two little children and two peanut butter and jelly sandwiches wrapped in wax paper were handed to Henry. Their first stop before leaving town was a liquor store where Henry bought a pint of blended whiskey and cashed his paycheck.

The three of them were aligned in a straight row on the bench seat with Gracey sitting between Henry and Tom. She often slept against the crook of her father's extended arm at the steering wheel. The first miles were always the best. Henry had a purpose. Tom and Gracey were with their father. But fear found them in the cab of the truck. It ate at them. "Maybe, maybe their lives would always be this way," it whispered to them.

Usually by the eighth mile marker, Tom vomited. He rubbed his stomach with both of his hands. He looked at his sister with desperate eyes and vomited again, not on the floorboard of the truck, but on himself, sitting on the bench seat, crying for his mother.

Henry looked his son; he didn't say a word. He pulled into a gas station at the first exit. After helping Tom out of the truck, he locked Gracey inside the cab. Hand-in-hand the father and son walked to the side of the building to the men's room.

When they returned, Tom's face and hair were wet, and he was wearing Henry's long-sleeved shirt. Henry, wearing a tee shirt, handed each child a bottle of 7-Up and a bag of peanuts.

"Here you go, little buddies. This will help your tummies. Let's get the radio on and head to Grandma's. We're almost there." Henry started the truck, pushed the clutch, and shifted at the steering wheel. He smiled at his children balancing bottles of 7-Up between their legs and pouring peanuts down their throats.

"Look here, that's a good song. Sing it with me, Gracey."

The three of them saw the Dairy Dream sign together. The crunch of the oyster shell parking lot beneath the truck tires resonated in the cab. Grandma Viola opened the truck door and reached for the two children. The cab was immediately filled with the scent of Juicy Fruit gum and Youth Dew perfume.

Thirty minutes later, Henry was gone. Tom and Gracey stayed with Viola and their Grandpa Bauer. They did not see their mother. They did not see their father. For eight months, they lived with the daily anticipation of meeting Henry again at the Dairy Dream parking lot.

When Helen and Henry didn't show up for Christmas, Tom, with all the rage of a desperate and hurt nine-year-old, took the BB gun his grandfather bought for him and shot out the windows of Viola's car. His grandfather grabbed him by one arm and dragged him to the side of the house, removed the belt from around his waist and whipped Tom's naked legs and arms.

Gracey watched from the front door, crying.

"Don't hurt him, Grandpa Bauer, don't hurt him. He didn't mean to."

Afterwards, Tom walked inside the house, closed the door to the bedroom and wept on the loneliness of a cot, a temporary bed for a boy who lived in a temporary home.

"Tom, Tom, let me see. Let me see, Tom," Gracey cried on the other side of the locked door. Tom did not reply.

He remained silent in his anger for the rest of his life. He could not trust people, let alone the chance of ever being happy.

He was forever the nine-year-old boy throwing up, breaking

out car windows, and being whipped in public. His mother, father, and grandfather never showed him what it was to be a man . . .

At fifty-two, Gracey wondered if her brother would ever forgive any of them.

Tom, I know everything you know about this family. There's no secret, no rock unturned. I know them all. I've kept them buried for years in my gut. When they'd rise up to haunt me, I'd stomp them down with anger and resentment. You got nothing on me, brother. We're both eaten alive with resentment.

She reached for the light switch and darkness fell in her childhood bedroom. Stopping to look at herself in the dresser mirror in the dimmed light coming through the unshaded window, she saw her mother and father in her face. She saw Tom and Angela. She saw Viola, Patricia and Aileen. She couldn't help herself. She loved them.

Chapter Thirteen
Running on Empty

"I need to get back to the hospital," Gracey sighed.

She pulled her hair into a tight pony tail, grabbed a Diet Coke out of the refrigerator, and left her father's house.

Once she drove out of the small town traffic of downtown Loti, stopping for every truck and sedan making a left hand-turn into the Dairy Queen parking lot for an early lunch, she called Mark.

"I'm on my way to the hospital. Need to check with the nurses, maybe see the doctor. Don't know what I'll do from there. I'm so sad, Mark. I shouldn't be here alone. Too many memories in that old house."

"I know, baby. I can't stop thinking about you. Are you getting any sleep?

"I rest during the day. Little cat naps here and there. It seems like I've been here for weeks, but it's only been a few days."

"Well, you don't have your routine of work and home to mark up the hours of the day. You're just weighing out every minute of your life right now. Probably thinking about things too much.

"How could I not? I did get a phone call from Therese. She sounds so happy. She and Daniel have booked the reception at some castle in Darver. That picked me up quite a bit. Haven't heard from Will. I guess it's too hard for him to talk about everything. He's got school and work to keep him busy. I miss you. I miss my kids."

"Don't get upset, Gracey. I can't stand the thought of you driving down the road, crying. Pull over, and we'll talk."

"No, I can't. I've got to see this through."

"Look, your dad doesn't know if you're there or not. Where are Tom and Angela? Want me to call them? I have no problem with that. Do you want me to come?"

Gracey knew he didn't want to come. If he did, he wouldn't have asked her. He would already be there with her.

"I'm okay. I'm really okay, I think. I've talked to Tom. He may be here tomorrow. Hey, do this for me while I'm thinking about it. Make sure you have a clean suit. See about Will's, too. Make the cleaners do a 24-hour turn around. I don't think things will change here. No one is expecting miracles, much less praying for them. I'm sure you'll be pallbearers with Tom, Henry's nephews in Houston, and John. Handle the household stuff for me and get those suits taken care of. That would help a lot."

"You still didn't tell me where Angela is?"

"Well, I left her a message. They're travelling on business, Mark. I think she and John are buying another pump and valve company in Oklahoma. Or was it Midland? Some oil city in some oil state, somewhere. Was it Waco? No, couldn't be. Hell, I don't know."

"Did you let her know things are urgent? That you need her to get to the hospital right away?"

"Why yes I did, Mark, in a way that wouldn't cause a heart attack or the shakes when she received it. Angela has a different relationship than I do with Henry. She loves him as if, as if, well . . . you know what I'm saying. I'm not getting in the middle of it. She'll see him when she gets here. I've got to keep things simple or I'll lose my mind.

"A text would keep it simple. You can write it and she can read it at her convenience."

"I'm doing the best I can here. You can't just leave crazy text messages on people's cell phones. Who could handle a text reading, DAD ON DEATH BED! GET HERE ASAP!"

"That's not what I'm suggesting."

"Help me out here. I'm too tired to decipher what you're trying to tell me. Just say it for God's sake!"

"Okay, be good to yourself, Gracey. Stop trying to hold it all together. You don't have to be in charge."

"Mark, I don't know how to handle this any better than I'm doing right now. I'm not going to call them up and demand they get here. They both have jobs and kids. Lots of responsibilities. We all do. It's just . . . each of us has a different kind of relationship with Henry. It's hard enough to accept my own relationship with him. I don't know what's the right thing to do. I'm, I'm all over the place with the past, the present, I don't know what to do with myself."

"Gracey, pull over right now."

Like a scolded child, frustrated by her own inabilities to improve her situation, she obeyed him and pulled the car to the side of the road. A tractor trailer loaded with bales of hay whooshed by her, causing the little car to lean temporarily on its right side.

"Are you there?"

"Oh yeah, right here on the side of Highway 77 in 100 degree heat."

"Let the car run, Gracey and stay in it."

"I just need you to be kind to me right now. I just need a little attention and some kindness." Gracey's voice cracked with a sob.

"Gracey, you know I love you. This time, this very bad time in our lives, is not going to last forever. We'll get through it. You're going to get through it, Grace. Like you always have. Yes, most of it is out of your control. You can't bend it, you just have to adjust to what comes your way. But there's a few things you can control, to make it easier on yourself.

"Like what? Please don't make me mad, Mark. I was just starting to fall in love with you, again."

"I'm going to say this as gently as I can, because, damn it, you need to hear it. Quit digging up bones. I bet you're in that house, digging through old photo albums, probably reading an old diary, and going through every bill, letter, birthday card your mom and dad ever wrote or paid. When's the last time you ate a decent meal?"

Gracey stared at the opened Diet Coke can between her legs and the grease-soaked Sonic bag on the floor board.

"Well, you caught me red handed. Juke food and caffeine are all I've got right now."

"No, Gracey, you have me, and Therese, Will. You have people who love you, love you unconditionally."

"Yes," she said slowly, allowing herself to enjoy the gift he offered her. The gift that had always been there, though she had so often refused it. "Yes, Mark, we do love each other. Our children . . . our home. I needed that. I need you," she said, feeling the balm of his words to the core of her being.

"Take it easy. Just slow down with everything. There's no reason to tear yourself up, especially driving down the road. Now, call me when you find something out at the hospital."

"I will. Love you."

The cell phone went blank and he was gone.

She pulled into the hospital parking lot, parking near three small post oaks to use as landmarks when she needed to find the car later. She walked to the elevator in the main lobby. The bird-like receptionist was no longer at her desk. Gracey imagined she flew home in a yellow hybrid to a wild, screeching flock of children who looked a lot like her and her accommodating husband.

She saw the nurse's station when the elevator door opened. She approached the first nurse who smiled and made eye contact with her. She seemed to be the most accepting of the three women behind the large, curved counter. When Gracey got closer, she noticed they all had the same sallow, lined faces from years of working indoors and comforting the sick.

"When will Mr. Mueller's doctor be in?" she asked.

"Dr. Pencik makes his rounds at 11, I'll tell him Mr. Mueller has a family member who wants to see him. Are you on the list for HIPPA purposes?"

"Yes. I'm Gracey Reiter, the oldest daughter."

"I'll let him know, Ms. Gracey. I just checked on your dad. He's resting, not much has changed." She gave Gracey a sad little nod of the chin. "The coffee's fresh in the reception area, if you'd like a cup."

"No, thank you. Appreciate it. Appreciate everything you've done for my dad."

"We provide grievance counseling. I can get you a brochure with a phone number if you'd like. Or, the hospital's chapel is open twenty-four hours a day. You can have your privacy in there."

"Oh, I'll be all right." Gracey wondered if she looked as bad as she felt, since the nurse seemed concerned about her mental state.

She went into the visitors' reception area in search of a restroom. Inside, standing in front of the sink mirror, she outlined her lips in mauve lipstick, and rubbed some of the color against her cheekbones. She gave a dissatisfied look into the mirror and retraced her lips in a final dredge of color, pressing down harder than she had before. She broke off the tip of the lipstick and threw it with a clunk into the metal garbage can at her feet.

She found her brush at the bottom of her purse. Removing the elastic band from the pony tail she made earlier, she brushed her hair furiously, stopped, gave it a quick fluff, then tucked it behind her ears. She looked at herself in the mirror.

The exact same. Absolutely no difference than when I walked in here.

She threw the brush into the bottom of her purse and pushed the door open with her right foot.

Room 605 was dark and cold when she stepped in. Irma wasn't there. She left for a cigarette break. Henry was still sleeping in the same position Gracey had last seen him in. Next to his bed, a dull hum escaped from the orchestra of tubes and machines pumping toxins in and out of his body.

She didn't sit down. She stood next to the drawn curtains, watching him sleep. She didn't know what to do with herself, other than stand there. She folded and refolded the newspaper she read from earlier. She threw away the unopened Copenhagen cans she had given him. Next, she placed the Astros baseball cap on top of the folded newspaper. She spotted the oversized gift bag, billowing with tissue paper next to the vinyl chair. She folded the tissue paper into neat squares, tucked them into the gift bag and placed it underneath the newspaper. With all that effort, the clock had only moved by a minute or two.

Things were different this time. When her mother was in the hospital, she slept next to her bed in a different vinyl chair. She didn't eat. She didn't sleep. She could hardly breathe, thinking it might waste time, time she wanted. Time she could never get back again. It would be too late, too late; she would be gone.

But Gracey was Helen's girl, her confidante and confessor, the protector of her secret. When Helen died, Gracey felt both liberated and bitter. Liberated from the responsibility, bitter for the wasted years. The one truth that made sense to her caused her the most pain. Their lives could have been better. She still believed that. Nothing through the years had changed that simple fact for her. Not time. Not her marriage. Not her children. Not Henry's illness. Nothing. Their lives could have been better.

When she was a little girl, she'd pretend her mother was married to someone else, someone other than Henry. She still would have been Helen's daughter, but their lives would have been different. Her mother would have remained young and beautiful. Cancer free. Wrinkle free. Care free.

Gracey's pretend family would be like all the other families she knew when she was a girl. The mothers were busy all day restocking the Dixie Cups in the bathroom dispenser and planting roses in the front yard, while their fathers came home driving shiny cars and wearing clean clothes. They swung their lunch pails as they whistled their way to the front doors of all the neatly trimmed, brick houses. Their wives met them at the door with a peck on the cheek and their children hugged their pant legs. Life could have been that simple, that ordinary. It would have made Gracey and her mother very happy to live that life.

But Helen gave up on taking reckless chances when Angela was born. When she needed a vacation from Henry, she visited her relatives in Louisiana. By the time she was fifty, she no longer looked for an escape route. Instead, a desperate existence, day-after-day, year-after-year, took the place of happiness. Gracey would never stop grieving for her.

God, help me. Help me forgive him. He's my father. Mama, you were easier to love. I don't know why. Maybe because you owned every mistake you ever made. You paid for it, every day. But Henry, he couldn't. He could not say it. I never heard the man say I'm sorry for anything he did. But he sure could let us all know how miserable he was. I have to forgive him or it will simply eat me alive, every day for the rest of my life.

She sat in the green vinyl chair next to his bed. She realized with Henry's approaching death came the conclusion to the story. In that story, Helen would forever be the broken woman desperate for absolution, and Henry would be the betrayed man, driving up and down the roads of South Texas in a truck, searching for something he would never find, a perfect marriage.

She stood up and leaned over the hospital bed, kissed Henry on the head, and put her hand over his. He didn't stir.

"Daddy." She bent down, closer to his face. "Daddy." The sound of her voice was of the little girl sitting next to him in the 1959 Chevy truck. He didn't open his eyes; he didn't flutter his lashes; he didn't reach for her hand, the hand of his little girl, Gracey. But Gracey reached for his hand and placed it in hers, and covered it with the side of her face.

Henry was lost, lost to this world, somewhere between death and an existence created by the medical industry, fed by the pharmaceutical industry, and documented by the insurance industry. Limbo, limbo, limbo repeated the machines, as the death march played on.

The door opened to the hospital room, and Gracey turned to see the doctor enter the room.

She was struck by how young he was, or maybe she hadn't realized how old she had become. She was sure he was at least thirty, maybe mid-thirties, but it was hard to tell. He was wearing a pair of sunglasses, which she found very odd. He took them off, before speaking to her, and placed them in the front pocket of his lab coat.

"Mrs. Reiter, Dr. Pencik." He extended his hand and she shook it. It was smooth, soft, with neatly trimmed nails. He wore a Mariner Rolex with the brilliant nautical blue face. "I'm afraid not much has changed. Your father sleeps mostly. We're giving him some oxygen to help him breathe easier. We are dealing with pneumonia now, and your father is retaining quite a bit of fluid. We're making him as comfortable as possible. It won't be much longer, I'm afraid. You should call your family."

"My sister should be here today. I'll leave her name at the nurse's station, my brother's, too," she said looking at him, then turned away to look at Henry.

"Let me know if there is anything we can do for your family. Just let the nurses know. They'll get in touch with me." He touched her shoulder and walked out the door.

Gracey might have stood next to Henry's bed for an hour. She didn't know. She couldn't tell. Nothing had changed in the room; all the sounds and the smells were the same. Sunlight did not creep through the closed blinds in the window. The tomb was sealing itself.

"I'm not going to stay, Daddy. I have to go. You keep on sleeping. The worries of this life, all its heartaches and disappointments are almost gone for you. I'm sorry for all of it. So sorry everything had to be so hard all the time. I know you suffered, Daddy. You suffered for your daddy, your grandpa. No matter how we all tried, so much good just seem to turn bad. I'm even sorrier we hurt each other. I wish I could take every unhappy time away. But I can't. I can't," she whispered in her father's ear then kissed his forehead. "I love you." The only sound she heard in return was the maddening drone of the machines.

She felt herself running. She didn't want to, but something pushed her, past the nurses' station and the lone nurse reading charts, past the coffee station with a tower of Styrofoam cups, until she reached the elevator. The door opened and swallowed her inside, where she caught her breath, leaning against the control panel. She ran out of the elevator, past the receptionist desk, past the opened-mouth of the receptionist, past the cafeteria entrance with people standing in line, holding plastic red trays, running, running, never stopping, with her purse banging against her right hip.

She spotted the three trees in the parking lot.

Where's the car? Where's the car? There, there, next to the trees.

She ran wildly, hair flying, purse dancing against her side, across the parking lot. She unlocked the car door and started the engine. A blast of hot air from the air conditioner greeted her. She strapped herself in, looked in the rearview mirror, and pushed the accelerator.

She didn't remember backing out of the hospital parking lot. She didn't remember leaving the familiarity of Highway 77 or the entrance ramp at Highway 59 toward Houston. She wasn't conscious of the radio or the hum of the wheels on the asphalt. All she knew was to keep both hands on the wheel and to urge the car forward, driving farther and farther away.

She missed her exit three times in the I-10 exchange in downtown Houston. Rush hour traffic and a driving rain pushed her onto 45 South to Galveston, before she could maneuver the car toward an exit and a nearby convenience store.

How can I be lost? I've driven this highway a million times.

Through the rain, the neon signs of massage parlors and taquerias beckoned her into another existence. She sat staring at the entrances, rubbing her forehead with the back of her hand. She went into the convenience store for a cup of coffee. Back in the car, she sat drinking it. Its rising steam, like the slightest of ghosts, rising, rising, until it became a defroster against the rain covered windshield.

In that moment, she heard it. It was the tiniest thought escaping, mingling in the steam of the coffee.

I abandoned my father. I left him alone in that room. No one he has known or loved in his life is there with him. He is alone. Alone like he was as a boy. Alone. What kind of person am I? What did I do? What did I just do?

Gracey started the car, turned on the radio, pushed the car to eighty miles an hour on the entrance ramp. Veering right, she made the I-10 East exit. She was finally in the direction that headed home; she knew this route, the same road, the same interstate she had driven all her life. Biloxi to Loti. Loti to Biloxi. She was headed home.

Her cell phone rang an hour out of Port Arthur, amidst pampas grass growing in the freeway medians and eighteen-wheelers controlling the flow of traffic. She cradled it against her right ear and shoulder.

"Hey, I'm finally here at the hospital. Sorry I didn't come to the house first and pick you up," said Angela.

"Angela, I'm on my way home.

"Which home? Dad's? Biloxi? Which home, Gracey?"

"I talked to the doctor before I left. I'm an hour or more outside of Baton Rouge."

"Don't do this, Gracey. Get back here. You have no right to punish me for being late. I tried my best to get here."

"I'm not punishing you, Angela. Dad is sleeping a lot, really doesn't come out of it. I'm glad you're there, now. I'm glad he's not alone anymore."

"I can't believe you're leaving. Don't leave me here by myself to watch Daddy die, Gracey."

"Is John there with you?"

"Yes, but I want you here."

"I need to go home. Tom and I, the kids, will be back for the funeral. I found the burial policy. It's on the kitchen table. I've already called the funeral home. Got his suit ready. I straightened the house. The yard. I picked up the mail. I did those things. They're done. They're done."

"No, Gracey."

"I loved him. I loved him the best I could, but you. Angela. You loved him with the best heart. The kindest heart. I just couldn't do it; I tried. I substituted being dutiful for loving him. I'm not the one he needs right now. He's been asking for you. It won't be much longer now. You should have that privilege Angela, to be with him in the end. I don't deserve that."

"He loved you, too. He loved you, too."

"It's not easy being alone in that house, alone with all those years closing in on you." In her choking guilt, she offered her sister a simple plan. "Let me go home now. I'll call you tonight."

"I'm calling Tom when I get off the phone with you."

"Okay, call him. He's not going to tell you anything different than I have. Tom, Tom, is having a hard time. Let him be."

"We need to be together now, as a family, all three of us."

"Yes, like a family. I'll call you tonight," Gracey said and hung up.

She turned on the radio and allowed herself to think about Angela's last sentence. *We need to do this as a family. What family would that be? Would that be Henry, his father William, or great-grandfather, Jonas Mueller, a South Texas legend of abandonment, ice house brawls, and week-long drunks? Who could blame Henry for being anything other than what he was with a family tree like that?*

Gracey remembered her two great aunts, Grandpa Mueller's sisters, and the stories they told about their father, Jonas Mueller. Evelyn and Dot were widows who lived in a grey asbestos-sided house on the outskirts of Point Comfort. They had worked their entire lives at the WB Seafood Processing Plant on Lavaca Bay . . .

The two sisters were as different as the morning and evening tides, forged from the same gravitational pull that controlled and swept them into the crushing undertow of a broken home.

While Dot would laugh at the perceived antics of her drunken father, Evelyn, taller and thinner than Dot, would look away, transporting herself to the little girl who was afraid of her father, whether he was there or not. "I remember Daddy being gone when that hurricane 'bout washed us all away. That was after the Spanish-American War. It didn't last long, but Daddy came back from it plumb crazy. By the time that hurricane came through, we didn't see much of him. That storm tore up most of the coast and drowned out Hallettsville. I was about seven, no more than eight. Mama and I looked out in the morning, and almost everything we owned, cups, clothes, the coffee pot, an ironing board, were all floating in Lavaca Bay. I don't know what was worse, the rain or the wind from that storm. Mama made a tent out of sheets for us, so there was some kind of shelter between us and the sun burning down through the ripped tin on the roof. Three days later, Daddy showed up with a few cans of food. We had been eating beets and pickles Mama canned earlier that summer. I won't touch a pickle to this day."

"Did we ever tell you about the time the Klan came looking for him?" Evelyn asked.

Like a rehearsed vaudeville act, Evelyn would launch the second act with the dramatically whispered word, "Klan." Dot, taking her cue, began her soliloquy. Gracey had heard the story throughout her childhood. As an adult, she thought it odd her aunts would tell a young child such a disturbing story. But for them, it was not disturbing, it was the only childhood they had known.

"Some would call Daddy a jack of all trades. After the war, he did all kinds of things to make a living. Sometimes he painted houses, fished, and even boxed in beer joints up and down the coast, from Houston to Corpus. I guess the one thing you could count on with him is he never went without that fifth of whiskey. When he sobered up between jobs, he'd come home to us. One time it got really hard for us. Mama was pregnant with William. Evelyn and I were trying to go to school, but missed a lot of it to help Mama with the baby.

"We lived in a little rent house on a dirt road outside of Port Lavaca. Our neighbors were real good to us, giving us eggs, and sometimes fresh milk. There was a hole in the kitchen floor of that old rent house." Dot laughed. "It was an old pier and beam house off the ground. Evelyn and I tied the last piece of bacon scraps to that string and put it through that hole. We thought we were going to catch a chicken from the neighbor's yard," she laughed out loud, took a sip of coffee, gasped for air, and started again. "With oil being found all over Texas in the early 1900s, the Klan moved into the Matagorda and Lavaca Bay areas. With money and all those men working in the refineries, prostitution, beer joints, and wild living took over the little towns. The Church of Christ and Baptist Church started meeting, talking about how to get the little towns back from the Devil. Some even said the Klan members were deacons in the Baptist Church. I guess it took the devils we knew in the Klan to get rid of the Devil himself in South Texas.

"Well, it wasn't long before the Klan found out what a no-count Jonas was as a husband and father. The Klan back in those days had little patience with colored folks and Mexicans, and even less for a white man not acting like a Christian. I guess our neighbors were talking in town about our situation. The closer Mama got to delivering William, the more we saw the neighbors. It seemed they were always coming over to talk to her, asking about Jonas, and how me and Evelyn were doing.

"Mama delivered William, and she had a hard time of it. She stayed in bed maybe a week, it could have been longer. She lost a lot of blood and didn't have enough milk for the baby. The neighbor brought over some goat's milk in a glass bottle with a little homemade nipple on top, hoping this would help Mama and the baby out. Evelyn and me did our best. We washed diapers and cooked. I don't know where Daddy was. We was too busy tryin' to survive to even think about him. Before we knew it, he had come home to us. Had a little money and some tins of food. He was home maybe a day or two, when the Klan came.

"It was just like the movies. They were wearing white sheets and their faces were covered. Evelyn and I were scared to death. Mama hollered for us to stay in the house. They knocked on the door and when Jonas opened it, they grabbed him, all of them. It was like a huge swarm of locusts, avenging God. They descended on him, all at once. It seemed like there was a hundred legs and arms, flaying and flying at him on the ground. Mama and the baby didn't go out there. She walked away from the front door and came in the bedroom with us. She didn't cry, but only prayed louder and louder, drowning out Daddy's screams and the curse words of the men beating him as he lay in the middle of that dirt yard. 'kill me. Kill me. I don't care. God should have done it in the war.'

That's all Daddy could say to those men. Over and over. The words still haunt me to this day. His crying, cussing, praying, kicking, after a while became one sound, like a machine. It was real bad for us." Dot reached out and touched Evelyn's hand trembling in her lap . . .

*   *   *

Similar to the sound of the machines in Daddy's room, a finale they were all forced to hear, repeating over and over, take me God, why won't you take me and have it done with, thought Gracey as the traffic slowed in East Baton Rouge, allowing chemical refinery workers to merge onto I-10.

I'm part of those people, and no matter how I tried all these years, I didn't fool anyone. Not even myself. Scratch below the surface and you find me, like them, begging for a decent wage, desperate for happiness, replacing alcohol with the sham of perfection. Perfect? A good girl? Oh, my God. I am no different. No matter how far beyond reproach I thought I had become, I could never control any of it. It was always there, in the back of my mind, the shame of who I am and my family. But, I love them. I love all of them, the criminals and the saints, the drunks and the broken soldiers, the abuser and the abused. God, I love them, because, because they loved me.

As Gracey crossed the Mississippi River into Baton Rouge, the cement umbilical cord of I-10 connecting her to Loti and the Mueller family broke. Henry took his last breath in a hospital room in Victoria, Texas. The last of the Mohicans, the last poor boy from a small town in South Texas died as hard as he had lived.

Chapter Fourteen
Found in the Wreckage

When Gracey parked the car in front of her home in Biloxi, Mark met her at the front door.

She looked at him and knew. *He got the call. Henry's dead. It's over. It's over, now.*

"Gracey," he said, reaching to hold her.

"You don't have to tell me. I already know."

"Let me get you something to eat. You don't look well. Take a shower. I'll scramble you some eggs. Toast."

"I don't want any food, Mark. I want to sleep. Sleep for an entire year. Wake me up when it's over. The funeral. The family. All of it. Let me sleep through every bit of it."

She placed her purse on the kitchen table and walked into the bedroom. Removing her shoes, she lay in bed staring at the wall until she fell asleep. She slept through the night, waking at 4 AM with a heaviness, a tightening at the throat, a black weight on her chest. *What is this? What?* Then she remembered. Henry was dead.

Quietly, she slipped out of bed, careful not to wake Mark as he slept the dreamless, sound sleep of the guiltless. She turned to look at him. The closed eyes and soft mouth of her husband.

This bed. This man. Mark. We haven't loved each other in years, like we once did, like we deserved. I was so busy at doing nothing. Nothing of importance. Twenty-four-hours-a-day, speeding through my life, your life, my family, never stopping to see any of it, except... My interpretation of it, my version was what mattered. Got to go, got to do . . . and what I got in return for all the empty doing I did was nothing.

Dressing in the closet, trying not to make any noise, she put on a pair of shorts and a T-shirt and slid her bare feet into flip-flops. Tip-toeing out of the room, hoping the shoes would not slap her heels, she opened the front door to the porch facing the bay. From a rocking chair she viewed the new day, the morning, hopeful and quiet in its first hours.

She could see the Biloxi Bay Bridge span across the Mississippi Sound. Early August dawn provided the glimpse of a quarter moon faint in the late summer sky. She stared at it as she rocked in the chair.

I don't want to think and I don't want to feel. I'm just going to sit and do nothing.

But as the sun climbed higher in the sky, the day with all its expectations and disappointments was rising around her as the traffic increased across the bridge. A delivery truck moved along First Street, turning onto Beach View Drive. The newspaper, delivered by a 1993 black Pontiac Firebird, was tossed in the driveway by a large, hairy arm and a male voice calling out, "Mornin'!"

She smiled and waved back.

"Want some coffee," Mark said, stepping onto the porch and handing her a cup.

She barely heard him. It was as if the sound came from another room. She strained to hear, leaning toward where he stood.

"Gracey?"

"I don't know if I want to be that awake. Just put the coffee on the porch railing," she said nodding her head toward it. "Let's go for a walk."

He reached for her hand, but she had already set the pace for the day, hopping off the porch steps and walking toward the beach. He followed her to the water's edge, walking across the cracked sidewalk next to the sea wall. A light southwest wind blew across the sea oats. A wooden boat with a sputtering motor drifted across the Sound, occasionally stopping to check crab traps.

"Wonder if he got anything?" Mark asked.

The sound of the motor drifted to her as if from a cave, a shallow sound, far away.

Gracey looked at the boat. "I don't know why he couldn't love me like he did Angela."

"Gracey, let's sit here and talk." He took her hand and guided her to the three-foot seawall. Together they sat, staring at the water.

"Henry loved you; he simply spent more time with Angela than he did with you and Tom. Life finally got better for him after she was born. Your mom stayed home; he wasn't out looking for her anymore. As for Tom, I don't know if a lifetime could've healed the pain between him and Henry. It's different for men. A woman can cry and forgive openly. A man turns his heart completely off when the pain is too much. You have to become a cold bastard to survive it. That's why Tom kept his distance all those years. It was how he dealt with it. You might not like this, but it's the truth. Angela took Henry for who he was. Right or wrong. She loved him without reserve. Henry knew that. He didn't have to fear judgment from her, like he did from you and Tom."

"I know it was easier for him to love Angela than Tom and me, or even Mom."

"Your mom, he never stopped loving her. Where do you think all that rage came from? It's a fine line between love and hate. Passion fuels both. He loved Helen more than anyone, but when a man loves a woman with everything he's got to give, and it's not enough, especially if she looks for love outside the marriage, well, sometimes a man can't get over it. It broke him. And you know when you look at it, it broke your mom, too. Don't let it break you. Don't you think you've given up enough of your life?"

"I tried to be good to him. I guess I thought cleaning up the mess and keeping my mouth shut was a fair exchange for love. I should have sat with him; sat with him and talked, loved him for who he was instead of who I wanted him to be."

"It's hard to live with a saint, Gracey. You can be exactly like your Grandma Viola. It's like we all fall short of being what you want us to be. Without you saying a single word, we can see the disappointment in your face, so we pretend to be what you want us to be. Sometimes, it's too hard to live up to that expectation."

"I'm sorry. Pushing you away, making you feel inadequate was the last thing I wanted to do."

"All I ever wanted was for you to be happy. Happy with me and what we made of our lives. I didn't know how to help you, so I worked. I worked too much. It was easier than seeing your disappointment. I felt like I couldn't make you happy. All I know is that you let the first eighteen years of your life damage the next thirty-two. I never could understand why you couldn't let it go."

"I couldn't let it go, because, because I love them. I love my family. And I really believed if I tried hard enough, I could change all of it." She buried her face in her hands and cried.

"Oh, baby." Mark pulled her closer to him, putting his arms around her shoulders.

"I held on to that damn pain like it was a life raft. I didn't know I was drowning and taking everyone down with me. I was waiting on some sort of perfect life, waiting thirty-two years for something that would undo all the bad. It never happened. But that didn't take away my right to be indignant. Oh, no. I was so sure of it that I became a self-righteous bully, judging everybody in my martyrdom. What a fool. What a stupid fool." Gracey searched in her pocket for a Kleenex. When she didn't find one, she pushed her shirt sleeve across her eyes and nose.

"Why, why did I think I was so special? Like I was the only kid in the world who had a drunk for a father. The world is full of kids like me."

Mark hugged her tightly. He felt her shoulders drop against his chest.

"I don't think you understand. Henry did the best he could, loved you the best he could. Life is about loss and pain. And it will break your heart in two, but you can't let it. You got to face it and call it exactly what it is, not what you want it to be. If you don't, honey, listen to me." Mark raised her face to his and looked in her eyes. "If you don't, you are going to bleed from that pain every day, for the rest of your life."

She grabbed his shirt with both hands, making fists with the fabric, and cried with her head buried in his chest.

"It's not too late to be happy. I know I work a lot. We can slow that all down, Gracey, and enjoy each other. Let the dead bury the dead. Let's do some living."

He pulled her to her feet and kissed her. She stepped back and looked at him, smiling. "Mark, you haven't kissed me like that in years. Let's be in love together, let's get that time back and make things good, again."

"Want me, Gracey. That's all you have to do. Just want me. Smile at me when you wake up in the morning and when you close your eyes at night, lying next to me in bed." He kissed her forehead and her mouth.

Together, they walked home holding hands.

Gracey stopped before walking up the porch steps. "Go on in. I'll be a minute," she said, turning to face Mark. "I want to talk to Father Thomas."

She walked along the sidewalk of Second Street, one of the oldest streets, in one of the oldest towns, Biloxi. A port town founded by French sailors in 1699, its past and present were entwined with pirates, immigrant fishermen, boat builders, mad artists, and casinos—all gamblers searching for the one break that would make the suffocating humidity and annual hurricanes worth it.

Four-hundred-year-old oak trees created a natural canopy against the stifling morning heat. The grand trees that survived the deadliest of hurricanes, Katrina, were a daily testimony to the endurance of the Mississippi Coast. As each new leaf sprouted, as each branch reached higher, a collected sigh was heard: "It's coming back. It's coming back. It's coming back."

She walked past the Creole Cottages, abandoned store fronts, and empty lots Hurricane Katrina had wrought ten years earlier. St. Patrick Catholic Church was located on the corner of Second Street and Porter Avenue, on a spit of land between the Biloxi Bay and the Gulf of Mexico. The church was nearly washed away by the two bodies of water during Katrina. A water mark of seventeen feet left its permanent stain on the white brick structure.

Father Thomas was alone in the church when Gracey opened the door. As he prepared for 8:00 Mass, she sat on the back pew watching him.

The crucified Christ, a God who became human, stared down at her.

She looked in sorrow at the humility of Jesus.

Jesus, you told the world, 'Love Your Neighbor.' The world responded by nailing you to a cross.

A small wooden table, scarred with years of use, held votive candles lit by the parishioners. Faded photographs of the dead and scraps of paper were squeezed into the rows of candles. They were the recorded anguish and hope of the Faithful, praying for lost souls and lost causes.

Gracey thought of those prayers, whispered in every language, repeated through the centuries, swirling in the smoke of the candles. Prayers infused with incense and tears, crying, "For I know my transgressions, and my sin is ever before me."

"You're early for Mass this morning, Gracey. How are you?" The old priest's voice startled her.

"I'm not doing so good today, Father." She turned away from him and cried.

The priest walked away from the altar and sat next to her.

"I have such a heavy heart. My dad died last night. All I could think of is how much more I should have loved him. I should have stayed with him until the end. I should have held his hand until he died, but I didn't. I'm guilty of hurting my mother, the same way, the exact same way. I knew she suffered. I saw her many times, sitting alone and worried. But I didn't sit with her. No, I knew her pain and walked away from it. I remained silent and thought of my own hurt."

"Let's go into the confessional. We'll have our privacy there."

Gracey followed the priest to the rear of the church. He pushed aside a long, black curtain revealing a small room with a desk and two wooden chairs on each side.

"Do you want to use the other confessional?"

"No, Father. I'm comfortable facing you. You've seen me at

my worst, like right after Therese moved to Ireland. No use hiding from you now. We've known each other a long time."

"In the name of the Father, Son, and the Holy Spirit." The priest and the woman spoke and touched their hands sequentially to their forehead, chest, and each shoulder as they made the sign of the cross on their bodies.

"O my God, I am heartily sorry for having offended you." Gracey began the confessional prayer, stopping to catch her breath and wipe her eyes with a ragged Kleenex she held in her hand. "I detest all my sins . . . because of your just punishments, but most of all . . . they offend you, my God, who art all-good and deserving of all my love. I firmly resolve, with the help of your grace, to sin no more and to avoid the near occasions of sin."

"Amen," the priest said, handing Gracey another Kleenex.

"I left my father alone to die. I left him in his shame and loneliness when he needed me the most. All I could do was judge him. All I could think about was how he should have been better, a better parent to me. God, forgive me. I have done this to everyone in my life. When they don't measure up, I cut them off. I may be there in presence, but my love is not there. I guard that like a weapon.

"My mom and dad were kids when they married. My mother was only seventeen, a girl really. They were both from poor homes. My father was from a broken home, himself, with years of fighting and abuse. But, that didn't stop me from judging them. I've given complete strangers more allowance for their shortcomings than I did my own family." Gracey gasped for air and placed a hand over her mouth, shocked by the horror of her own words.

"I want you to think of the true nature of mercy and forgiveness, Gracey." The priest held her in his eyes. "We are reminded that Jesus' very nature is to have compassion for us and to forgive us. He asks us to do the same for others."

"It's hard to forgive myself. I've let so many years slip away in resentment. I could have loved my brother and sister more in their pain. I could have loved my husband more; I should have grabbed him, held him, and let him know how much he meant to me, but I filled my day with things that did not matter. None of those things meant anything compared to what these people are worth to me. I was capable of loving them all. The way they deserved to be loved, but I only thought of myself.

"I was not my dad's favorite, Father. I was more of a sister to my parents than a child. They confided in me. They told me things I didn't want to know. I didn't want their pain. I wanted to be their child, to be loved like their child. They taught me not to trust happiness, because it was only a matter of time before I would be shipped off to live with a relative, because my mom and dad couldn't . . . they couldn't take care of me." Gracey covered her face with both hands and cried bitterly.

"It's hard work to forgive someone who has hurt you, even harder to not let it change who you are. Do not be a slave to that injury. Pardon it, and Christ's mercy will heal that pain. You must remember there are many ways to love someone. Your parents saw your strength, even when you were a child. They needed it and trusted you. The comfort you gave them in return was your gift. None of us are perfect. The disciples could not stay awake an hour for Jesus when he faced his approaching death in the Garden of Gethsemane. Imagine, Gracey, failing Christ who showed them the most perfect example of love. Yes, none of us are perfect. Let's pray in the words he taught us."

She closed her eyes, reciting the prayer she had been taught as a child.

"Our Father, who art in Heaven
hallowed be thy name.
Thy kingdom come,
Thy will be done, on earth, as it is in Heaven.
Give us this day our daily bread,
and forgive us our trespasses,
as we forgive those who trespass against us,
and lead us not into temptation,
but deliver us from evil.

She cried bitterly for the years she recited the prayer, never knowing, never comprehending its meaning.

"God, the father of mercies, through the death and the resurrection of His Son has reconciled the world to himself and sent the Holy Spirit among us for the forgiveness of sins: through the ministry of the church may God give you pardon and peace, and I absolve you from your sins in the name of the Father, and of the Son, and of the Holy Spirit," said the priest.

"Thank you, Father. You know I hate coming to confession. You can't imagine the things I torture myself with." Gracey laughed. "But now, well, I feel like I've lost twenty pounds."

"Confession is not a torture chamber. You should look at it as a second baptism. You are forgiven."

"Yes, Father."

"Remember the Lord's Prayer, Gracey. Say it as part of your evening prayers, before you go to bed. It will help you to remember we are all sinners. We must pray every day for each other."

Chapter Fifteen
Family Gathering

The day of Henry Mueller's funeral brought continuous rain for the residents of Loti. The parking lot of Clegg Funeral Home was sparse at 8:30 Saturday morning.

"Not too many of us left. The family reunions get smaller and smaller every year," said Jimmy Mueller, Henry's nephew from Houston, as he leaned against the door frame to the front entrance of the funeral home.

"You're right, man," said Tom. "Only time we see each other is at funerals."

The two men stood next to each other as Henry Mueller's family and friends guided sedans and trucks into the asphalt parking lot of the funeral home. Umbrellas emerged from the vehicles first, followed by feet, arms, hats, and walkers.

"Looks like people are starting to show up."

"Yeah, there'll be a lot of local people now that the rain is slacking off. Hard for the old folks to get in and out of the weather," Jimmy said, blowing cigarette smoke in the direction of the parking lot.

A woman in her eighties was barreling up the sidewalk as if the two men standing at the sidewalk's end were designated targets. Wiry grey hair pinned with black bobby pins and blue eyes, Fran Ernst supported her 5'8" frame by leaning and lifting in sequential movements a walker supported by punctured tennis balls. She stared straight ahead at them, causing Jimmy to toss his lit cigarette into the grass. She came to an abrupt halt with the walker ending its dance in a thud of rubber and concrete.

"Y'all ought to be ashamed of yourselves, burning up your daddy like that to save a few dollars." She didn't wait for a reply, but pushed her way past the two men, determined to sit on the front row, a place reserved for those who were closest to the deceased.

"What the hell?" Tom asked.

"I think she's Henry's cousin, Fran from Tivoli," said Jimmy.

"How did she know about the cremation?"

"Brother, like a one-horse town, this is a one-funeral-home town, and those old women have been on the phone talking since they saw the funeral notice posted at the grocery store and gas station."

"It's a hell of a way to start."

"Forget it. Let's just get through it."

Together, the men walked into the sanctuary of perfectly aligned rows of folding chairs. They sat next to Gracey and Angela's families. Tom gave a nervous side glance at Fran, who was sitting at the end of the front row. Her walker was placed in the open aisle next to her in case she needed a ready weapon or a speedy exit.

Irma entered the room as a recording of "Amazing Grace" piped its way through the ceiling speakers. Angela got up and helped her walk to where the family was sitting.

Gracey stood to greet her. "Hello, Irma," she said, moving over a chair, so Irma could sit next to her.

"I'm sorry for this day. I know you will miss Dad. You were there every day with him."

"He was my friend, a good friend to me." Irma placed her hand over Gracey's hand resting in her lap. "I'll never forget him."

"I once was lost, but now I'm found. Was blind but now I see," concluded the recording above their heads.

The service began. Henry Mueller's children sat upright, straight as arrows, as he had taught them. They looked onward, past the open casket, past the empty words of a eulogy given by a man who never knew their father. They saw past the automated air freshener that "psst" a fine mist into the room every ten minutes, past the falseness of a scripture that was read as Henry's "favorite," and past the wreaths of lilies and mums with well-meaning cards.

They weren't really there. Years of practice had allowed them to separate the body from the heart. The three children of Henry and Helen Mueller were in a place where Tom was eleven, Gracey was five, and Angela was everyone's baby. They were sitting at a table, laughing. Henry and Helen were sitting at opposite ends of the table. They smiled at their children as they placed food on their plates. The curtains in the open window fluttered. The ceiling fan hummed above them. They were a family. A long time ago, three little children, a man, and a woman were a family.

"Turn your hymnal to number 364, 'The Old Rugged Cross,'" announced the funeral director. Family, friends, and the curious stood to sing.

"At least they got this song right," Tom whispered to Gracey.

The tears of Tom, Gracey, and Angela fell, merging with the voices of their family and friends who sang this song for Henry Mueller, as they had for his wife, his mother, his father, his grandmother and his grandfather before him.

They all came. Henry's domino buddies with their broken teeth and polished shoes sat together on the back row of folding chairs. They shared their stories quietly amongst themselves.

"Henry didn't like to lose at dominoes. No siree! He'd let you win enough to give you a little hope, then he'd throw down a double six. If you hesitated the slightest on your next play, he'd say, 'Columbus took a chance, and he was on water'," Joe Bures laughed quietly, rubbing his sweating palms on his pressed slacks.

"Yes sir, yes sir, Henry sure hated to lose. If you got upset with him about a smart aleck play he'd make, cutting everybody out of the game early, he'd laugh and say, 'Better than a sharp stick in the eye'," said Raymond Novak.

Henry's relatives, the nieces and nephews who shared the joy and the burden of the family history, smiled with sad eyes at their three cousins sitting near their uncle's casket. They remembered the stories their mothers and fathers told them as children, stories of Uncle Henry driving all over Texas and Louisiana looking for Aunt Helen. They didn't believe it as children, and they didn't believe it as adults. They loved Aunt Helen.

"I remember when my dad died . . . Aunt Helen sat with me all day. She told me about my dad when he was young. What he liked to do. She kept getting up to fix me something to eat and drink. She never left my side. Uncle Henry? Hell, the only thing he ever said to me was 'Boy, get your ass up. We're going to work.' What else could I do? I was a high school dropout and my dad was dead. I went to work," Jimmy whispered to his wife, standing next to him in the receiving line after the service.

"You sure showed all of them." Sheila squeezed her husband's arm and smiled down at the three carat diamond ring on her finger.

"Henry taught me to work. I'll give him that. But I kept working, long after he hit the bottle at closing time. I worked and worked until I didn't have to work for that old man ever again."

The small town merchants, whom Henry and Helen borrowed from for sixty years, came. Now retired, they had nothing else to do but read the obituaries in the *Victoria Advocate* every morning and attend funerals.

"Tom, there's old man Preston in the receiving line," said Gracey looking at a man in his late seventies dressed in a 1980s pin-striped suit.

"Don't recall why he's important to us."

"Remember when he built that McMansion on the edge of town? It was a brick fortress on a postage stamp yard. Dad did all the sheetrock on that house. He even subcontracted the framing and roofing. Old man Preston never paid him. You know, Dad paid his guys when they were done with the job. It ended up putting him in a hole. Mom sold the only decent car she ever had, that huge Ford LTD. We ate a lot of chicken leg quarters then."

"I don't remember all that."

"Yeah, it was tough for a while. You might have been out of the house by then. Anyway, I went to school with his daughter,

Janie. She was homecoming queen when I was a sophomore. The next year I wore her homecoming dress to a school dance. Mom had picked it up at a garage sale. Janie was such a brat. She came up to me and said, 'Hey, that's my dress you're wearing'."

"Well, the old man's got big cojones to come to the funeral."

"I doubt he even remembers any of it, Tom. He probably doesn't even know he's at Dad's funeral. Look at the way he's shaking. Bet it's Alzheimer's. In his mind, he's standing at the checkout line in the grocery store. Look at all of Dad's crew behind him. Bet they remember the story."

The men Henry had employed when he got a "big" job, painting a church or a doctor's house, had come to pay their respects. The day laborers were long gone and forgotten, as quickly as they had shown up to work and left with a $50 bill in their pockets. But the men who painted and patched sheetrock alongside Henry, stood patiently in line with his relatives and friends, for a chance to tell their story.

"I was sorry to hear about your daddy, Ms. Gracey. Mr. Henry was real good to me when I was goin' through a hard time back in the late Seventies," said a grey haired black man with dried paint on the sleeve of his shirt. "I had got out of the pen. He gave me a job, some tools, and a draft on my first paycheck. I'll never forget that. Your mama would always have a cup of coffee for me while I waited for your daddy in the morning. I walked through the front door and waited in their house, like a man. They treated me like a man."

Before Gracey had a chance to thank the man for attending the service, a local merchant was hugging her tightly around the neck.

"It was real nice, Gracey," said seventy-year-old Evelyn Hopkins, wearing ropes of pearls and diamonds accentuated against a black silk dress. Opium perfume bathed the air around her. "Y'all did good, you, Tom, and Angela. I knew your folks for a long time. Your mama was always coming into the store for y'all."

"Thank you, Mrs. Evelyn." Gracey fought the urge to grab her and cry within the warmth and elegance of her dress and demeanor.

"You know, darling-girl, life was not meant to be easy. It

seems that we have a lot of hard roads at times. I think God intends for us to have those rocky times, to make better people out of us."

Gracey threw her arms around her. The old woman returned her hug with the same intensity.

"Honey. Now, I want you to always remember that you gave your mama and daddy a nice send off to heaven. You come see me before you leave town." Evelyn Hopkins walked away, still beautiful, still glamorous, still a woman, untouched by age.

"Who was that?" asked Tom. "She's got chandeliers in her ear lobes."

"Mrs. Evelyn. She owned a little jewelry store for years, next to the bank. That's where we bought our high school graduation rings, birthday gifts, all sorts of little trinkets. The Hopkins let you charge, so you basically paid $5 a week for a $40 piece of jewelry. Imagine, no interest! They gave us the chance to be ten-cent millionaires," Gracey laughed and turned to greet the next person in the receiving line.

Judith Martin shook her hand.

"Gracey, so sorry for you-all's loss. Gene would be here if he could. Had business at the bank this morning."

"Yes, ma'am. It was nice of you to come. I still see Connie now and then when I'm in Houston."

"We all miss Connie. Gracey, hon, what did your daddy do?"

The question stopped her heart. She didn't know what to say.

What did my father do? What did he do? You knew Henry for over sixty years. Your daughter and I were best friends. I slept in her bed. I ate your food. In fact, I think you still owe him from all the holes in the sheetrock he patched for you. Did you throw that flower vase a little bit too hard, Ms. Judith?

Gracey swallowed her anger and hugged the old woman.

"Daddy was a jack of all trades, like his daddy and like his grandfather. But he mostly did painting and sheetrock work. "

She seemed satisfied with the answer and walked away.

"Hi, Grace. So sorry to hear about your dad," said Andrew Bellows.

Gracey recognized him immediately. The last thirty years gave him a paunch and thinning hair, but his eyes were the same. His voice was the same. But she was no longer a humiliated eighteen-year-old girl.

"Thank you, he had been sick awhile."

"It's good to see you. You look the same, really. How you been?"

"We're doing okay. Still a married lady with a daughter about to marry and a son in grad school. The years slip on by, don't they? I've been lucky, Andrew. How 'bout you?"

"I'm living in my grandfather's house full-time now. You remember that old house. I got a divorce last year and moved out of Houston for good."

"Yes, I remember your grandpa's house. Doesn't seem that long ago, but in some ways, it was a million years ago." *I hope to God my face isn't red.* "Well, thanks for coming, Andrew. It was nice of you to remember my dad," she said offering her hand. She noticed both of his hands shaking when she touched him. They were the hands of an alcoholic before the first drink of the day.

In the reception area, they ate pimento cheese sandwiches on white bread, cut in triangles, and potato chips. Old women in flowery dresses poured endless cups of coffee and lined the counter tops with Styrofoam cups of iced tea. They ate too much. They talked too much. They hugged tightly, promising a better time. As quickly as they had poured into the funeral home offering memories and condolences, they were gone. Irma was the last to leave.

"I'll stop by the house later on," said Irma. "I'll give you the keys I have. Guess y'all will want to sell it."

"Please do, Irma. We'll be there a couple of days, sorting through things," said Angela.

Irma hugged Angela then made her way to the back door for her cigarettes and car keys.

Gracey watched them together.

"You were much better with her, Angela, than I was," said Gracey.

"She bathed our father. She cut his fingernails. She probably placed him on the toilet and wiped his butt. That's something we never had to do. She did it, because we weren't there."

"I begged Dad to move in with me."

"He didn't want his daughter to change his diaper."

"I know. I know that now," Gracey said, walking away from her sister. She walked outside and stood next to her husband and son at the front entrance, watching the cars and trucks back up in the parking lot and drive away.

The rain had slowed to a light shower, as the dry heat returned quickly, erasing any trace of moisture from the dying grass next to the parking lot. A lone blue jay sat on the branch of a pin oak watching the cars come and go.

"Mark, I'm going back to Dad's house with Tom and Angela."

"Right now?"

"It's better to clean it out and get it on the market before anything breaks or the forty-year-old roof caves in."

"You don't have to do that right now. Come home with us and rest."

"No. I don't want to drive back here by myself. Let Will take my car back. Tom can drive me to Hobby and I'll fly home when it's all over."

"How long do you think you'll be?"

"It shouldn't be too long. Tom and Angela will be with me. There's really not that much stuff. It won't be hard."

He hugged her. "Therese has been calling my phone all morning. I'll call her back once we get on the road."

"I'm sure she feels bad for not being here. Well, it's the new life we're going to have to get used to, and it's only the beginning. There's more funerals to come. We can count on that. It's hard on everyone, but I certainly don't want her feeling guilty for living her own life. Tell her it will be okay. I'll call her when I can. I need to call work, too."

Gracey took off her shoes, letting her bare feet spread against a patch of unmowed grass next to the asphalt. She felt very tired.

"Bye, Will." She hugged her son tightly. "Take care of Dad. Don't be sad, honey. Grandpa was sick for a long time. I'll be home in a few days."

The two men who loved her with the kindest of hearts climbed into the truck cab and watched her on the edge of the sidewalk. She waved at them, forcing her swollen feet back into the shoes, and walked away. Mark backed the truck out of the Clegg Funeral Home parking lot and waved goodbye to his wife.

"Dad, it's not right that we didn't bury Grandpa at the cemetery."

"They'll put his ashes there, Will."

"I saw Mom and Angela arguing right before we left, Dad. Tom didn't say much to anyone. Did all this have anything to do with not taking Grandpa to the cemetery?"

"Will, funerals are just hard. Unfortunately, you'll have a lifetime of going to them. It's just a part of life. I don't know why they were arguing. Emotions are running very high right now. Your grandpa was sick a long time, and that's stressful. Then, everyone's got an opinion of how things should be done. But most of all, people think about how a life was lived once it's over."

"Mom was always so uptight around Grandpa. She wouldn't say anything, but you could see it all over her face."

"Your mom had a lot of hurt feelings, Will. So did Tom. I think they thought, right or wrong, that Angela had it easier than they did when they were kids. That's just old-fashioned sibling rivalry. There's been a lot written about the birth order. If you're the first born, you tend to expect more of your parents, because you had more time with them before the other children came along. The middle child never got enough time, having to adjust to an older sibling and the new baby. The parents were busier tending to a larger family. Some say the middle child will do anything to avoid a fight, but resents having to deal with being the peace maker in the family."

"That's Mom. Oh my God, it's like she wants you to read her mind, know exactly what she's thinking then adjust your behavior according to her will. When you don't, weeks go by and, out of the blue, she blows up, mad, that you hurt her, took advantage of her kindness. Therese can be like that, too."

"You and Therese have done a good job defining sibling rivalry all by yourselves."

"Dad, she's the baby and gets away with murder. You and Mom are a lot harder on me than you were with her. It's obvious."

"Okay, so there's how the first born views the last born. The youngest always has it easier. Will, being a parent is the hardest thing in the world. We love you and your sister, equally. How you handle people is based on their individual personalities. Think about it. What works for your sister doesn't always work for you."

"I get it, but why were they mad at Grandpa?"

"They just wanted him to be different than he was capable of being."

"Was it his drinking?"

"It was about the choices he made, Will. There's a parable I remember hearing when I was a boy. It might help you make sense of this. In fact, it's a good lesson for all of us. It was told to me by an uncle when I was in high school, my Uncle Wallace, my father's brother. I've never forgotten it. It's helped me make a lot of decisions as I've become older, in work, in relationships, it's got a lot to say about what makes people tick. Supposed to be a Native American parable, I'm unsure of what tribe it comes from. Could be Eskimo or Apache. Who knows? But it's a good parable about choices we make.

"The story begins when a young Indian brave is brought before the tribal elders. They are concerned about his anger and aggressive behavior. One of the elders takes the young brave aside and tells him his anger is understandable, since all humans have within them two dogs. One dog is good and peaceable, and the other is evil and angry.

"The elder tells the brave, 'The two dogs are in constant battle with one another, since neither is strong enough to destroy the other.'

"Thinking about this for a while, the brave then asked the elder, 'If they are of equal power, which dog will win?'

"The elder replied, 'The one you feed the most.'"

Mark looked at his son, sitting next to him in the truck cab, and continued.

"Grandpa Henry lived a hard life. He grew up poor; he didn't have the opportunities you and I have had. He didn't get to finish high school. Think about that, Will. It's a given for your generation that high school is just a stepping stone into the world. No different than eating three squares a day or having clean clothes to wear every morning. Henry didn't have that. On his back, from the time he was a kid, he carried more than you and I ever had to. Yet, he took care of his family the best he knew. He made some bad choices in life, Will. We all do, at one time or another. That's just life. The important thing is don't continue to make the same mistakes over and over. I didn't grow up with the problems Henry had and neither did you. There was a lot of pain in his life. It is not my place or yours to judge him."

"Dad, I loved Grandpa. I loved his stories. He taught me to like country music. He forced that issue, but the other things . . . he taught me the names of birds and plants and trees. He was good to me."

"I loved him, too. Henry and I had a lot of fun playing dominoes. Your mom, Angela, Tom, they all loved him, but it's hard to let go of regret and disappointment. It just takes some time. It takes some people longer than others. Remember, everyone is different. You have to treat them accordingly. You don't know what someone has been through just by looking them in the eyes. People tend to hide what they're ashamed of. Your mom, Tom and Angela have a lot more history there, a lot more pain, and happiness as well. We didn't grow up dealing with the things they had to deal with."

Will watched his father driving the truck for a awhile, then he laid his head against the truck window and closed his eyes. He felt empty of words and feelings, and fell asleep listening to a country song on the radio, while his father drove toward the I-10 East entrance ramp.

*   *   *

Gracey overheard Forest Clegg talking to Tom in the funeral home reception hall.

"Mr. Mueller, if you'll come with me," he said.

Tom followed him.

"I guess he's getting Dad's ashes," said Gracey.

"Where are we going to put them?" Angela asked.

"I think we should scatter them next to Mom's grave in the cemetery."

"Is that legal?"

"Does it matter? We can scatter the ashes on the plot Grandma bought for him years ago, or we can let the ashes sit on someone's mantle. There's enough room on Mom's headstone to put his name and the date. Forget about what is legal or what others think is appropriate. Actually, I don't even care what anybody thinks. Dad should be with Mom."

"I know. It's hard, it's really hard for me right now," replied Angela, staring at the floor.

Tom approached his sisters holding an urn of brass and alloy. He held it slightly extended from his body, as if he wanted one of the women to take it from him. Angela sighed heavily.

"Tom, Gracey is going to ride back with me to the house. Before we go, we'll pick up the flowers, plants, and guest book from the service. I'm going to pull my car around to the front."

"Do you want me to pick up anything before I get back to the house? There's nothing to eat, much less drink."

"Good idea. Get some wine. No 'Pinkie's Wine of the Week.' You might try something that comes with a cork."

"Why does she have to talk to me like that?" Tom asked Gracey.

Chapter Sixteen
Mending the Broken

"Angela, I'm not letting these plants sit in the living room until they die, then throw them out," said Gracey, before turning into the driveway. "There's nothing worse than a dead plant from a funeral. Let's drop them off at the nursing home."

"Go on, then. I'll go in and start cleaning the house. I need to work off the white bread and processed cheese I ate."

Gracey wasn't gone a half an hour when she returned to her parents' house and heard Tom and Angela arguing. She placed her keys and purse on the table in the foyer, straining to hear each word.

"I'm keeping Dad's walking stick," Tom said. "Did you know it had a secret compartment?"

"I know. I bought it when we were dove hunting in Argentina two years ago."

"Is the secret compartment for storing dove?"

"Don't make her mad, Tom," Gracey whispered in the hallway.

Angela didn't respond. Tom took the baiting to the next level.

"Since we're out of Argentinian dove, how 'bout I put Henry's diamond ring in here?"

"Damn it, Tom, you're going to lose that ring."

"I'm fifty-eight years old. I think I can be trusted with a walking stick and a gold nugget ring with chipped diamonds. If you didn't want me to have the ring, why did you offer it?"

"Really, Tom. Is that all it is to you—a cheap ring? It was

everything to Dad, because he never had anything . . . But you do what you want, you always have."

"No, that's where you're wrong. I've never done exactly what I've wanted. Henry taught me a long time ago to be a good soldier and fall in line."

"What? What does Dad have to do with the way your life turned out?"

"Everything," Tom exploded.

"Save it for someone else. I loved him. He was my friend. But you, you never gave him a chance. You're a cold man, Tom. Couldn't even call him. Forget about stopping by. All he wanted . . . all he wanted was for you to love him. Why couldn't you? Why?"

"That's easy. Because he didn't try for me. Not one time. I work my ass off every day for my kids, because I want them to have better lives. It comes natural to want that for your own flesh and blood. But for Henry, it was a death march to be around us, maybe not you, but for me and Mom, even Grace. Had to force himself to come home every night. He was better to a stranger in the street than he was to his own family."

"No, he wasn't! No, he wasn't!" Angela screamed and shoved Tom into the refrigerator. "He was a good man. He gave it all he had, yet it wasn't good enough for you. It hurt him. Maybe . . . maybe that's why he didn't come home until we were asleep. He couldn't deal with the look of disappointment on our faces."

Angela walked out of the kitchen and met Gracey in the hallway.

"What?" Angela said, glaring at her. Gracey grabbed her arm.

"I don't need you to make me feel better." Angela pulled her arm free and walked into the living room.

Gracey followed her, stopping in the doorway to watch her. Angela sat in Henry's recliner and stared out the window at the dead grass in the front yard. She began to cry with her head in her hands.

"What am I going to do? You were my go-to-guy, Daddy. I'm going to miss my friend."

Gracey was frozen by Angela's grief for Henry. She could neither walk forward nor leave the room. She simply watched her from the doorway, feeling a bitter jealousy, a reminder, that the bond between Henry and Angela was something she would never know.

Gracey watched Angela push herself from the recliner.

"Enough." With one proclamation, Angela buried her grief and pulled her hair into a pony tail. She quickly removed the Patek Philippe watch from her wrist and deposited it in the cut glass candy dish bought from the dollar store.

She surveyed the room with a hand on each hip. Her eyes rested on the large book case lining the living room walls. It was Henry's trophy case, bulging with a fifty-year history of dust, ball caps, coffee mugs, and Encyclopedia Britannica.

"Tom, do we have any large garbage bags?" Angela hollered.

Tom placed the walking stick with the secret compartment on the kitchen table. He found a stack of paper grocery store bags folded under the kitchen sink next to three cans of Comet, a can of bug spray, and a bottle of Pine Sol.

"Here." He stacked the bags on a lower shelf of the book case, where Angela was balanced on a vinyl foot stool, reaching for a tower of Houston Astro ball caps.

Gracey observed the two from her self-made confessional. All she could think of was her place between them as the uncelebrated, predictable middle child.

There they are, the oldest and the youngest, the first and the favored. And then there's me, the kid in the middle, still hiding from them in the same damn house.

A loud knock at the door interrupted her thoughts, putting all three of Henry's children in motion for the front door.

"I'll get it," hollered Gracey.

Forty-eight-year-old Beverly Abel, holding a sixteen-ounce beer can, greeted Gracey on the other side of the door.

"Hey, cuz," she announced and strode into the living room taking a seat in Henry's electric wheelchair parked next to the flat screen television.

"Thought I'd stop by for a short visit before heading back to Austin. Didn't get a chance to talk to y'all at the funeral. Too many people standing around saying the same thing over and over again."

She removed an electronic cigarette from her shirt pocket and took a puff, turned the switch to "on" and moved the electric wheelchair closer to Angela still perched on the vinyl foot stool. "An hour in Loti with the family, and you remember why you left in the first place. You doing okay, Angela?"

"Yeah. We're starting to pick up the place. Need to get it on the market, before we all go back to our lives."

Tom looked at Angela then at Beverly. "We're putting it on the market before it falls on our heads. The roof is over forty years old. You can't flush the toilet and run the washing machine at the same time. What else? Oh yeah, the air conditioning unit was new in 1983. Duct tape and a prayer are keeping it going."

"Right," said Beverly, taking a sip of beer and easing the electric wheelchair by the combination TV and stereo cabinet. "Poor Uncle Henry. Does this thing still work?" she asked, setting the beer can on the cabinet.

"All of it works except the TV; that tube blew when I was in high school," Gracey said kneeling in front of the albums stacked inside the cabinet.

Henry elevated his status in the entertainment world by switching to a high-end Magnavox and later, a flat screen. No money was spared when it came to Henry's TV. Like an altar, its top was decorated with John Wayne memorabilia and photographs of his grandchildren.

"Look at this! It's that album Mom listened to when we were kids, *Ebb Tide*, even the title is romantic and sad. She'd sit at night in the living room without a lamp on, alone in the dark, listening to that song over and over again. All you could see was her silhouette and the red glow of her cigarette."

"What about Red Foley's *Peace in the Valley* album? Is it still in there? Remember how I changed the words to 'Peas in the Valley.' Put it on first."

Angela turned around and looked at her brother and sister. Gracey returned her look.

She's mad at me and Tom, because she doesn't remember the music. She thinks we're purposely leaving her out. She could be mad because she thinks we're not working as hard as her; we're shooting the breeze with Beverly while she does all the heavy lifting.

"Dad listened to a lot of Willie and Waylon on the Bose system I bought him. It's in the kitchen. I'm sure the sound quality is better if you want to listen to music," said Angela.

Well, there you have it. She's jealous. I'm not fixing it either!

"The other big album for the family was *Nat King Cole's Greatest Hits*. Remember, Mom would pour herself a glass of Mogen David and hold on to every word of 'Nature Boy'," said Gracey, ignoring Angela's offer.

"I don't think my kids know records used to come in speeds, 78, 33, and 45 . . . think about it. Crazy to remember, really. Are the Zydeco albums still there? Mom would stack Clifton Chenier records, three at a time on the little stereo arm. Barefoot and legs everywhere, we'd dance right here in the living room . . . She never really stopped being that little Cajun girl, did she?" asked Tom.

"Okay, I'm done with the built-in. Help me move this Baker's Rack by the sliding glass door," Angela said loudly.

Fighting the urge not to cry when thinking of their mother and happier times, Tom and Gracey picked up the Baker's Rack and moved it. Underneath was a film of dust, a pack of rolling papers, and a tightly rolled joint.

"What? Is that a joint?" said Tom, bending down to pick it up.

"It is," said Gracey.

"Whose is it, I'd like to know," said Angela.

Beverly moved the electric wheelchair closer to where the three were standing. "Does it matter whose it is? Let's fire it up!"

"I'm throwing it away," said Angela, taking it out of Tom's hand.

"Hell, if you're going to throw it away, give it to me," said Beverly, sticking the electronic cigarette into the large, oval shaped bun on the top of her head. "I'll smoke it on the way home, if it offends you."

"I wonder where it came from?" asked Tom.

"I bet Dad was smoking pot with the next door neighbor," said Gracey.

"What?" Angela said.

"You know, Irma's brother, Robert Kaspar, the gay guy," said Gracey.

"That's too funny," Tom laughed. "Dad was smoking pot with the guy he hated for years. I guess they were smoking the peace pipe."

Beverly threw her head back and howled with laughter. She grabbed the beer can sitting between her legs, took a deep drink, coughed for a few seconds, and started laughing again.

"What makes you think it was Dad smoking pot? It could have been any number of people. Home health care personnel or the cleaning lady."

"I doubt if sixty-seven-year-old Minerva was smoking pot and watching soap operas while she vacuumed once a week," said Gracey.

"Angela, an occasional joint is more mainstream than *Wheel of Fortune*," replied Beverly. "It's not just for tattoo artists and Harley owners, anymore."

"Really, Beverly?" said Angela, turning her back to all of them. She picked up a dust rag and swiped furiously at the forty-five-year-old encyclopedia set.

"Dad and Robert became friends, Tom. I think they started playing dominoes together last winter. Robert would come over in the afternoons, and they'd play until the evening news. Dad mentioned it a couple of times to me when I'd call."

Angela turned around and pointed the dust rag at Beverly. "You're going to have to get out of that chair. It's making me crazy."

"No problem. I need to get going, anyway. Hey, wanted to see y'all one more time." She picked up the beer can and placed it on the cabinet without looking at Angela. She hugged Tom then Gracey, slapping each of them on their backs, followed by an open-palm rub back and forth, back and forth.

"Love you, too, Angela." She put both arms around her and squeezed for a moment before opening the front door.

"Damn, it's hot" were the last words they heard from her before she slammed the door closed.

*   *   *

The afternoon sun burnt through the curtains, gradually becoming long shadows on a house sanitized of living. Angela scrubbed and scoured the surfaces, removing all traces of who they had been. Tom filled garbage bags with all the things they had owned. Gracey vacuumed footprints from where they had walked, run, and danced.

As they worked, each child remembered who they had been many years ago in their parents' house. Tom found the cigar box Henry used when he played dominoes at the kitchen table. Inside the cardboard box was the stub of a number 2 pencil, sharpened by a pocket knife, and scraps of paper for keeping score. Tom's and Henry's names were written at the top of the page. A line was drawn down the center, separating each player's score.

"That cigar box has lived a lot of lives. Think the first time I saw it was in a beer joint when I was, what, maybe nine or ten," Tom said to Gracey.

Tom remembered the day his father gave it to him. Henry had taken him to an ice house on Telephone Road in Houston one Saturday afternoon. He could remember sitting on an aluminum bar stool with a red Naugahyde seat . . .

"Get my little buddy here a Coke," said Henry. The female bartender, a middle-aged woman with her hair tied in a pink sheer scarf smiled at Tom. She put a six-ounce bottle of Coke and a bag of Fritos on the scarred bar surface in front of him. "Here you go, sug," the bright red lips said.

Henry stood next to Tom, his hands on the bar. Henry had a beer and made small talk with the other patrons while Tom finished his Coke. Henry would stop in mid-sentence and smile at Tom, grabbing his small boy shoulders and squeezing them.

"Kay, you got any cigar boxes? My boy gonna be startin' another school year. He can put his treasures in there."

"Sure do." She returned to the bar holding a box with the words TAMPA NUGGET in red block lettering. Around the box were little golden haloes with brown cigars in the middle . . .

"Man, that was a good day with Henry," Tom said aloud, surprising himself when a tear fell on the box he found. "Damn thing must be fifty-something-years-old."

Later that night, Tom took the cigar box with the pencil and paper and placed it in his suitcase, under a pile of tee shirts, so no one could see it. By all rights, it was his. Henry's only son was the rightful owner.

While cleaning downstairs, Gracey found the aluminum Christmas tree with its color wheel in its original box in the hall closet. She remembered helping her mother stick the hairy, silver branches into the holes of the silver bark. She sat cross-legged with sponge rollers in her hair on Christmas Eve, mesmerized by the changing color wheel of red, blue, and green on the silver glow of the tree. She carried the box to her bedroom upstairs. She was bringing it home. She didn't care what Tom or Angela thought.

In Henry's bedroom, Angela found the tintype photo of Patricia Mueller's sons. She looked behind her to see if anyone was watching. She quickly wrapped it in a white, cotton handkerchief Henry had kept in the top dresser drawer. She put it in her jean pocket, along with Henry's gold-tone Elgin watch.

"Daddy," she said out loud like a prayer. She patted her jean pocket with her hand and closed her eyes.

A continuous stream of music, a compilation of the Forties, Fifties, and Sixties played while they worked. It was Henry and Helen's opera with the single refrain that life no longer mattered as it had the first forty years they lived together.

"Smoke, smoke, smoke, that cigarette. Smoke it till you smoke yourself to death." Tom sang along with Tex Williams, while packing the chipped dinnerware of the family in a cardboard box.

"Straighten up and fly right. Straighten up and do right."

Gracey sang from the upstairs bathroom, throwing Henry's prescription pills, insulin bottles, and syringes in a green plastic bag.

"I wish to God they would shut up," Angela said, hoping they heard her, while she pulled the sheets off of Henry's bed. She placed the pillows in the middle and tied the sheets around it in a tight knot.

The music played. The children worked. The house that Henry and Helen made was reduced to boxes, plastic bags, and bulging garbage cans. But in suitcases and a pocket, each child kept a coveted jewel from the home that once was theirs.

"I need something to eat. We've been at this for a while," said Tom. "Let's stop and eat."

"Why don't I get a pizza or Red Rooster fried chicken? I need something with a drive-thru, looking like this." Gracey picked up her purse from the kitchen counter.

An hour later, the three sat together in the living room. The coffee table served as a dining table with a box of fried chicken and Styrofoam containers of mashed potatoes, gravy, and fried okra opened for serving. Two bottles of wine anchored the box of chicken.

Tom sat in Henry's recliner, eating, and staring at the TV in front of him. The sisters sat on the carpet with elbows resting on the coffee table. *Dancing with the Stars* filled the need to make conversation.

"I'm going to bed," Angela said suddenly, rising from the floor.

"Come on, Angela, stay up a little longer with us. We can look at pictures together. I'll open another bottle of wine."

"There's not enough wine in the world to make me feel better tonight."

Tom and Gracey watched her walk out of the room with her shoulders slumped forward, wiping tears from her face. Gracey felt Angela's sadness slowly rising to engulf her. She stood up from the coffee table and sat closer to Tom.

"You want some more wine, Tom?"

"Okay, Sis."

He reached for the remote control and turned off the TV.

"You know, she thinks she's the only one suffering here. We're all suffering." He took a long drink from his glass of wine. "I'm glad it's over. Every day I kept thinking how many more years of my life am I going to have to deal with this? Every single day of my life I felt that way."

Gracey turned to face him. She didn't say anything.

"Mom and Dad dropped us off and picked us up, like we were luggage. Put us in the car and down the road we drove. A new house, a new school, and never an explanation on why our lives were so screwed up. Along comes Angela, and everything is different. Mom's different, Dad's different, but not me." Tom looked at his sister and picked up his wine glass. He drained it. "I remember what it was like before Angela. Not having any money in the house; we ate ketchup sandwiches then, Gracey. Two pieces of white bread with ketchup! With the two of them at each other's throats! When I think of some of the things they said to each other."

"Oh, Tom," Gracey said, looking down at the floor.

It was as if he didn't hear her or even know she was there. He continued talking to himself, explaining the unexplainable to the little boy he was, while defending the middle-aged man he became.

Tom, the bystander, waited his entire life for an action or word that would make life different for him. Life before Angela's birth. Life after Angela's birth. Life before Henry died. Life after Henry died. He had spent his life waiting to hear an answer to every late night "Why?" he whispered in the dark.

"I can't forgive him. I can't. I was a kid, a boy . . . He humiliated me, the man ruined me." Tom began crying, placing his head in his hands.

"It's okay. It'll be okay, Tom." Gracey stood next to him, touching his bent shoulders.

Tom did not look at his sister, but continued talking.

"Everybody was at the house. Drinking in the back yard, standing around the barbeque pit. People he worked with, some relatives were there, the neighbors. I don't know where Mom was. That was around the time she stayed in the house mostly, walking around in a robe with a wet rag on her forehead . . . always sick. I was wrestling with one of the cousins. Kid stuff, ya know? I might have been ten at the time. We weren't but a few feet from where everybody was standing." Tom stopped to catch his breath and wipe his palms against the thighs of his jeans. "I barely touched him. It was a little karate kick on his butt. Dad must have been watching the whole time. He ran toward me. Yanked me by the arm and pulled his belt off around his waist. It happened so fast, I didn't even know why Dad was mad.

"He whipped me with that belt. Right there. With everyone standing around the barbeque pit, he whipped the back of my legs, my ass. When I tried to put my hands across my backside, he whipped my hands, my arms. I fell down . . . Oh God." Tom stood up and turned his back to Gracey. "I can still hear that belt being pulled from his waist. Called me a pussy for kicking my cousin. He wasn't having a pussy son. He'd beat it right out of me. Kept hollering, 'Get up or I'll hit you harder, boy'."

Gracey stood next to her brother. The room held an awful silence. She didn't think either one of them was breathing or their hearts, beating. She reached for his arm to steady herself.

"No one tried to take that belt from him, Gracey. No one said anything. All I heard was the belt against my skin and his heavy breathing. He exhausted himself beating me; he only stopped long enough to tell me to get the hell away from him. He didn't want to see my face. But you know, that wasn't the worst part. That was the next morning. And then I knew . . . I knew that man never loved me enough to get past his own misery. He made me a full breakfast the next morning. Sausage, bacon, eggs, and biscuits. The works. Poured me a glass of milk and called me his 'Little Buddy.' Like nothing had happened . . . like dropping us off with strangers when Mom left. We were lost, lost to them, Gracey."

"I'm sorry. I'm sorry," Gracey cried with her brother, standing over him, touching his shoulder.

"I finally figured out why running came so natural to me. I mean, even when I was fifteen, no one could touch me in cross country. I could run for hours. The sound of my heart and the pounding of my feet on the track drowned it all out. After a mile, sometimes it took two, I could run Henry completely out of my mind." He looked directly at Gracey. "I'm going outside. Don't wait up for me."

He walked away from her into the kitchen. She heard the screen door slam back against its frame. She sat in the living room alone, listening to the sounds outside the window. She told herself he was thinking things through on the back porch.

She cleaned up the remains of dinner, turned the lights off, and lay down on the couch. She waited for him there in the dark.

She woke up as early morning light came through the living room window. She met it with panic, realizing she had fallen asleep on the couch and had forgotten about her brother.

He struggled for years wanting to tell someone. And when he finally gets the guts to do it, I leave him alone with it. Why didn't I follow him outside? What's wrong with me?

She rose from the couch with the anxiety of yesterday's troubles seeping into the morning. She peered out the window to see if his truck was still in the driveway. Relieved to see it, she put the coffee maker on and sat down in the kitchen.

Oh God, help me. Help me to make this day better than yesterday. Please help me to love my brother and sister through this.

At once she thought of Henry's bird bath on the side of the house. Imagining it to be bone dry in the heat of the day, she let the back door slam behind her as she walked outside.

The water can was still hooked on the fence where she last saw it. She filled it at the water hose on the side of the house and poured it into the cement bird bath. Patches of grass near the bird bath were covered in hundreds of dried nettles from the cedar tree bending over it.

She turned and looked at the house, thinking of Angela and

Tom, tucked into thin quilts, the same blankets that covered them as children, in the same beds they had slept as children. Her big brother. Her little sister. Her Tom and Angela. She whispered a prayer into the morning light that fell on her father's house.

"Lord, make me an instrument of your peace,
where there is hatred, let me sow love;
where there is injury, pardon;
where there is doubt, faith;
where there is darkness, light;
where there is sadness, joy;

O Divine Master, grant that I may not so much seek to be
consoled as to console;
to be understood as to understand;
to be loved as to love.

For it is in giving that we receive;
it is in pardoning that we are pardoned;
and it is in dying that we are born to eternal life."

Chapter Seventeen
My Brother's Keeper

Gracey walked back inside the house, stopping to wipe the wet grass and cedar nettles off her bare feet with an old towel Henry kept on the railing of the back steps. She walked into the kitchen and poured herself a cup of coffee at the counter, drinking it at the sink, staring out the window.

Tap, tap, tap-tap-tap. There was no mistaking the sound of high heels on a linoleum floor. It was a sound she always associated with this house, and all the comings and goings, throughout its existence.

"Good morning," Gracey said to Angela, who at 8 AM was fully dressed with make-up, jewelry and a purse the size of an airline carry-on bag.

"I'm closing out everything at the bank and going by Allen's Used Cars to sell Dad's truck. We'll need all the cash we can get once the medical bills arrive."

"How about some breakfast? I can scramble some eggs with tortillas."

"I'll get coffee in town."

"We need to think about scattering Dad's ashes sometime before we all leave. Tom and I can finish the house today. We'll go by the dump, take some things to Goodwill. If you want something, better get it now. Maybe tomorrow morning we can go to the cemetery."

"Have you and Tom already discussed this?"

"No, we haven't. I'm discussing it with you right now."

"We'll go tomorrow morning, before it gets too hot." Angela's heels made a determined, solid click on the cracked linoleum floor as she walked to the back door.

"Wait a minute, Angela. You don't have to do all that right now. Let's eat breakfast together. Talk some. I know we all got our lives somewhere out there, away from this place, but, you know, this is really the last time, it will just be me, you and Tom in this house. The last time."

Angela sighed and put her purse and keys down on the counter with an unenthusiastic clunk. She sat down at the kitchen table and folder her arms across her chest.

Gracey walked to the foot of the stairs and called her brother.

"Tom, coffee's on."

She heard the toilet flush upstairs, followed by his footsteps on the stairs.

"Hey," he said, sitting down at the kitchen table.

She placed a cup of coffee in front of him, touching his shoulder when he leaned forward for a sip.

"Tom, I've been thinking about last night. And I haven't said anything to Angela besides good morning. I want us all to sit here, just a little while and try to be good to each other. We need to do this for each other. We got to leave here with some kind of buoyancy to get us back into our other lives or, you know, I'll just spend the next years regretting . . . regretting that I never told you, either of you, how much I love you. You mean everything to me. You, too, Angela."

Angela got up from the table and poured herself a cup of coffee at the counter, holding her breath and wishing she could evaporate into the coffee fumes.

"Tom, I'm sorry I didn't wait up for you. It wasn't because I didn't care. There's just nothing I can do. I can't make it right for you. Wish I could, but the words don't exist and I can't fix it for you. If I could, I'd do it every day for the rest of my life. You're the only one that can fix it." Gracey sat next to her brother and reached for his hand. "I'm not saying what you feel isn't real. What I'm trying to say, Tom, is my heart breaks for you. I wish I could have helped you with this a long time ago. You got to let it go now. You got to let go of the shame. We all need to, even you, Angela. It never was ours to feel. It was Dad's shame. Mom's shame. They're gone. So is the shame."

"I wasn't ashamed of them. I never was," Angela said, walking toward the table and pulling out a chair. "I loved them. They loved me. It's really that simple for me. I just can't understand, I can't, why it can't be for the two of you."

Tom didn't look up from the table. With each minute that passed he seemed to become smaller and smaller in the chair, as small as a nine-year-old boy, insignificant and unheard.

"Yes, but you know Angela, that's how it is with a family, with people in general. Three little kids can be walking down a sidewalk, and there's an accident; someone gets hurt. All three are going to have a different story. Whose fault it was . . . every one of us is going to have a different hero and a different bad guy. There's no bad guy here. And if you think about it, there never was. We all have a different sort of hurt. It's a different sidewalk for each of us."

"I don't know if I can let it go," Tom said, still looking down into his cup of coffee, searching for phrases and words that would float to the top of the cup and save him. He didn't need two women to help him fight his private war, his guarded hurt. He had years of experience of burying casualties deep within. It was none of their business.

"It's not something that's going to happen overnight, Tom. You're going to have to pray about it. Pray for your peace. Pray for yourself. You deserve that. You are worth that. You were a little boy who was hurt by his father, who was hurt by his own father, and so on and so on . . . It's a redundantly long line of pain. Maybe it's time to let it go. Maybe you can forgive him."

"Well, it's out there now, isn't it?" Tom looked away from his sisters, focusing through the parted curtain in the kitchen window. "What's hideous and unspeakable eases a little bit when you say it aloud." He looked at Gracey and smiled faintly. "You know, I feel like I can breathe easier. Isn't that crazy? All that crap was in my head, sloshing around. I got pretty damn good at torturing myself. I kept reliving it over and over again, trying to find a reason, trying to make sense of it. It was a scab I kept picking at, never letting it heal."

"What's the big bad secret? Dad drank? Mom was unhappy? What was it Tom, what the hell was it?" Angela said, beginning to cry.

"I never told you, Angela, or even you, Gracey, until last night, because . . . because I didn't want to burden you. I didn't want to make any of you sad. Especially you, Angela. You loved Dad so much. It was the one good thing in this house; that love you two had for each other. Gracey, you had Mom. I didn't want to take any of that from you. I loved you that much. I just didn't belong, you know?"

"No, Tom. You're wrong." Angela got up from the table and put her arms around her brother. "Every time I came to see Dad, every single time, or if I called, he'd asked for you. For you. He wanted you. And he wanted you, too, Gracey. He would ask me over and over, 'Have you heard from them? What's Tom been doing? How's Gracey and the kids?' He never stopped asking."

Gracey stood next to Tom and Angela, putting her hand on each of their shoulders.

"I wish I would have known . . . I wish . . . but, that's passed. Gone. Does it even matter that we try to make sense of it? Tom, Angela, even Mom and Dad, every one of us deserves some mercy. And maybe mercy is purely the start of a new day. Maybe it's burying the past. Maybe it's forgiving all the pain. Sometimes, that's enough. Sometimes that's all we need."

Tom stood up from the kitchen table, scraping the chair across the floor. He pulled Angela and Gracey next to him, hugging them tightly against his chest. After a moment, he stiffened and pulled away from the two sisters. "I don't want to talk about it anymore, okay?"

"You don't need to, Tom. Let's get our day going. Angela's

'bout out the door to take care of Dad's finances," Gracey said as she slowly rubbed her brother's back with her open palm.

"Yeah, let's get the house done."

"We should probably take the ashes to the cemetery tomorrow morning, before it gets too hot," Gracey said.

"We can do that. As far as the furniture in the house, it's a ride to Goodwill and the dump."

A knock at the kitchen door interrupted their conversation. Before Gracey could open the door, Irma let herself in.

"Y'all up and at it this morning?" asked Irma, wearing the usual visor with matching capri pants and a striped blouse.

"Come in," said Gracey. "We're finishing breakfast."

"Morning, Irma. I was about to get dressed. Got some errands in town later today," said Tom, quickly leaving the room.

"Want some coffee, Irma?"

"Nope. Been up since four o'clock. Drank my three cups then. Wanted to come by and see how y'all were doing. Drop off my house keys. How you doin' Angela?"

"Morning, Irma. I've got business in town. Maybe I'll see you when I get back." She gave the old woman a peck of a kiss and closed the door behind her.

Irma stared at the door, whipped her hands against her thighs, and looked at Gracey rinsing out the coffee pot at the sink.

"Gracey, I'd like to have a few things. Not much. Maybe a few pictures of your daddy and me. Maybe his coffee cup. I need to gather-up all my stuff, too."

"Sure."

"I know we didn't always get along, but I want you to know, I did love your daddy. You might not believe that. I did love him and did my best to take care of him."

Gracey put her dish towel on the counter and walked toward Irma.

"Irma, I don't want to hurt you, and I don't want you to hurt me. Let's let the past go. Let it go. It doesn't matter anymore. I'm grateful Dad wasn't alone. You did a lot for him, a lot of hard things, especially for a woman your age. It would have been hard for anyone." Gracey reached out to hug the old woman. "You take whatever you want. I'll get a bag for you. You ought to take some of the music you and Dad listened to as well."

An hour later, with a plastic grocery bag full of ten-cent memorabilia of an old man and woman's friendship in her hand, the rest in her car, Irma Novosad lit a cigarette in the front yard and squinted into the morning sun. She walked to the side of the garage and pulled up a rusted tomato stake with a vegetable can clipped to it. It was the ash tray Henry had made for her when she smoked outside. Gracey smiled at her from the screen door.

"We sure could use some more rain," Irma said, looking at Gracey.

"Yes, we sure could." Gracey let the door slap back against the house and walked toward her. "Dad left you some money. We'll call you once the attorney goes over the will with us. It may be a couple of weeks, but I wanted you to know that."

The old woman began to cry, pulling the plastic bag in front of her face, so Gracey couldn't see her tears. In the other hand, she held onto her cigarette. "He didn't have to do that. He didn't. I would have loved him anyway. I would have loved him if he didn't have two nickels to rub together. He wasn't an easy man to love, but I loved him."

"I know you did, Irma."

The old woman stepped into the gold Oldsmobile. She backed out of the driveway and waved goodbye. When the car paused at the stop sign on the corner, she honked the horn in two short blasts. The car slowly turned left, and Irma was gone forever.

"Hey, let's load the truck up for the dump. I think we can get a few more bags in there." Tom stuck his head out from the screen door. "You ready?"

"I guess. I can't believe how stinking hot it is at ten in the morning."

Tom and Gracey drove past the hospital on the farm market road to the county dump. Neither one spoke. The sun created a haze across the land, void of water or even a blade of green grass, no sign of the downpour from the day before. The grass died in May. Only people in air conditioned vehicles and snakes made their way across this land in August.

The gate to the dump was open as the truck pulled in front of it. Tom drove to a pile of household garbage to the right of the gate.

"I'm going to back-up to this pile. You use the hoe in the back of the truck and push it out. I'll get the big pieces."

She got out of the truck. Grabbing the hoe resting on top of the plastic bags, she pulled it back, ripping the bags open. Coffee grinds, soured fruit, and rotting meat created a gaseous white ooze that fell to her feet. Above her, the seagulls screamed in their mad circle of flight.

"I hate this. All of it! It's too damn hot to be working like this! What are we doing here?"

"Slow down. Slow down or get in the truck and wait for me to finish. You're going to hurt yourself if you keep jerking around."

"Why do we always have to do it like this? It doesn't make sense."

"It's not that much, Gracey. Get in the truck if you're tired."

"That's not what I'm saying. I'm trying to tell you, tell you that I'm fifty-two and still working like I'm twenty. I don't know if it's arrogance, thinking I can do it, or I'm used to working like this. But it's how they taught us, Tom. They taught us to work. Put your head down, put your ego in your back pocket, and work. Remember when Mom died? That same day we went back to the house and started working in the yard, cutting grass, trimming trees. Why did we do that? Why?" Her tears fell hot across her face as she kicked the side of the truck.

Tom watched the lone back hoe owned by the county dump separate the garbage into categories: abandoned TVs and furniture to the left, household trash and yard clippings to the right. Back and forth, back and forth, all day long. He never looked at his sister, only at what was in front of him. That, he could understand. The anger and tears of a frustrated woman, he'd never understand despite the years of hearing it.

"We did it, Tom, working like fools after Mom died, because there wasn't anyone around us who loved us enough to say 'stop, sit down and cry; grieve for your mother.' Poor kids work, so they don't have to think about things; they don't have to see the obvious; that no one, including yourself, thinks you're worth anything else but mindless work."

Tom turned from the direction of the back hoe and looked at her sister. Her hair was drenched in sweat and her face was bright red.

"Why didn't we want more for ourselves, Tom? I'll tell you. It took me years to figure it out. Because when you put your head down and accept all the work they can give you, you don't have to think. You don't have to think how do I make Mama love Daddy or Daddy love Mama, or maybe even love me. There's the crazy irony of it all. It's easier to work than accept you're not worth much. It's the legacy of the poor. It's the Mueller legacy—too many children, too many hardships, never a plan for something better, only living day by day, praying things will get better. Why didn't Mama and Daddy want anything more? Didn't they think we deserved better?"

Tom took his sister's hand, opened the truck door, and put her in the cab.

"Gracey, that's enough. Get in the truck and stay in it. Mom and Dad did the best they could, just like you and me. We're all doing the best we can right now. That's it for today. Let's be quiet and rest awhile."

She sat in the truck, staring through the windshield at the mounds and mounds of garbage piled into a rancid mountain before her. She thought how those mounds of garbage had once been someone's treasure, Christmas gift, birthday present; once loved, now discarded, no longer wanted.

"I'm tired. I'm really tired today," she said aloud. She watched the seagulls fly in circles outside the truck windshield as Tom started the truck. She closed her eyes when she heard the engine rev.

Chapter Eighteen
Breathing

"You ready, Angela?" asked Gracey, standing at the foot of the stairs.

"Yeah. Get Dad's thermos, I want some coffee once we get there. Still don't know why we have to do this at seven in the morning."

"Let's get it over with."

The three siblings sat side-by-side in the cab of their father's truck. The oldest drove, the youngest sat in the middle, cradling her father's urn close to her chest, and the middle child held her great-great-grandmother's Bible on her lap.

They didn't speak. Each child was lost in his or her separate memories of their mother and father. Each child was sure no one had ever loved and suffered at the hands of their mother and father as he or she had.

They drove in silence to the Loti Cemetery located between the Highway 59 overpass and the American Legion Hall in a grove of oak and cedar trees. A gravel road separated the cemetery between the burial plots of Catholics and Protestants. The three of them could drive there with their eyes closed. It was a familiar place, with a familiar pain.

Tom parked the truck under the shade of an oak tree. The early August heat had not burnt off the morning's dew as Tom and Gracey walked to their mother's grave. The droplets misted across the tops of their shoes, leaving the smallest of grass blades clinging to their shoe laces. Angela remained inside the truck with both hands pressed tightly on the urn. Gracey turned to look at her, but she did not call her name.

"Come here, Angela," Tom said, looking toward the truck.

Angela got out and walked toward her brother and sister, tears falling with each step she took.

Taking the urn from Angela, Tom pulled her closer to him and Gracey. The shoulders of the brother and two sisters touched as they stood together at the grave site. Tom began speaking, all the while looking at his mother's headstone.

"I'm sorry for all your suffering, Dad. I'm sorry for all the things that hurt you and disappointed you. Our only peace is knowing we're passing through this life, and when it's over, we'll see each other in heaven. We'll be together then and love each other with all the strength we weren't able to find while on this earth. You gave us the best you had to give. We love you. We love you, Mama." Tom removed the lid of the urn and turned it upside down. Its contents sprinkled across Helen Mueller's grave. He placed the urn next to her headstone.

Gracey opened Patricia Walsh's Bible and turned to the chapter she had marked and began reading.

"If I speak in the tongues of mortals and of angels, but do not have love, I am a noisy gong or a clanging cymbal. And if I have prophetic powers, and understand all mysteries and all knowledge, and if I have faith, so as to remove mountains, but do not have love, I am nothing. If I give away all my possessions, and if I hand over my body so that I may boast, but do not have love, I gain nothing.

Love is patient; love is kind; love is not envious or boastful or arrogant or rude. It does not insist on its own way; it is not irritable or resentful; it does not rejoice in wrongdoing, but rejoices in the truth. It bears all things, believes all things, hopes all things, endures all things.

Love never ends. But as for prophecies, they will come to an end; as for tongues, they will cease; as for knowledge, it will come to an end. For we know only in part, and we prophesy only in part; but when the complete comes, the partial will come to an end. When I was a child, I spoke like a child, I thought like a child, I reasoned like a child; when I became an adult, I put an end to childish ways. For now we see in a mirror, dimly, but then we will see face to face. Now I know only in part; then I will know fully, even as I have been fully known.

And now faith, hope, and love abide, these three; and the greatest of these is love."

"Goodbye, Mama and Daddy. I'll never forget you. Every time I look at my daughter, her eyes, and sweet smile, I see you. She's got Daddy's eyes, Mama, but she's named for you. She's beautiful like you were," Angela said touching the tombstone. "I can't believe you're both gone. I didn't have you long enough." She turned and walked back to the truck.

Tom and Gracey followed her.

Tom put the tailgate down on the truck. Together, the son and daughters of Henry and Helen Mueller sat on the tailgate of their father's truck, drinking coffee in the silence of an August morning in South Texas.

"I could use a little something in my coffee," Angela said.

Tom stood up, opened the truck door, and felt underneath the driver's seat. His raised hand showed a fifth of Canadian Club wrapped in a paper bag. The two sisters offered their coffee cups for filling.

"Dad kept the same hiding place for years," said Tom. They bent their heads to the cup rims, swallowing the liquid warmth of coffee and whiskey.

The mid-morning sun rose through the land, creating a lushness of sky, earth, and oak. Its smell was as familiar to the three children sitting on the tailgate as breathing itself.

Chapter Nineteen
Goodness and Mercy

Gracey couldn't tell if the day would bring rain or sunlight in the damp September morning outside the hotel pub in Forkhill, Ireland. There was a strong possibility there could be rain and sunlight. Ireland was like that. Unpredictable.

The door to the pub was unlocked. Gracey found a table near a large window facing the street. As she sat down, the slightest of rain began to fall against the window, sliding sideways until it disappeared in the window frame. The smallest of droplets, crystalline and pure, driven by wind from the Atlantic, danced like colorless ribbons on the window.

The rain and wind increased. Now, the leaves flew from the tops of the ash and sycamore trees, joining the dance. Underneath their boughs, the wet earth was covered in a blanket of yellow, orange, and brown confetti. Then, as quickly as it began, the rain and wind stopped. The sun spread thin each cumulus cloud, its light pouring in through the rain-streaked window. "Come," the day whispered its beginning.

She sat silently in the luxury of the moment, then she remembered why she got up at 6 AM and came downstairs.

I can't believe the wedding is tomorrow. Have I forgotten anyone or anything? She grabbed her pencil and yellow pad of paper out of her purse. *First things first, I need some caffeine.*

She found last night's bartender mopping the tile floors.

"So sorry to bother you. My God, do you live here? You were keeping the bar last night."

"No bother, no bother at all, miss. I stay here when I work late. The owner keeps a room for the workers when there's a wedding. Let me get the kettle on to wet your tea."

"Thanks. I want to get started on the weekend's events. Hard to imagine a wedding lasting for three days. It's almost biblical."

"It'll be grand. Nothing like an Irish wedding. The cook comes in at eight if you want an Ulster Fry, but I can get you a wee bun for your tea."

Gracey offered him a smile.

If I were in the States, he would've told me to come back at eight when the cook arrived; that the kitchen is closed. Then the litany of excuses: "It's not my job. I don't get paid to do that. We could be sued." The Irish, they were tough. Like any people subjected to centuries of servitude, they could serve you with a smile on their lips and murder in their eyes.

Gracey understood the Irish capacity to suffer. A cup of coffee, a glass of iced tea, a shot of whiskey were solaces taken by her mother and father, her grandmother and great-great-grandmother, against the bitterness of everyday life.

She watched the bartender wipe down the bar with his back to her. He plugged in an electric kettle on the cleaned surface and began preparing her tea.

The poor of America are no different than the poor in Ireland, or anywhere else around the world; like my own family who worked and waited for their pay, accepted half the amount owed them, and died realizing their bodies were nothing more than tools used by others. But that didn't change them, no. Grandma, Mama, Daddy, they all continued to get up every morning and try again, knowing the odds were stacked against them the day they were born.

What was it that Henry always said? Oh, yeah! 'I'll stand and be counted same as any man.' That's so Irish. Fightin' Irish! They never offered cheap sentiment or an excuse, only the iron will to survive.

"Here's your tea, miss."

The waiter sat the tea cup in front of her. She couldn't decide how old he was. He looked to be in his early twenties. She wondered if he was like so many young men and women of the Eurozone, destined to fly from borderless country to borderless country, working on construction crews or serving the vacationing rich of the world. It saddened her to realize he was probably no different than the generations of Irishmen before him, destined to leave home, searching for a fair wage elsewhere.

The great exodus never ceased for Ireland. Like a wildfire tendered by the bones of the starving in 1845, emigration continued to bleed a nation that could not employ its own. As they did in the 19th century, they travelled to America, Australia, and Canada in the 21st century.

The Irish are all over the world. Sending those letters back home to their crying mothers, missing their babies. But you got to eat, so off you go, leaving your home and family, hoping for the day you've got enough cash to go home to die.

Gracey held the warmth of the tea cup in her hand.

Am I here in Ireland for my daughter's wedding or in Texas sitting on a tailgate of a truck, dangling my legs, like a girl, a girl of fifteen? Where did that time go? It's a cruel thing to grow older and remember being younger. To be that fifteen-year-old girl again, on a June day in Texas, would be everything, everything imaginable. What I'd give to hear one of my childhood friends call my name from a distance. 'Hurry, Gracey. Hurry.' We'd hold each other's hands and jump off the Francitas River Bridge, swimming together to the river's bank, only a few miles from where my great-great-grandmother lived as an Irish immigrant.

She thought of Patricia Walsh, raising her sons and growing cotton on their small dirt farm.

Did she ever dare to think her great-great-granddaughter would return to her homeland? The years go by, centuries really, to find me, Patricia's granddaughter, sitting in a pub in Forkhill, Ireland on a cool September morning. My God, the changes, the grief, the joy, the living.

She scribbled the timeline of the events for the next three days on a memo pad in front of her:

      1) Tonight at the country pub in Creggan

      2) The wedding in the cathedral with the reception in Darver

3) Sunday, a bus-load of Texans converge with the Irish in Carlingford for oysters and beer.

"Looks like there'll be clear skies for the wedding. Thanks be to God." The waiter placed scones, butter, and jam on a plate next to Gracey's tea cup.

There were clear skies for the last summer of Henry's life. It was the third summer of the Texas drought with temperatures in the low hundreds and months without a drop of rain. They all had prayed for rain, the ranchers and farmers. The poor prayed the most. They could not afford to water their yards or plants. They prayed their trees would not die . . .

Henry's lawn had died, but he'd continued to water a few plants and vegetables he kept in assorted pots near the garage.

"That weatherman don't know shit from shinola," Henry had said, as he pushed the wheelchair down the plywood ramp in the garage and filled an empty coffee can with water. The first cigarette of the day was balanced on his lower lip. Refilling his can, he added fresh water to the bird bath on the side of the house. Next, he refilled the bird feeder with thistle seed . . .

It's not humanly possible to say goodbye to those images. They play over and over again in my heart. I feel that staggering heat, and I know that waterless land. And my father, Daddy had the guts to sustain life around him, although he was dying.

Gracey whispered a prayer for him, crossing her breast with the words she was taught as a little girl, by her mother.

"God our Father,
Your power brings us to birth,
Your providence guides our lives,
and by Your command we return to dust.
Lord, those who die still live in Your presence,
their lives change but do not end.
I pray in hope for my family,

relatives and friends,
and for all the dead known to You alone.

In company with Christ,
Who died and now lives,
may they rejoice in Your kingdom,
where all our tears are wiped away.
Unite us together again in one family,
to sing Your praise forever and ever.

In the name of the Father, Son, and Holy Spirit."

After making the sign of the cross, she opened her eyes to see the waiter looking at her. He smiled. She returned the smile, then placed a twenty-pound note under her tea cup as a measure of thanks for his kindness to her.

She was travelling on Helen and Henry's money. Money they left her in the will. It had purchased three round-trip tickets to Ireland, a first edition copy of Ulysses for Mark, and two gold Celtic crosses for her daughter and son.

It saddened her to accept it. It was money Helen and Henry saved by denying themselves anything that could have made life easier. To Helen and Henry, leaving their children money and a house free of a mortgage were gifts they could never imagine for themselves. Gifts they could have never imagined they could offer.

Gracey took her mother's tea set, wrapped in *The Victoria Advocate*, and mailed it back to Mississippi on the last day she was in Texas. The only time it had been moved from the curio cabinet was the day after Henry's funeral.

It must be 8 o'clock.

Gracey heard the kitchen staff arriving at the hotel entrance. Soon her family would come down from their rooms.

They came in stages: the oldest first, the youngest arriving late, each seeking a quiet table and a hot cup of coffee to nurse their hangovers. Gracey watched them as she sipped her tea. Her cousins, her brother, her sister, her mother-in-law, her brother-in-law, her friends, her husband, and their two children, Therese and Will. They were an image of the love Mark and Gracey knew when they were young, and nurtured as they grew old, together. She watched them and loved them with her eyes until its perfection hurt.

"So what's on today's agenda?" Will sat in a chair next to his mother.

"Well, hon, we'll take a bus from the hotel lobby about 6 PM and head to The Cabin, a little country pub in Creggan; it's just down the road a piece. I'll get a passenger bus and driver to take us there. Daniel's best man has promised food, drink, and live music. Once the manager comes, I'll get a printed agenda of the next three days; that way you can come and go as you please until the bus shows up."

"I got out a little yesterday. Went to the liquor store across the street."

"How was that?"

"Uncle Bryan went with me. It was a bit retro. The guy was about your age that waited on us. The Boom Town Rats were blasting away in there. Uncle Bryan knew the song. We got some Kilbeggan to keep in our rooms."

"I bet Uncle Bryan did know the song," Gracey laughed. She thought of Mark's oldest brother, and the fun they knew in college, dancing in the New Wave Clubs of Lower Westheimer in Houston. Bob Geldof was also young then, dancing in his underwear and flirting with civil disobedience. He grew up to feed the world. The world took his wife and daughter in return.

"I think Bryan pissed the guy off, though. He didn't mean to. He was only trying to be friendly. He told him we were with a bunch of Americans in town for a wedding. Then he clarified it by saying Texans were in town for a wedding. I was watching the guy's face. That seem to make him really mad because his face turned red. Bryan told him we were getting an early start on the drinking, so we wouldn't be outdone by the Irish reputation for drinking."

"Oh, no."

"Yeah, it gets even better. The guy looked at Bryan and me and said, 'Yous Yanks are in good form with yous drinking.' We just paid for the whiskey and got out of there."

"Keep an eye on your Uncle Bryan this weekend," Gracey laughed.

The men of Ireland and South Texas had much in common, thought Gracie, proud and stubborn. Both knew what it meant to cause a row. She didn't want any brawls at the reception once the whiskey and Guinness blew caution out the door.

She thought of a fight she saw at a dance in the Knights of Columbus Hall in El Campo, Texas when she was fourteen. Two roughnecks, drunk on Lone Star Beer and Jack Daniels, were a ball on the ground, tangled in their drunken anger, scratching, clawing, and gouging. An occasional loose leg allowed a sharp kick with a cowboy boot to the spleen. The fight ended when the winner bit the ear off of the other man. At the time, Gracey didn't think an ear could bleed that much; no less than she could believe that a fundraiser for the church ended in a drunken brawl.

"Mornin', Gracey." With her hair piled into an enormous cylinder-shaped bun on top of her head, Beverly looked for a friendly face.

"Hey Bev, sit down and have some breakfast with me."

"I heard you tell Will we'd be going to an authentic Irish country pub tonight."

"Yeah, it'll be fun. I hired a driver and a small bus to take us back and forth, so people can enjoy themselves without worrying about drinking and driving."

"So it's like the pubs Rick Steves visits?"

"What do you mean?"

"You know when he travels on his PBS shows? He always visits the pubs with the Union Jacks hanging all over the walls, where people are singing with their arms around each other, drinking giant mugs of beer. I even remember some of the words to their song, 'And now my song is over, I've got no more to say. Just give us eggs and brandy and we'll be on our way'."

"I don't think we'll see any Union Jacks in this pub, Beverly. You might not want to mention that to the bartender or Daniel's family when we get there."

"That's cool."

By 6 PM, the cast of characters had assembled in the hotel lobby for the bus ride. The in-laws, out-laws, assorted kooks, and faithful friends stood in a mismatched circle of stories, assumptions, pecking orders, past wrongs, jealousies, successes, failures, yet loved beyond measure and held by the bond of family and lifelong friendships.

Gracey and Mark stood on the sidewalk and watched everyone get on the bus. The last of a slow sun warmed the late afternoon before sinking behind the hills covered in multiple shades of a green quilt called Ireland.

The Irish loved the land, like the South Texans. They worried about the weather, the tomato plants, the cattle, and the price of feed. They loved their coastline, the marsh and sea, fishing the same waters as their fathers and grandfathers, knowing each oyster bed, each seasonal tide, each grass the fowl rested in at the shore. The land, to the Irish and Texans, was sacred; their people had died for it.

The old ladies tending the shops in the town square of Forkhill picked up the door mats and placed the "closed" signs in the front windows. The young girls of St. Anne Parochial School, in their white shirts and navy green tartan skirts, had walked home hours ago, after spending the last of their money on pastries at Gran Martin's Fine Irish Bakery and on magazines at McNamee's Corner Shop.

The day was ending, and the night was beginning. In Ireland, they were distinct times. For the night was for family, lovers, and friends. The day's work was done. There would be no interrupting the evening to make a sweaty pound for the Crown.

Gracey stood watching life all around her, squeezing Mark's hand in hers.

"Get on the bus," everyone yelled.

"Right, right," Gracey laughed, letting go of Mark's hand. She squeezed in between Angela and her mother-in-law. The lorry driver pushed in the clutch and shifted into first, lurching the bus forward. Into the dusk of September, into the foot hills of the Ring of Gullion, they travelled.

Chapter Twenty
Life's a Song

"Did anyone get food at the Cabin?" Gracey asked, walking into the hotel pub after paying the lorry driver.

"No, but we got a lot to drink." Beverly raised a margarita glass to her cousin.

"Please don't tell me you're drinking a margarita?"

"Yep, and it's a good one."

I got to get some food into these people. Tomorrow starts early with the Wedding Mass at eleven.

Gracey surveyed the crowd and the empty shot glasses stacked at each table.

"Bartender, is the kitchen closed?"

"Yes, miss, but my cousin has a pizza take-away. It's open 'till eleven. Let me call for yous. You can eat it here."

"Perfect. Better get us six of the biggest they have with everything on it."

The pizzas arrived forty minutes later.

"Is that canned corn on the pizza?" Angela questioned, surveying the slice handed to her by Tom.

"Hell yeah, and it's good," Mark said taking a bite. "I'll have a Guinness, too. Hey, did anyone see the memorial in Creggan?"

"I saw it," said Will, reaching for a piece of pizza across the table. "It said, 'We are our brothers' keepers.' That's from the Bible, you know. Guess it was a dedication to the fighters during the Troubles. Right after that sign was one that said 'Stop the Strip Searches.' Doesn't look like it's over for a lot of people."

"How do you get over guerrilla warfare in your neighborhood streets? That was less than a generation ago. I bet Daniel remembers it," Tom added.

"Take it easy, y'all. We're here for a wedding. Nobody needs to stir the pot." Gracey motioned for a round of beers for the table.

"It seems crazy to me that this is one island with two different governments with euros and pounds, but a common language," Tom said, ignoring his sister.

"You know Scotland had a chance not too long ago to change that. I bet William Wallace is rolling in his grave," said Mark.

"Wonder if he's related to Big Foot Wallace, the ranger that fought in the Texas Revolution?" added Beverly, giving a nod to the bartender for another margarita.

"I doubt that, Bev. They were separated by a few centuries," laughed Tom.

"I'm begging y'all, stop it now," cautioned Gracey. "It's a lot of drunk talk for us, but not for the people here. Can't we talk about tomorrow? Like, we all need to show up on time and hopefully, without hangovers?"

"You heard the lady. Now, where's my beer?" laughed Mark.

The bartender followed the proper form for pouring the heavy mass of dark beer with its creamy white head. Like a religious ritual, the glass was held at the right angle, the tab was pulled slowly, and finally, presented to the customer like a fine gift.

The family gathered around the six boxes of pizza sprinkled with canned corn, eating, talking, and drinking. Tomorrow came closer and closer with each hour they laughed and ate together. They should go to sleep, but they were afraid. Afraid to let this moment go, afraid they would never know this much happiness, together, again.

"Was that the Irish National Anthem they were singing tonight?" Angela asked Therese.

"Oh yes, even the kids sang along. Their little faces showed every word. They're proud people."

"I think we ought to sing the Texas National Anthem right here," said Tom.

"I didn't know Texas had a National Anthem," Beverly said, thoughtfully stirring her margarita with her finger.

"Come on, Tom. Don't get her started." Gracey looked directly at her brother as she ran her forefinger across her throat.

"I just think we should do a little pub singing, like the Irish."

"Mama, why don't you sing that song you used to sing about the bluebonnets?"

"I'm surprised you remember that, Therese. I used to sing it when I was in the fifth grade at Loti Elementary School. It was the morning ritual to say the 'Pledge of Allegiance,' then sing the bluebonnet song. Mrs. Albritton made us stand up by our desk with our hands over our hearts, reciting the pledge and singing that song. Oh, honey, I don't know, I've had a lot to drink and I'm really tired . . . Oh, why not?

"Bluebonnets, Bluebonnets, bonnets oh so blue.
Your bright eyes are shining, through the silvery dew.
I know you're a dolly, offered for the rain.
I know you'll return again to Texas in the spring."

Gracey surprised herself when tears filled her eyes while singing. She looked at the smiling faces around her. Their eyes were glistening and brimming, too.

"Aren't we a sight?" She laughed, wanting to elevate the mood. Her family clapped, raising their glasses to her.

She turned to her cousin with her finger still in the margarita.

"Well, Bev, did you hear any songs or see any Union Jacks in the pub we were in earlier?"

"No. But I saw a man with sunglasses on, just like Bono's."

"I don't think he was with the groom's group."

"I bought him a beer. He asked me what the craic was."

"Oh, Bev, what did you tell him?"

"I told him about Therese and Daniel, how they met, and the family being over here. You know? We kept drinking beer and talking. Could have stayed all night. He was even a musician. His band plays in Dublin all the time."

"Wonder if that's a pick-up line for middle-aged women travelling in Ireland?"

"Huh?" Said Beverly.

"Never mind," Gracey laughed. "Bartender, put this train wreck on my tab. I'm going to bed."

Chapter Twenty-one
A Ring of Gold

"Please tell me that is not a permanent tattoo. Got to be some kind of henna thing for a joke. My God, it's a huge frigate sailing the Pacific across the maid of honor's back. She doesn't even own a boat!"

Gracey dropped the armload of curling irons, flat irons, and hair spray on the floor when she saw Tiffany Smith's back, a human canvas, from the open bathroom door in the church.

"Mom, she'll hear you!"

"What? I'm out of line, here? She could have said something before we bought the strapless dresses. She had a vote. God knows I circled that jpeg for months seeking everyone's approval."

"It's not that big of a deal, Mom. Let it go."

"She's going to have to put make-up over it. There's no way she's walking in the church with that across her back. All people will remember is the tattoo, not the dress, not the couple, but the huge ship sailing across Tiffany's back."

"Would you relax? Look, we're all drinking champagne in here. Let's have some fun." Therese moved away from her mother in search of a champagne flute as a peace offering.

"Here," Therese said, handing her mother a flute of champagne. "Let's go into the priest's study, and you can help me with my dress."

Mother and daughter were alone in the priest's office. Gracey sat in the overstuffed chair near the window and surveyed the room. A small image of Mary cast in white marble stood on an oak pedestal; at her feet lay fresh cut red roses.

Gracey drank the glass of champagne, admiring the icon. She then looked out the large bay window and saw a rose bush growing against a white trellis; its stems bursting with red blooms.

Then Gracey felt her mother standing next to her. They all were with her. The women who loved and nurtured her, the women whose blood coursed through her and her daughter's veins.

"Helen, Viola, Patricia, and Aileen," she whispered their names.

"Mama?"

"Oh honey, I feel so fortunate to be here; that my life led me to this day. I can hardly take it all in." Gracey reached in her purse for a Kleenex. "Spent a fortune on this make-up to ruin it before the wedding even starts."

"I want you to know, Mom, you've been the best to me— not just now, with the wedding and everything, but as long as I can remember. You gave me a happy childhood. I've never taken that fact for granted. If I'm lucky enough to get pregnant during the honeymoon, that first child, that little girl, will be named after you and our Irish grandma, Patricia. That brings it all together for us, Mom—all the years, all our journeys—it finally makes sense now, doesn't it?"

Gracey looked at her. The late morning sun came through the window in stark white and gold streaks that rested in her daughter's hair. She could hear the cars outside in the parking lot, and the people laughing and talking in the church's vestibule. She felt the closeness of her daughter's breath on her skin. This was the moment she had prepared for her entire life.

She clipped the pearl-beaded headpiece to the crown of her daughter's head bathed in sunlight, smoothed the lace veil against the side of her face and shoulders, then pulled her close and smiled.

"Therese, this is for you." Gracey placed the linen handker-chief with the cross-stitched M in her daughter's hands. "It was Grandma Patricia's."

"The granny from Ireland? The Galway girl? Oh, Mama,

it's perfect," Therese hugged her mother tightly. "I've got almost everything now . . . let's see, 'Something old, something new, something borrowed, something blue, and a silver sixpence in my shoe.' "

Gracey laughed. "Where are we going to get a silver sixpence?"

"Forget it, Mom, Thatcher took it out of circulation years ago. The only thing that remains is the little song. I might have a few coins in the bottom of my purse."

"Let's do an American coin. Just as good, if not better. How 'bout a quarter? Got to feel better in the bottom of a shoe than a penny. Too small. Here, take my wallet. There's got to be one in there. Last time the quarter could really be of use was in the days of pay phones. Grandpa would give me four quarters before I went on any date. It was my safety net. I'd call him and he'd rescue me. Thank God I never had to put the theory into practice," Gracey laughed.

"Found one, Mom. I'll put it in my right shoe. Grandpa will be walking down the aisle with me today. I miss him. It was hard being here when he died. Nobody knew how much it hurt."

"He knew you loved him. That's all that matters. It's how we love people while they're alive, not the regrets when they're gone. Best to let that go. He knew you cared."

"Let's not be sad today, Mom. Let's be happy we're together and will be in the years to come. My children will know who you are, Mama. All the beautiful names from our families, my children will carry those names."

"It's our way, isn't it? We name our children after our fathers and mothers, grandmothers and grandfathers, our loving aunts, because the greatest thing we can give them is our shared story in this world; that each generation did its best to make life easier for their children. You and Will are the best things that ever happened to me."

"Oh, Mom, we'll never make it to the wedding at this rate. Please don't cry."

"I know. I know, but you'll see someday. That little Irish girl you'll have, she'll complete the circle. Life's a mystery, Therese. You've got to hold on through the bad and enjoy all the good, knowing God is there all along. Nothing is ever broken, nothing is lost. The same human race that is capable of horrendous acts is also capable of tremendous love. You may be far from me, but an ocean is simply something to cross. Exactly like it was for Grandma Walsh and will be for my granddaughter."

"I love you, Mom." The mother and daughter held each other tightly.

"Now, let's find your dad. He won't believe how beautiful you are. I've got to get to the church and sit down before I collapse," said Gracey, pulling away from her daughter.

The two-hundred-year-old church, with interior wooden beams and arched columns, was filled to capacity with Americans and Irish. Cousins spilled into the outer areas of the church, sitting in the balcony, above the altar. Outside, in the silence of the church's ancient graveyard, Therese, Mark, and the three bridesmaids held their breaths when the massive, wooden doors of the church were opened to them.

Bright sunlight filled the nave of the church; its intensity temporarily blinding the congregation. The smell of peonies and altar candles enfolded the wedding party as they walked into the church. The families of Therese and Daniel rose to greet them as the organist began the ascending notes of "Ave Maria."

Gracey grabbed Will's hand and held it tightly in hers, as only a parent could reach and hold their child's hand. The same hand, though much larger and stronger now, she and Mark held when he was a baby, teaching him to someday live without them, *Small steps, bigger steps, walk, walk . . . Oh, we all fall down, but you must try again. Now, stand. Stand and reach for a star . . .*

Will held his mother's hand, as firmly as she held his. The unspoken words of their bond, *comfort me, reassure me, love me, forgive me*, linked them through the trials, the laughter, the living and the dying.

Mark and Therese approached the altar and the waiting groom. The father kissed his daughter and placed her hand in the hand of her husband-to-be. *I am placing the most precious thing in my life within the palm of your hand. Love her, protect her, defend her, care for her, just as I have, just as my wife and I have.*

Grace looked across the pew at Tom and Angela sitting together, with their spouses and children. They met each other's eyes, laughing, loving the beauty of this single moment in their lives. She closed her eyes, squeezing her son's hand in hers.

This . . . this must be what heaven is like.

Chapter Twenty-two
Faith, Hope and Love

The November sky above the Gulf of Mexico was cast the same hue as the water below it. Gracey couldn't tell where the sky ended and the water began as she drove along the coastal road from Pass Christian to Biloxi. She slowed the car to thirty-five mph, stunned by the palest of blues that washed the delineation between land, water, and sky.

The Neap Tide, just after the first quarter of the moon, erased the depths of high and low water along the shore line. Perhaps it was the season's first cold front creating the visual illusion of heaven and earth as one.

She had left the house early that morning to interview an oyster fisherman for the *Biloxi Times*. She met him at the Pass Christian Harbor at early dawn, just as the first orange and red rays of the morning sun pushed the moon aside.

He was an old man; poor like all people who make their living off the water. Between the price of fuel and a dwindling seafood population, the work had become that of gamblers or those who simply hadn't the guts or skill level to start working in any other field. This was all they knew, just like their fathers and grandfathers before them. For generations, they had taught their sons how to feed themselves and their families.

He was dressed in a paint-spattered sweatshirt, jeans and white rubber boots. She smiled at him as he loaded the flat bottom boat with wooden-handled tongs of metal teeth. He then connected the oyster dredge with its metal chain at the back of the boat. Slowly the little motor would drag it, netting oysters asleep on reefs in the warm Gulf waters. Oystering and its opening season for November was a ritual on the Gulf Coast. It was observed by every oystering family and the commercial fisherman, from Florida's Apalachicola Bay to Galveston Bay in Texas.

The old man stopped to drink coffee from an aluminum thermos after loading his boat with the day's tools. He held the thermos in two gloved hands and looked at her.

"How long have you been doing this, Mr. Debouys?"

"Since I could walk, in all kinds of weather. I've been catching 'bout anything you could eat the Gulf provides," he answered her, setting the thermos on the deck of the boat, he began checking his lines.

"It's cold this morning. Feels to be a northern wind of about fifteen knots. Will it affect the catch?"

"Cold, ain't nothing. Won't be a problem. A problem is when I go out and don't come back with anything to sell. This is the first of the season. I hope to come back with sack-after-sack of fat, salty oysters. Would be good, really good for my family if I caught my limit in the first day of the season. I'd be selling to every restaurant up and down Highway 90. Took us awhile to recover after Katrina. Damn 'bout knocked us all out of the game."

"Well, I wish you a lot of luck. I'll buy some from you when you're ready to sell."

"Lady, I'll give you a sack if you make sure to get a good picture of me in the paper. I ain't never been in the paper before, not even for perfect attendance in grade school or for making the honor roll."

"I can do that for you," Gracey laughed. "Give me your address and I'll mail you the article when it's printed. I can email it if you prefer."

"Lady, I ain't got no computer. Hell, I can barely pay the electric bill."

"Of course, tell me where you live. I'll get it off to you right away. Couple of copies for you and your family."

"'Preciate that." He started the trolling motor, waved to her with his one free hand and steered the little boat into the white caps of the gulf water.

Gracey hadn't eaten oysters since the Sunday following the wedding in September. The Irish and Americans climbed into a passenger van, winding their way through the Ring of Gullion until the land flattened itself into the coastal flats of the Irish Sea and Carlingford. It was a day of oysters and Guinness. The foamy white head of the beer, with the thickness of molasses, was dessert after eating the salty oysters. She smiled when she remembered the day; her family sitting with her in the tiny pub.

Today had been a good day as well. She enjoyed the writing assignment and was thankful to return to the routine of the newspaper, despite the monthly bantering to get her paycheck. Some things would never change, but she had a job and she could still do what she loved, talking to people and telling their stories.

She parked the car in front of the home she shared with her husband in Biloxi, put the cell phone in her pant pocket, leaving her purse, camera and notebook behind on the passenger seat. The weather was too perfect to go inside the house and do laundry or sweep a floor. She had to take advantage of the day and its weather. It was the rare time of the year when people could be outside on the Gulf Coast without sweating or swatting mosquitos.

Early November also brought the high school ritual of Homecoming to the little towns up and down the Gulf Coast. She thought of Loti and of being sixteen; the simple joys of a Friday night high school football game followed by a dance in the school gym.

The week leading to the event was one of high school boys and girls buying mum corsages and boutonnieres, as well as new clothes and shoes to wear to the dance. Who was going with whom? Who changed their minds at the last minute, followed by the caustic decision of either going with a group of friends or making a last minute, desperate phone call to the girl who smiled too much?

They'd gather in the high school gym, under the glow of

a rented mirrored ball, and dance. They'd fall in love with each other, promising everything in the future, for that one moment, on that November night.

It's a good thing we don't know much of anything when we're young. The species would quickly become extinct, Gracey mused.

She walked to the beach, following the meandering sidewalk along the water's edge. The magic of late fall that cooled the earth, touching the row of cypress trees along the path, caused their airy leaves to change from evergreen to crisp orange and red.

A young mother and her toddler sat at a nearby picnic table with paper bags anchored by bottles of water and sandwiches wrapped in paper towels. Occasionally, the toddler threw a piece of bread to the ground, despite his mother's repetitive, "No, no." A circle of seagulls quickly dove toward their feet, fighting each other, screeching for their share of lunch.

An elderly woman walked past Gracey with a border collie on a leash. The woman and the dog both looked at her and smiled. Yes, Gracey was sure the dog smiled at her with its pointy white teeth, the same quick, toothy smile the woman had given her. She'd always thought dog owners and their pets were one entity after so many years of owning each other.

She continued her walk, past the volleyball players on the beach, past the middle-aged man on the bicycle with a crab trap tied around the front basket of the bike and a little American flag hoisted from the back fin of the tire rim. She sat down on the sea wall and took her shoes off.

Her cell phone rang in her pocket. Gracey hesitated to answer. It was probably her boss wondering when she'd finish the story about the fisherman. "Deadlines, Gracey. Our work is about meeting deadlines. I'm not paying overtime to the production staff because you can't tell time."

She needed the job, because she needed air fare, so she slid her index finger across the phone's surface, and instantly, she was back in the world.

"Mom?"

"Therese. honey, oh my gosh, it's so good to hear your voice."

"I've been trying to call you on the landline since early this morning, your time. It's late here. Where have you been all day?"

"Got a little writing assignment, not much money involved, but it was good to get out and see some things. How are you? Daniel? It's must be really cold there."

"Well it's raining, but that's not unusual," her daughter laughed.

"Tell me everything that's going on with you and Daniel. I don't want to cost you a fortune, but do tell me everything."

"I have some good news, Mama. We're just driving back from the clinic in Newry. I'm pregnant. Eight weeks. I'm going to have a baby."

Gracey felt a lightness, a quickening of breath, and a rush of blood pumping through every vein in her body.

"Therese, a baby . . . I'm so happy for you. For Daniel. Oh my God, I'm so happy for me! I knew it. When you sent me the jpegs from your honeymoon in Florence. That picture of you in the wide-brimmed hat and the little red sundress. Your face, honey, you had this ethereal look on your face. I knew it then. You were just so beautiful and happy, and sweet and young, everything, all at the same time."

"I don't know about all that," Therese laughed.

"You might have gotten pregnant the night of the wedding reception," Gracey laughed. "I was watching everybody, all that dancing, hugging, kissing, champagne. I knew someone would end up pregnant that night."

"Mom, you're embarrassing me," Therese laughed.

"I'm marching home right now to tell your father and to book a flight. He's going to be so happy. Wait. Do you want to tell him? It's your special news. I'll have him call you. Then we'll need to tell Will."

"Slow down. I can make some calls tomorrow. I just wanted you to be the first one I called."

"Oh, honey. I didn't even ask you how you were feeling. Are you throwing up? 7-Up and saltines will cure that."

"No, just queasy and tired, really tired. I haven't been sleeping so well; I guess the newness of it all. I did the in-home pregnancy testing kits for a couple of weeks, so we had some idea of what was happening, but I didn't trust it a hundred percent. The Newry doctor confirmed what I thought. It's amazing. Daniel and I are on a cloud right now."

"I bet, but you will need to get your rest and put your feet up as much as possible. You don't want your ankles swelling. Welcome to the world of varicose veins and stretch marks. Got 'em all with Will. You shouldn't be watching any TV at night, either. Bad for you and the baby. Just relax with a good book in bed. Maybe a little herbal tea after dinner. What are you wearing now? I'm sure the maternity clothes are outrageous there. I'll start shopping tomorrow. You'll need a lot. The baby will need—"

"Don't worry about that now. We'll sort it later. Listen Mom, Daniel and I already have a name picked out if we have a girl. Remember? You and I talked about it before the wedding. When you were helping me with my veil in the priest's study."

"Therese, that day was a blur for me. I just know I was incredibly happy and my feet were killing me."

"Mama, our baby's name will be Patricia Grace, after our Irish grandma and you. She'll have black hair like both of y'all, but her eyes, they'll be blue like Daniel's and like Grandma Patricia. Black hair and blue eyes just like the little Irish girl from Galway."

"Therese . . . what an honor. Thank you. It's just wonderful. Wonderful to hear every word of what you're saying."

"It was one of the easiest decisions of my life, like marrying Daniel. I'm exhausted from all that's gone on though, all the excitement. I better let you go. I'll call Dad tomorrow. You can tell him if you simply can't help yourself, Mom. I know how you are. Love you, bye."

Gracey stood up and put her phone back in her pocket. She looked at the Biloxi Bay in the afternoon sun, reflecting light on the water like a million pieces of glass, a perfectly defined prism of violet, blue, cyan, green, yellow, orange and red bouncing off the water's surface. Therese, pregnant, would soon be asleep across this body of water, across a thousand rivers, a hundred lakes, and finally, across the Atlantic Ocean, on the other side of the world.

Gracey thought of the two sisters, Patricia and Ana Grace, with black hair and blue eyes against the fairest skin, walking hand-in-hand from Galway to Dublin. Sleeping hand-in-hand in the bowels of a ship crossing the Atlantic. Searching for a home, hand-in-hand on the docks of Indianola, Texas.

Patricia Grace. Patricia Grace. My granddaughter. A baby girl, precious hope for all of us. Patricia Grace, I've known you before you were in your mother's womb. You were always there in my prayers. Through every year of my life, your name was written on my heart.

About the Author

A former English teacher and journalist, Johnnie Bernhard lives with her husband in Ocean Springs, Mississippi.

Her work has appeared in the following publications: University of Michigan Graduate Studies Publications, *Heart of Ann Arbor Magazine*, *Houston Style Magazine*, *World Oil Magazine*, *The Suburban Reporter of Houston*, *The Mississippi Press*, the international *Word Among Us*, and in anthologies with the Gulf Coast Writers Association. Her essay, "The Last Mayberry," received over 7,500 views, nationally and internationally, on the NPR-CowBird production on small town America.

A Good Girl received top ten finalist recognition in the 2015 Faulkner-Wisdom Creative Writing Competition. Her essay, "Ignorance or Innocence," received "Equal Runner-up" in the 2016 Faulkner-Wisdom Competition.

Johnnie and her husband, Bryant, reside in a 19th century cottage surrounded by ancient oak trees and a salt water marsh near the Mississippi Sound. They share that delightful space with their dog, Lily, and cat, Poncho. All residents eagerly await weekend and holiday visits from the Bernhards' adult children and their granddaughter, Frieda, the Belle of Crossmaglen, Ireland.